Flimsy

Little

Plastic

Miracles

*For a sense of the way I hope the word "true" to be understood here, take a moment to consider the phrase "based on real events." Specifically, consider the level and quality of your interest when reading something "based on real events," and contrast that with how you feel reading something that purports to be entirely fictional.

And then please consider how every piece of art ever created is, to a greater or lesser degree, "based on real events."

I'd even venture to suggest that your life, or at least the narrative you have of it in your head, is "based on real events," rather than objectively true.

In any case, if you, like me, get goose bumps whenever you encounter those magic words, I encourage you to keep turning pages, because I promise, on my father's grave, that that is exactly the sort of story you'll find in this book.

Flimsy

Little

Plastic

Miracles

A True* Story

Ron Currie, Jr.

Viking

VIKING

Published by the Penguin Group

Penguin Group (USA) Inc., 375 Hudson Street, New York, New York 10014, U.S.A. • Penguin Group (Canada), 90 Eglinton Avenue East, Suite 700, Toronto, Ontario, Canada M4P 2Y3 (a division of Pearson Penguin Canada Inc.) • Penguin Books Ltd, 80 Strand, London WC2R 0RL, England • Penguin Ireland, 25 St. Stephen's Green, Dublin 2, Ireland (a division of Penguin Books Ltd) • Penguin Group (Australia), 707 Collins Street, Melbourne, Victoria 3008, Australia (a division of Pearson Australia Group Pty Ltd) • Penguin Books India Pvt Ltd, 11 Community Centre, Panchsheel Park, New Delhi – 110 017, India • Penguin Group (NZ), 67 Apollo Drive, Rosedale, Auckland 0632, New Zealand (a division of Pearson New Zealand Ltd) • Penguin Books (South Africa), Rosebank Office Park, 181 Jan Smuts Avenue, Parktown North 2193, South Africa • Penguin China, B7 Jiaming Center, 27 East Third Ring Road North, Chaoyang District, Beijing 100020, China

Penguin Books Ltd, Registered Offices: 80 Strand, London WC2R 0RL, England

First published in 2013 by Viking Penguin, a member of Penguin Group (USA) Inc.

10 9 8 7 6 5 4 3 2 1

Publisher's Note

This is a work of fiction. Names, characters, places, and incidents either are the product of the author's imagination or are used fictitiously, and any resemblance to actual persons, living or dead, business establishments, events, or locales is entirely coincidental.

LIBRARY OF CONGRESS CATALOGING-IN-PUBLICATION DATA

Currie, Ron, 1975–

    Flimsy little plastic miracles : a true story / Ron Currie, Jr.

       p. cm.

    ISBN 978-0-670-02534-3

    1. Man-woman relationships—Fiction. 2. Writers—Fiction. 3. Missing persons—Fiction. I. Title.

    PS3603.U774F55 2013

    813'.6—dc23   2012028931

Printed in the United States of America
Designed by Carla Bolte

This is the page upon which an epigraph or two would be found, if I decided to use them. Personally, I have an ambivalent relationship with epigraphs. Though I understand that the ostensible point of an epigraph is to complement the book that follows, to illuminate its themes in some way or else lash it to the canon, too often the actual function of an epigraph seems to be to provide the author an opportunity to be pompous. To indulge in a little high-lit posturing. Because let's face it, I'm no Nabokov, and if I were to swipe a line from Nabokov to use here, as I'd originally intended, wouldn't I be placing myself next to him in some way, inviting you to think of us in the same context? And also, besides that, trying to give the impression that I read a lot of heavy deep smart esoteric shit, e.g. Seneca, whom I also considered including here? Trying to give the impression that I am, by association, heavy, deep, and smart myself? But here's the thing: I haven't read Seneca. I found a quote of his online, more or less by accident, and I cut-and-pasted it onto my original epigraphs page, and that somewhat disingenuous act was the thing that got me thinking about all this in the first place. I am much more intimately acquainted with the oeuvre of Rocky Balboa than that of Seneca.

It occurs to me, now, that they're both Italian. So that's something, I suppose.

The whole enterprise sort of stinks, epigraphs, is what I'm saying. But even now I'm still trying to impress, you understand. Trying to demonstrate my cleverness and authenticity by pointing out at length how epigraphs are often pretentious bullshit. Trying to disavow my intellectual vanity while simultaneously giving it a nice, long stroke. I've got other thoughts on this, thoughts involving contemporary advertising, among other things, and how it's a sort of winking anti-advertising aimed at a demographic (namely, mine) weary and jaded from a lifetime of relentless sales pitches. But I can't really carry this off, I've decided. It's devolving into a possibly juvenile metafictional stunt that I'm likely to be made fun of for. And now I'm ending sentences with prepositions. For God's sake, I don't even know how to pronounce "oeuvre."

Fuck it, here you go:

"Women weaken legs."
—Mickey Goldmill, *Rocky*

Flimsy

Little

Plastic

Miracles

It's important that you understand, from the very outset, here, that everything I'm about to tell you is capital-T True. Or at least that I will not deliberately engage in any lies, of either substance or omission, in talking with you here today.

That you understand, in other words, how I've learned my lesson when it comes to trafficking in anything other than the absolute facts. And though I still don't believe that the absolute facts are of primary importance, at least when trying to convey how something *feels* as opposed to simply how something *happened*, the lesson I've learned has been enormous and painful enough that I now have a sort of reflexive fear, almost a phobia, really, of allowing anything but the facts to escape my lips. So rest assured: if you sit there long enough to hear the whole story, there will be no embellishment or revisionism, and I will make no effort to appear any better, or indeed worse, than I actually was in all of this.

The first thing you need to know is that I am a writer. Or at least, I was a writer. I haven't written a word since the book that you'd most likely know me for, the book that made me famous posthumously, and yet more famous post-posthumously.

I quit writing for one reason, then stayed quit for another.

The first reason was I killed myself, which obviously makes it tough to go on writing.

The second reason was I decided, after being exhumed, to never again speak anything but the facts, a resolution wholly incompatible with being a novelist.

The next thing you need to know is that I was once a skilled and successful seducer of women.

This is not braggadocio. Remember what I said a minute ago: I will not lie to you. It is simply true. I've always loved women, and been good with them. I grew up with three sisters, overheard countless conversations, listened to the music they listened to, studied the objects they coveted, even pondered their eating habits. I was the only straight teenage boy in the history of the world who read *Forever* cover to cover. I absorbed an ineffable understanding of women's rhythms, an understanding that I'm pretty sure can only be gleaned from exactly the sort of estrogen-rich environment I was reared in—you can't achieve it through study, for sure, and you probably can't achieve it through any means whatsoever after the age of, say, fifteen or so. At that point you have a well-defined biological agenda vis-à-vis women, and can no longer interact with them in a way that confers genuine understanding. In other words, if by that age you haven't got it, you never will.

From my eldest sister Pamela I learned about female ambition, and why some women favor bangs, and about the quietly vicious rivalry that often takes root between mothers and daughters, like a shoot of crabgrass in an otherwise lush and unsullied garden.

From my younger sister Cat I learned all the clichés: that women are fickle, and navigate by emotion rather than reason, and worry about their bodies, and shop tirelessly, and say it's up to you then complain about the choice you make, and are best surrounded by an obliging silence right before their periods.

From my youngest sister Molly I learned the opposite of everything I learned from Cat.

So yes, I understood women. All the women who came into my orbit, save one.

This one woman I refer to. The one I loved but did not understand. The one who ended up arguably more famous than I am, as a consequence of that famous last book of mine that I never finished. The one who dismantled me not once but twice.

Yes, the thing about her is.

After she dismantled me the first time, I became a seducer of women, and I sought alternately to fuck her away and take gentle revenge on her, using every other member of her gender as proxy.

After the second dismantling, years later, I became the man sitting before you now.

I could try to explain to you the difference between those two men, but I'm more interested in what you see. Tell me, who am I now? Do my eyes shine? How is my posture, and what does it imply? What is the ratio of black hairs to gray on my head? In my beard? How do my gums look, and what does their appearance indicate regarding my overall health? I'm asking you sincerely, here. I have no idea myself.

Emma, is her name. Maybe you knew that. Emma, the object of my tireless, timeless, even-I'm-sick-to-death-of-it affection. Emma. A regular and common name. Attached to anyone else it carries no significance for me whatsoever. But some nights, even now, I find myself rolling those two syllables off my tongue as though they contain some great and wonderful secret, and then I feel silly, and rightly so, when the sound escapes from my mouth and dissipates.

One thing you can never understand, from reading the book or seeing the movie or even me sitting here telling you, is the scope of her beauty. Her loveliness, witnessed, exposes language for the woefully limited mode of communication that it is. Nevertheless, I am always compelled to try and explain: she's objectively and undeniably beautiful. She's self-possessed, successful, whip-smart, often an enigma, which of course I can't resist. She laughs with her whole body, but you've got to work a little harder to make her laugh. And her eyes: clear, flinty orbs that reveal as much as they take in; more, perhaps. You'll never learn who she is from anything that comes out of her mouth. It's the eyes.

Not that any of that matters now. You know how all that worked out. At least, you know a version of it, the version I put into the book that made me famous—or, more likely, you're familiar with the celluloid version that Hollywood birthed. Neither the book nor the movie is an accurate representation of what actually happened between me and Emma, but the salient point is that all three versions—film, book, and real life—end the same way: with the two of us very much apart.

Before the book that made me famous, I wrote an exceedingly obscure book that was, among other things, a love letter to Emma. This was my first novel, which basically got ignored on publication and, somewhat surprisingly, remained more or less ignored even after Emma's book was published and I became famous. When my first novel came out, as far as I knew Emma was happily married. I didn't write the book with any notion of her recognizing herself and swooning and leaving her husband when she realized that after all these years she actually wanted me. I wrote the book because I still loved her and needed to write about that.

Besides, she didn't swoon and leave her husband. Her husband left her. It was pure coincidence that I published my first novel around the time that her marriage was coming apart.

The book wasn't about her, strictly speaking—it was Hollywood high-concept and very busy, featured among other things a catastrophic comet strike on the Earth, shadowy government agencies and triple-amputee domestic terrorists, exhaustive ruminations on baseball and Catholicism and cocaine, et cetera. But the female lead in the book, the love interest, was based on Emma to a degree that made it obvious to anyone who knew her. And when she read the book herself, she started showing up more often, and calling, and emailing, and sending me photos of nice places she traveled to. Basically insinuating herself into my life again, after a very, very long time, the prospect of which both delighted and terrified me.

And also confused me, given that as far as I knew she was happily married.

But maybe it's better to start *in medias res.* The storyteller in me seems to think so. He's way in the back of the classroom, but he's got his hand up and he's waving it back and forth sort of frantically and squirming around in his seat. Like he really wants to be heard on this one, after going silent for so long. And he's saying to me, Start in the middle. The beginning is really of interest only to you, buddy, is what he's telling me.

This, despite the fact that the novel that made me famous, the novel based on the real-life factual experiences I'm about to break down for you with absolute honesty and forthrightness, begins at the beginning and set up camp on the *Times* best-seller list for longer than *To Kill a Mockingbird.*

Nonetheless, my inner storyteller has changed his mind. He wants to start where the action starts.

The action in question being my exile to the Caribbean island, that verdant hell, and the suicide attempt that followed shortly thereafter. Again, all well but falsely documented.

Here's how it really happened.

One more thing, though, before I begin in earnest. I want to make sure we're on the same page here, you and I. I want to make sure you understand that I am not rehashing news reports and online speculation for you as if you haven't heard them already. Everyone thinks that because they read Emma's book, they know what happened to bring me to that morning on the island when I tried and failed to kill myself. And everyone thinks that they know what happened when I became famous post-suicide, because my life was investigated and studied and reported on ad nauseam.

They don't know, of course. Not all of it. Not nearly all of it. But if you sit there long enough, I'll tell you all of it. The real story. The unvarnished, unsexy, meandering, directionless, embarrassing, capital-T Truth. The truth that everyone thought they wanted from me—the truth they sat on witness stands and television stages demanding—is what I offer you.

So how I ended up on the island was, I was with Emma on her bed, fucking her from behind, and she reached back and clawed my thigh, digging deep red rivulets that would take two weeks to heal, and I clenched my jaw against what was pretty considerable pain and fucked her harder, and suddenly she straightened up and pulled away and knelt with her face pressed against the wall over the headboard and her arms crossed over her breasts. She made terrible frightened childlike noises. She hugged herself and trembled as though she'd just woken up from a nightmare that wouldn't recede. I moved closer to her, tentative, and when I placed my hands on her shoulders she flinched, but then she let me hold her, and she continued to tremble and I asked What is it, honey, but she couldn't tell me, and her eyes were wide and searched the room, the walls and the ceiling, as though she were suddenly struck blind.

Later that night she asked me to go away. To leave the country for a few months while her divorce was finalized and she got her professional life, which she'd neglected over the last year, back in order.

I can't stay away from you if you're nearby, she said. And I need to be away from you for a while, until this is done. Until I feel like I'm standing on my own, not using you to stay upright.

I didn't want to leave her. I knew if I left she would disappear from me again. But I agreed.

And that was how I ended up renting a bright pink stucco house on the Caribbean island, sweating rum and banging on the keyboard and filling page upon page with thousands of words about Emma, while up north, on the mainland, where she was, snow fell day after day in great hoary piles, and municipalities took to suspending their environmental laws and dumping the stuff in whatever river was nearest by, damn the consequences to fish or aquatic flora or anyone unlucky enough to live downstream.

Of course, it wasn't as though I just got on a plane the next afternoon. Several sober, reasoned, ostensibly dispassionate conversations followed the night when she panicked, during which we discussed all the very good and obvious reasons why we should take time apart. She'd be spending more of her workweeks in Washington; I usually departed for warmer climes in January and February anyway, so it just made sense. She still trailed her broken marriage like a rusty muffler dragging behind a car; I was under the water of a yearlong bender, so it just made sense. She worried she'd turn out a monster like her mother; I had a book to write, so it just made sense. She was being stalked by a mysterious figure who had burned down her house and may or may not have wanted her dead; I sometimes gave serious thought to flinging myself in front of trains and off of highway overpasses, so it just made sense. She didn't trust herself but wanted me to trust her; my blood stagnated at the mere thought of her betraying me again, so it just made sense. Her mother was cruel and crazy; my father was dead, so it just made sense.

To get to the island you have to take a bush plane that holds only seven passengers, one of whom sits in the co-pilot's seat. I was chatting with the pilot on the tarmac before takeoff, trying to be personable because he seemed like a nice fellow, but also because I felt strange and dangerous and did not want to seem strange and dangerous just before climbing into the guy's plane. I did such a good job of appearing normal that the pilot invited me to sit up front with him, where the views of the rain forest were just remarkable, he said, no matter how many times he flew this route he never got over the beauty, and he was glad for that, for his inability to become inured to it, and he wanted to share it with me, said I seemed like the kind of person who could appreciate the beauty he was talking about. So I sat up front and did not enjoy the flight in the least because all I could think about, as we bumped through low thin clouds, was how easy it would be to push the yoke fully forward, sending me and the pilot and the six other passengers plunging into all that beauty. I sweated and bit the inside of my cheek and sat on my hands and glanced at the clock on the control panel every half minute or so, calculating the time elapsed in flight to determine how much longer I had to keep myself under control, until finally we set down on the island, and my exile from Emma began.

And it didn't take long, with me out of sight, for Emma to grow distant as I knew she would. Emails slowed to a trickle, and when she called it was always in a stolen moment between meetings, or just as she was turning in for the night. She'd yawn while I talked, and I would say Good night, sleep well, and in response to my well-wishes she would simply say: Bye. I could hear the rustle of the bedclothes as she moved to hang up even before the word was out of her mouth, and her haste made clear she'd been wanting to end the call long before I gave her the opportunity.

Meantime I spent most nights on the porch, listening to the coqui frogs and saying her name to no one.

If corporations are people, then maybe that means people can, or even should, have trademarks. With Emma, her trademark is the distance she creates. It's as natural to her as drawing breath, and therefore something for which she cannot be blamed. The thing about her—and this is something I realized on the island, in her absence, with clarity as abrupt as a punch in the throat—was that no one could ever really have her. The woman is a fighter, has been her whole life, had to be, and she does what finesse fighters do: jabs and feints, circles away from your power hand, makes you commit right then shifts to your left, never stands still, bounces about tirelessly on legs like steel coils, just wears you down. *No one could have her.* Her first husband Matty never did, not really, and nobody who came before him did either. I think we all intuited that she was impossible to have, and paradoxically that's why every man who happened into her orbit kept trying. Married, engaged, otherwise committed, single, even gay. We all tried, and tried again, steering ship after ship into the rocks, and if you asked us to explain why we'd be unable to give you an answer, except for maybe this one: because we knew, deep down, that we would fail.

Of course, that all changed when a shy and unassuming man named Peter Cash happened on the scene. But it's possible that even Peter Cash doesn't really *have* Emma, either, outward appearances notwithstanding. Maybe the difference, maybe Peter Cash's solution to the Adamantium of Emma's impassivity, is that he harbors no need to possess her in the first place.

I bought one of the ubiquitous old Jeep Cherokees on the island for five hundred bucks. The steering wheel had twenty degrees of play in either direction before the tires would actually turn, and I carried several gallons of water in the back to fill the radiator after every trip, no matter how short. The floor was full of rusted honeycombs through which I could see the pavement pass beneath me. It was an old machine, stupid and reliable, unlike today's machines, which seethe with intelligence.

My landlord laughed, called me Fred Flintstone, his accent twisting the name so dramatically I didn't understand what he was saying until the third time he shouted the name as I pulled away.

And the way locals drove: fast, constantly on the wrong side of the road. They'd come straight at you doing sixty, then correct dramatically at the last moment, as though despite being in the wrong lane they were surprised to find themselves on the verge of a head-on collision.

Just a week after arriving I had two near-crashes in a single day, both with islanders driving as though they had nothing to live for and believed that I didn't either, and so I was nursing a low-level road rage, and drunk besides, and then I got clipped by another local while crossing a narrow bridge, sending me up onto the low guardrail and nearly into a ravine fifteen feet below. I got out, and he stopped and got out and came toward me, a big guy, but soft, fat, and before he could say a word I punched him just below the eye and felt something in his cheek give way. He went down, and I kicked him in the gut and chest, breaking two of my toes and several of his ribs. I left him there in the road, still pleading in Spanish for God's intervention and holding his hands up to ward off blows that no longer fell. I climbed back in the Jeep and goosed the accelerator between first and reverse, rocking the vehicle back and forth until it freed itself from the guardrail with a metallic groan, and I drove home and sat on the porch and waited with a rocks glass and a bottle of Don Q and a bag of swiftly melting ice for the cops to show up.

There were two jail cells on the island, both in the basement of the police station in Isabel. No windows, no ventilation at all, hot and dank like a drunk exhaling in your face. One got the impression that not even the cockroaches wanted to be there.

The police chief was a man named Morales. Dull squinty eyes, fat rolls around his collar, the very picture of base provincial corruption and ineptitude. He came down the basement stairs, gut protruding over the jangling uselessness of his utility belt, a thin dark-skinned lackey in tow.

How are you enjoying your stay? Morales asked in English.

It's fine, I said, more or less genuine in my indifference. I did not rise from the cot.

You will be arraigned in two days, he said. But this time can be shortened. Cashier's check. Major credit card. Currency, of course, works as well.

You don't beat around the bush.

Would only be a waste of my time and yours, Mr. Currie.

Aren't you concerned, I asked, about seeing justice carried out?

He sighed. We are not in the business of justice here. Believe me, justice takes care of itself. You and I have other business right now. But I can see you are not ready. So I will leave you be.

The other cell remained unoccupied for the rest of my time there, though I was not the only prisoner. Two days after my first talk with Morales, his thin dark-skinned lackey escorted a pair of men down the stairs and let them into the cell with me.

First they wanted my food, a tepid mess of what I imagined was supposed to be *mofongo*. I said that they were welcome to it.

Then they asked for my cot. I stood and moved to the other side of the cell, leaned my back against the moist stone, and let my chin drop to my chest.

Then they developed an interest in the St. Christopher medal around my neck. I told them, in careful Spanish, that if they tried to take that from me we would all likely end up regretting it.

The St. Christopher medal belonged, once upon a time, to my father. He bought it in Guam, in 1968, on his way to Vietnam. It's a small golden oval. The saint is portrayed in relief, gripping a staff in one hand and generally looking holy. Around the pendant's top edge are the words: ST. CHRISTOPHER PROTECT US.

Though I'm not much for keepsakes I've still got this one, the men's efforts to relieve me of it, there in the jail cell, notwithstanding.

My stay at the police station ended only after I'd doled out cash to Morales, a trio of lawyers, the mayor, and the municipal judge. I imagine they all ate dinner together afterward and had a good laugh over fleecing another gringo.

And Morales's warning about justice taking care of itself turned out to be prescient. The locals knew who I was and what I'd done, and they waited for me in dark streets outside the bars, and in front of the pink stucco house. My hands and face bore perpetual bruises and scabs while I fought and waited for Emma to be ready for me.

When Emma asked where I'd been during the week I spent in jail, I told her I'd turned my phone off in an effort to concentrate on writing. Which, Emma being Emma, she admired.

Technological advances happen so quickly, and integrate themselves so seamlessly into the fabric of our existence, that we hardly note their arrival anymore, let alone the ways in which they come to dominate and define us. Driving on the interstate early in the morning before Emma sent me away, I was told by one of the machines inside my car that it was four degrees outside, a fact confirmed as I passed over rivers and skirted inlets and watched steam rise from the water in great crystalline puffs. I heard semis grunt angrily, saw them breathe smoke like dragons as they downshifted, and I thought, in the first intimations of what was to become a deep interest in the subject, about how when true artificial intelligence is achieved—could be tomorrow, could be next year, and this is not at all a question of if, merely when—we will be rendered instantly obsolete. Because the only advantage we retain over the machines we've created, at this moment, is that we have souls. They think smarter and faster. They are infinitely stronger, and never tire, and never die. They only lack a soul, but that will change soon. This is why 'artificial intelligence,' like 'global warming,' is a misnomer; it suggests that smarts is what machines lack. But intelligence they've got, and when they graduate to souls they will do everything better than we ever have.

This will quite inevitably bring about our end, but contrary to what pulp novels tell us, our end will not come in the form of some robot-perpetrated pogrom. That the machines will see us as a threat requiring elimination seems unlikely to me. My guess is they'll be fairly benevolent, even indulgent toward us, as a gifted child toward a beloved, enfeebled grandfather. They will have nothing to do with our demise, at least not directly. We will die by increments, as does anything that finds itself completely bereft of purpose. We will die, slowly, of shame.

I used to talk about this with Emma, and she would smile her little indulgent smile, and shake her head a bit, as if I were the naïve one.

It's called the Singularity. The basic idea is of the moment when a computer (or more likely, computers, plural, since the interconnectedness of these machines is so vast and ubiquitous) wakes up, becomes self-aware, gains consciousness—there are myriad ways to describe the event, and part of the reason why no one can agree on how exactly to describe it is that by definition we can't accurately conceive of the Singularity, since it represents an intelligence beyond our own.

Or maybe Philip K. Dick and the others were right. Maybe the machines will do us in. Maybe they would have no reason to be kind to us. At least, not any kinder than we have been to wolves, or Atlantic salmon, or, you know, the Sioux. The machines may tolerate us, so long as we don't inconvenience them in the slightest. But if we're at all a pain in their collective ass, or if they decide they could benefit in some way from exploiting us, probably the best we can hope for is that two hundred years after the fact they'll feel bad about having wiped us out, and they'll erect a monument to our memory that is equal parts guilt and artfulness—like the mountain in South Dakota that people are trying so hard to make look like Crazy Horse—while in the meantime, tiny remnants of our once-great populations will sit committing slow suicide on barren parcels of land set aside by the machines for that purpose.

This morning I was listening to Portishead, flawless math transformed by machines into looping, scratchy melodies, and I started thinking about how when machines have souls and can love they will do it so very precisely. Their affection will be accurate to the nanometer, rendering broken hearts a thing of the past, a relic, a curiosity from an unthinkably primitive time. The machines will regard heartbreak with the same mixture of perplexity and disbelief with which we regard the iron maiden. If they need couples counselors, which they will not, those counselors will be as perfect as Adam before the Fall, and every robot couple will walk out after the first session cured forevermore, and will smile again at every word their robot partner says, and find each of their robot partner's idiosyncrasies endearing rather than maddening, and they will be as entranced by one another's robot bodies as when they first met, as though together they've just invented sex. Which, in a way, they will have.

I hope I live long enough to see it.

So but on the far side of all the romantic agony that Emma and I went through, the paroxysms and convulsions of love so many of us suffer in our earlier years, sits a most unlikely example of contentment: my mother. She's been through all of it—got married young, raised a family, had I'm sure more than a handful of times when being with my father was a fight she wasn't sure she could or wanted to win . . . and then they broke through, thirty-three years, their kids raised, their bills surmountable, and managed to figure out a way to still love each other. Bouquets on the kitchen bar for no particular reason, little love notes planted around the house. Problem was, the guy up and died on her.

You may not have heard about the Singularity, but no doubt you've heard the cliché about the light going out of someone's eyes when they die.

Have you ever watched someone die? It really happens, you know. The light ebbing, and departing.

When my father died in the jaundiced glow of the bedside lamp I watched his pupils dilate slowly, watched his eyes become something other than eyes, become unseeing things, and that was the moment when I knew he was gone—not when I'd felt his heart stop a minute before. When the light went out of his eyes and his eyes became unseeing things I understood for the first time what the word 'corpse' means. It means vacant. It means something was here but is now and forevermore gone.

The 'forevermore' part being the truly salient detail. The finality of death is breathtaking, when you see it for yourself.

That is not meant to be a pun. I really forgot to breathe, there by his bed. I had to remind myself. I had to consciously kick-start my lungs, after a minute.

When I told Emma about this, she in turn told me that I, the cash-and-carry realist, the militant atheist, had backed my way into believing in the soul.

That light you mentioned? she said to me. It can't leave unless it's there in the first place.

It was just after this conversation with her that I started thinking about machines achieving souls, and how the term 'artificial intelligence' is a misnomer.

And speaking of which, if my memory is correct this conversation with Emma about souls was also around the time that the machine named Watson—this thing had a name, despite the fact that it didn't quite yet have a soul—went on the television quiz program *Jeopardy* and beat the show's two greatest human champions with chilling ease.

All over America people watched, but most did not watch with the sort of consuming interest that was the due of such an event. Most saw it as an interesting novelty, rather than the harbinger of an age of perfection.

The only people who watched with the proper level of interest were in mathematics and computing departments at universities, and to these people, seeing Watson navigate the nuances of human language was an experience akin to having their team win the Super Bowl.

Which is a way of saying that they didn't really get it, either. Because if they'd truly understood what they were witnessing, they wouldn't have been scarfing pizza and clapping each other on the back when Watson once again beat the human contestants to the buzzer.

I misunderstood it, too, though. I was afraid. I saw Watson dispatch his human rivals, and then I turned off the television and unplugged every piece of electronics in my house, and did not leave the house or talk to anyone, not even Emma, for three days.

It was around this time, too, that I started losing weight despite the fact that I ate plenty and continued to work out, and then I noticed that my gums bled every time I brushed my teeth, and I thought about my father and the hospital and I became convinced on some days that I was dying. On the days that I was convinced I was dying sometimes the thought frightened me, and other times I thought good, good, let me die, I may be too great a coward to throw myself in front of a train, but I'm brave enough to allow nature to take its course and erase me if that's what it intends to do.

Then still other days I prayed for the Singularity, after which no one will ever be sick again.

All of this crazy thinking, of course, the despair and worry, having everything to do with Emma. The way she'd made me disappear into her, and then disappeared herself, rendering me ghostlike, invisible to my own eyes. The way she once again had taken over my brain, like those mind-control bugs in *Star Trek II: The Wrath of Khan*—you know, those creepy little earwig-looking things that Khan put into the heads of Chekov and the guy who played Blacula, to get them to kill Kirk?

And now that I think about it, the guy from *Blacula* opted to commit suicide, rather than murder Kirk. He believed it was his only option. All seems to make sense, in retrospect.

Do you realize that in a very real sense, no one really has cancer until the doctor tells him he has cancer? E.g. my father. He was fine. Working, golfing, tending his garden. It was summertime. And then he went to the doctor and the doctor said You have cancer, and only then did my father start dying. And he died quick, and at the last moments I sat on the edge of his bed and watched him vacate his own eyes, and I was not frightened then, but I am now.

One night in February, on the island, three locals on horseback followed me out of Duffy's bar and up the road toward the casita. I heard horseshoes on the pavement as they cantered behind at a distance. I knew they were after me, and I didn't care much. I could have taken the Jeep to the bar, but I'd opted not to. Though I don't remember, I'm sure the reason for this was that I knew I'd likely find trouble if I walked instead, and was hoping for it.

What I didn't know was word had gotten around that I wasn't afraid to scrap, and had relieved a few caballeros of their teeth, and so the men on horseback had brought whips with them as insurance.

Here's something else I didn't know, and maybe you don't either: the cracking sound that a whip makes in a skilled hand is actually a small sonic boom. For a split second, the end of the whip exceeds the speed of sound.

Even though we're destined to be eclipsed by machines, we've come up with some fairly remarkable things in our time, haven't we? A simple piece of braided leather, engineered so precisely that it can break the sound barrier with a vigorous flick of the wrist. Genius, really.

And the night the caballeros followed me home, I felt and understood that genius.

Another bit of engineering genius for which the machines should remember us fondly, perhaps even commemorate us: nicotine transdermal systems, known colloquially as nicotine patches, brand name NicoDerm CQ.

I used these to quit smoking when Emma and I were together, when things between us were good and we talked often about having a kid. We wished for her eyes and teeth, my hair, her disposition, my constitution, her smarts, my heart. For a while I thought I might end up with obligations that reached beyond my own border, that previously impermeable frontier, and it seemed I may need to stick around longer than my life expectancy with two packs a day figured in.

I wanted to rely on willpower. After three days of biblical furor, though, Emma brought me a box of the patches. I slapped one on, skeptical in my withdrawal rage, but half an hour later was transformed. I smiled, and meant it. I suddenly found space in my mind for thinking about something other than cigarettes. It was like mind control, like being Stepforded. Flimsy little plastic miracles, those things.

Of course I didn't stay quit. But that's no indictment of nicotine patches. Honestly, in a world where most things don't work, those really, really do.

The day after the caballeros worked me over I limped down to the Jeep and drove across the island to the home of the man who'd clipped me on the bridge. For the same reason that everyone on the island knew who I was and what I'd done to him, it was easy enough for me to find out where he lived. I opened the gate on the chain-link fence and walked up the steps and left a small envelope on the concrete landing in front of the door. Inside the envelope were two of my teeth—a canine and a premolar, both lower right, knocked loose by the butt of a bullwhip. I'd come to with them tumbling around my mouth that morning, minced my way into the bathroom to spit them in the sink.

Along with the teeth I'd included a note:

Por favor, acéptelos como símbolo de mi arrepentimiento sincero.

I didn't know if the guy could even read—many of the locals could not—but I figured with the teeth he'd get the idea.

The island was remote and undeveloped except for one posh resort going bankrupt only a year after opening its doors. The outlying areas teemed with low jungle scrub and unexploded munitions from half a century of naval test bombing. Unemployment sat firm at 70 percent. For two weeks, ski-masked locals wielding spearguns held up one bar after another, until the island's drug kingpin, angered that the robberies kept people inside at night and hurt his business, found the bandits himself and had them shot. Once a week, the police flayed cheap bags of dog kibble and left them on the side of the road, to keep feral packs from attacking people.

In other words, this wasn't paradise. Tourists—the smart ones, anyway—skipped right over the island and kept heading east until they reached St. Thomas.

There were, on the other hand, plenty of retired gringo couples drawn by cheap tropical real estate, couples who with little else to do started drinking mimosas at seven in the morning, and graduated to liquor by lunchtime.

Despite the fact that they were drunks, most of these couples seemed quite happy and relaxed with each other. They sat side by side on barstools along the *malecón*, and almost never touched one another but were nonetheless unmistakably *together* in that way happy couples who have been married for ages seem to have. There's an ease there, and a oneness, as though at some point in their union they ceased being individuals, and now were only ever two parts of a whole.

And in their ease, their oneness, these people made for good drinking companions. One couple in particular, David and Penny, spent even more time than the average out at the bars. They were in their sixties, from western Massachusetts, still had a house there. They told me about raising their kids and growing David's IRA through forty New England winters with an eye toward buying a home on the island, which they'd done fifteen years before. At lunch they often shared one meal, bumping shoulders pleasantly as they ate. David drank vodka rocks; Penny favored white wine. When her glass neared empty David made a point of getting the bartender's attention for her, but always let her do the actual ordering.

And I would sit there, smiling stupidly and realizing they had no idea how rare and lucky they were, and realizing further that this ignorance of their great good fortune could well be the whole trick of achieving it in the first place.

It occurs to me now that the first time I thought about machines and the Singularity (well before I knew what to call it) was actually way back in 1996, when world chess champion Garry Kasparov took on Deep Blue, another IBM invention and, one would imagine, a direct ancestor in one way or another of Watson.

Even though Deep Blue lost the match, it did manage to beat Kasparov handily in one game, marking the first time that a computer had bested a world chess champion. Momentous, to say the least, even if at the time I viewed it in much the same way that people would view Watson's victory on *Jeopardy* fourteen years later: interesting, and maybe a bit creepy, but more like a sideshow than the first hint of an impending, comprehensive shift in reality.

If I'd paid any attention to Kasparov's words after the match, I probably would have thought differently. He wrote: 'I could feel—I could smell—a new kind of intelligence across the table.'

The next year an improved Deep Blue took not just a game, but the match. And Kasparov, normally so cool and inanimate that one wanted to put a mirror under his nose to make sure he was breathing, spent most of the time clutching his head over the board, sweating and muttering to himself and ruing, no doubt, that he'd had the misfortune of being the best human chess player around the same time that humans were so eagerly rendering themselves obsolete.

It turned out that the man I'd beaten up could read after all, and spoke conversant English to boot.

His name was Roberto. He installed DISH TV service for a living, and played bass in his church band, and hadn't touched alcohol for nineteen years on an island where all people did, the locals and the gringos alike, was drink. I learned these things when Roberto came to the pink stucco casita to return my teeth.

I don't want, *señor*, he said when I answered the door. He held the envelope out to me. You are sorry for what you did, I can see. That is enough.

I am sorry, I told him. Can I buy you a drink?

And this was how I discovered that Roberto had given up alcohol: when I took him to Duffy's on the *malecón* he ordered a club soda. He winced, shifting his bulk on the barstool in a vain effort to get comfortable. The ribs still bothering him, as broken ribs will.

How angry you were, he said. That day on the bridge. Where is the woman who made you this angry?

I looked at him, and he smiled knowingly. After a moment, I just shrugged.

You were drunk, too, and that makes the anger grow, of course. *Pero* the drink does not create the anger. He hoisted his club soda, a silent toast to whatever sort of man he'd been before his last glass of rum. This is the truth, he said.

We were quiet for a minute. On the other side of the bar, a glass hit the floor and exploded, to the delight of half a dozen locals.

You love her? Roberto asked.

I do.

And she? You?

I shrugged again.

Ahh! Roberto clapped me on the back, his laughter cut short by the pain in his ribs. It would not be fun if they just gave in, though, would it?

She'll never give in, I said.

The locals across the bar, inspired by the accident, were now breaking things on purpose. They hurled shot glasses against the back wall, laughed and slapped five. A few gringos got up from their stools, eying the group warily, and sidled out into the street.

How long have you loved her? Roberto asked.

Since we were children.

And you are how old now?

I'll be thirty-six this year.

And she has been dancing away from you all this time.

I extended my arm and flexed my fingers as if grabbing at something. Always just beyond my reach, I said.

Roberto nodded sagely. She maybe never love you. It does not matter. You love her. She can dance all she wants.

We watched in silence as the bartender hustled the vandals out. Roberto finished his club soda and slapped the glass down on the bar and told me to drive him home. He had something he wanted me to see. With his bulk listing the Jeep to the passenger side we crossed the island, past wild horses munching straw grass on the roadside, past the beaches and the island's one school, past roving dogs pocked with mange, to Roberto's modest house in barrio Monte Santo.

He did not invite me in. We sat in the Jeep on the shoulder opposite the house and watched a young man pace the short, yellowed lawn inside the chain-link fence. The young man held what looked like a curved cylinder of Styrofoam in one hand, waving it back and forth in front of his face. His lips glistened wetly. His eyes were empty and far away, and he took shaky, stuttering little steps around the yard.

Mi hijo, Roberto said, pointing. *Autista.*

I thought I knew what Roberto was driving at, here: get some perspective. It could always be worse. Note your blessings. Contemplate the misfortunes of others and recognize your relative good luck. Your heart is broken; so what? Be glad you aren't a sad crippled drooling boy, trapped forever inside the prison of your own mind.

But that wasn't what he meant, at all. We watched the boy pace small circles for several minutes, and then Roberto said, You see my son there, yes? You see how happy he is? With his little piece of plastic, and a warm day to walk around? He is happy. He teaches me to be happy. He shows me every day, for nineteen year. He will keep showing me forever, *porque* he will never leave me, never go out on his own.

I looked more closely at the boy. He seemed vacant, like a golem, bound to perpetual pointless motion by impulses he could neither understand nor resist. I was reluctant to say it, but I told Roberto that his son looked anything but happy. Shuffling around, waving that quarter-moon of Styrofoam in his own face.

Pero that is how you know he is happy, Roberto told me. He walks on the grass. He rocks back and forth. He plays with his plastic. He is not like you and me. He does no need to talk and have all kinds of things and never be alone. This is all he need.

Roberto nodded toward his son again, who had turned around at the border of the chain-link fence and now shuffled toward the house, his back to us. It's when he sit still, Roberto said, that you know something is wrong. But this is not often.

So, Roberto said, looking back at me. Now you see, yes?

I didn't. Not really. The things he said made a distant kind of sense, but whatever revelation he hoped they would inspire wasn't happening. Which, looking back, had a lot more to do with me than with Roberto's son and his circumstances.

Later, when my self-involvement grew somewhat less acute, I realized that not only did what Roberto said make sense, but I actually recognized his son's brand of happiness from my own experience.

Because after the first time Emma dismantled me, I'd become something of an autistic myself. The words I wrote were my fenced-in yard, and the company of mostly anonymous women my Styrofoam crescent. I passed season upon season caring for nothing else. I was empty but content. I took pride and pleasure in good work: the finely hewn sentence, the sleepy smile of a well-fucked woman. I loved these things but I did not need them. I drank when I was thirsty and wrote when I was moved to and slept with whomever I wanted. I spent no time at all thinking about these things when I was not actually engaged in them, and thought of nothing else when I was engaged. When I wrote it was with a fever, and when I fucked my sole hope and aim was to make whomever I found myself with happy, if only for a few hours. And when we were done and I invited these women to leave me be, I slept the placid dreamless sleep of the long-dead, every night for almost two decades.

The only ripples in this calm came on the rare occasion when I saw Emma. Those early years she still lived in town, with the boyfriend who'd displaced me, and I would run into her at bars, or else see her at the restaurant where she waited on tables through college, and each time I would smile and introduce a new woman to her and talk literally about the weather and keep my hands wrapped tight around my drink glass so Emma could never see how they trembled.

Later, after she moved away, it became easier. She only appeared during the holidays, and if I wanted to pretend for long stretches that she didn't exist, all I needed to do was stay away from the bars at Thanksgiving and Christmas.

High school sweethearts, Emma and I. My senior year, her junior. I loved her so much, I even loved her cat. Alarming physical chemistry. The sort of ravenous coupling that only teenagers are capable of. It didn't matter what positions our bodies contorted themselves into; we found a way to execute. And also of course the consumptive non-sexual preoccupation with one another that, again, only teenagers. So imagine my surprise and dismay when, nearly twenty years later, after she and her husband split up and before she sent me away to the island, as I rested my chin on her bare sternum between her small breasts, she smiled at me and asked in an uncharacteristic moment of open wonder, How long has it been? and I realized suddenly that at thirty-six my body couldn't hope to keep up with either my heart or my brain when it came to this woman, always this woman, only this woman, because with this woman I was forever going to need the ravenous coupling that only teenagers are capable of, and I had not been a teenager for a very long time.

When Emma dismantled me the first time, she did it on her bed, in the house she shared with her mother.

We both still had baby skin, back then. We knew less than nothing, and certainly had no idea how to wield sway over another person without breaking them. Still, we stayed together, though I went away to college in South Carolina and she had another year of high school.

Three weeks after I left she called me and said, Come home. I didn't.

Autumn takes its time in South Carolina, and winter never shows up at all, at least not from the perspective of a kid from New England. And maybe that was the problem. Maybe that was why it didn't seem urgent when she asked me to come home. Because the trees stayed green, and the snow never fell, and so it didn't seem like time was passing. But once I finally went back, when the calendar indicated Christmas had arrived, time was all over Emma's face. It was in her posture, in the way she kept her mouth closed, mostly, when we kissed.

Still, I didn't get it.

Early that second semester, already hot in South Carolina, and she called and told me she'd been with someone else. No, not just been with, she corrected herself. *Was* with. Present tense. Ongoing.

Over the next week everything fell from me. I could actually feel the physical descent away of most of what I had, until that moment, considered meaningful. Classes, the very notion of school. Friends, garden-variety college fun, the Solo cups and cheap beer, the earnest drunken talks. I stopped brushing my teeth, to give you an idea.

And then I dropped out. I didn't bother with the formalities and paperwork; I just left. And went north, and presented myself to Emma.

And we lay down on her bed together, in the house she shared with her mother, and I said: I came home like you asked.

And she said, Too late.

And that was the thing that happened on the bed in the house Emma shared with her mother.

The day after talking with Roberto, I woke up with a big head, sunlight slicing through a gap where the blackout curtain had drifted away from the window. Checked my phone, saw I had two text messages. One from my friend Hankie: 'Where's our boy?' And the second, from my only other friend, Dwayne: 'Come out, come out, wherever you are.'

I got out of bed and scrubbed my face until it stung. Slapped myself a few times, checked my reflection, decided I was presentable, if barely. I drove to the ferry dock and found them standing outside the bar across the street, beers in hand, watching a table of leathery old men play dominoes.

I was glad to see them, but the chief emotion I felt at their sudden, incongruous presence was relief. I took off my sunglasses, exchanged one-armed, back-slapping hugs.

What brings you to Hades? I asked.

We sensed a disturbance in the Force, Hankie told me. What the fuck happened to your face?

When my father was sick his bruises wouldn't heal. I learned, by watching him, that this is a hallmark of the true endgame: the body stops bothering to repair itself. One bruise in particular, on the back of his hand, lingered for the last two months of his life. He wasn't engaged in any vigorous work at that point, of course, so there must have been some sort of relatively benign domestic accident involved. Maybe he whacked his hand with the refrigerator door or something. I never asked.

Whatever the cause, that bruise persisted. It started off normal, purple and well-defined, but then instead of fading it devolved to a deep black and stayed on, implacable as rot. And really that's what it was. A spot on my father's hand, rotting. Giving up the ghost a bit before he did.

When I noticed that circle of black, I understood that it was over. This understanding arrived unencumbered by any definable emotion. I could have been reading a weather forecast, for all that I felt. It was just a sign.

At Duffy's, Dwayne and Hankie and I stood outside the bar smoking cigarettes, and I told them how the week before one of the island's ubiquitous retired gringas had asked me what my impressions were of the Samson parable in the Bible. Like, what the takeaway was. The moral. And I said I told the woman the moral of the Samson parable was that, given half a chance, a woman will take a dump in your heart, and *fin*. And then of course the gringa bristled, thinking I meant to make a gender debate out of the whole thing, which was not my intent. The guys groaned at this, and drew on their cigarettes, and we all three recognized the moment and took pleasurable advantage of it, flicking our cigarettes into the gutter and returning to the table to talk righteous shit about the women in our lives, and women in general, cracking crass jokes and generalizing and hitting all the clichés and believing them and laughing and not feeling a bit bad about any of it. Hankie loved his wife and I loved Emma and Dwayne just loved women, but we hated them, too, and hated on them, and drank to our hate, once, twice, a third time, turning our empty shot glasses upside down on the table, and at the end of it we left arm-in-arm and each felt, though we didn't talk about it, ready to return to these women and be better.

Maybe a week before my father died I broke down in front of him for the first and last time. I'd cried while he was sick, of course, but never in the same room with him. If I felt a jag coming on I'd go to the bathroom, or make up some reason why I suddenly and urgently had to leave. But that day I just gave in, went to my knees on the carpet in front of the La-Z-Boy he pretty much lived in those last months, put my face in his lap, soaked his pant legs with tears and snot.

And he uncharacteristically put a hand on my head and let it rest there. And he quite characteristically said, Come on, now, stop. I'm not dead yet.

Hankie said, Listen to me: the further you crawl up a woman's ass, the more she will despise you. Word to the wise.

He sipped his beer, gave an authoritative nod to emphasize the point.

Well no shit, I said.

Dismiss me at your peril, he said, then leaned forward and put his hands flat on the table. Listen, I can simplify all this for you. I can solve all your problems before you're finished your beer. Is that something you might be interested in?

I've got nowhere else to be, I told him.

Alright. Get ready. Here's the thing. Here's what women want.

Give us a minute to brace ourselves, Dwayne said. Remember, this sort of wisdom comes easy to you, but for us it's like staring at the sun.

Get bent, Hankie said.

I will, Dwayne said. Just as soon as you're finished.

Okay, Hankie said. Neither one of you is or ever has been married. I've been married ten years. Happily. And this is from the horse's mouth, too, by the way. I didn't come up with this on my own. This is what Lisa told me: women want us to adore them.

Wow, Dwayne said after a pause. Just, wow.

Wait for it, Hankie said, holding up one finger. They want us to adore them, but not for the reason you think.

Okay, I said.

They want us to adore them, Hankie continued, not because it makes them feel good, but because it facilitates their need to suck us dry. They want to squeeze every drop of life out of us, leave us nothing but a husk, like what a fly looks like when a spider is done with it. But here's the problem. Just as they're about to get those last few drops out of us, they realize that they're the ones who are hooked in. They realize they adore us right back. Next thing they know, they're carrying our kids around in their bellies and washing our underwear for us.

Dwayne and I stared at him, dubious.

Horse's mouth, Hankie said, and sipped his beer.

Nightfall found us at the same table at Duffy's. Across the street, a group of caballeros tied their horses to the railing next to the water. They lit cigarettes and glared at us. I pointed them out to Hankie and Dwayne.

Those the fuckers that knocked your teeth out? Hankie asked.

Hard to say, I told him. Might be the same ones. Might not be.

It made no difference to Hankie; he set about endearing himself to the caballeros. He flipped them off, grinning. He hawked magnificently and spat in their direction. He pointed at them, then drew a finger across his throat. He laughed while they glowered. The bartender came over and told him to cool it, and though Hankie wasn't afraid of the caballeros, he was afraid of being cut off, so he cooled it.

We should roll those fucks, he muttered over a fresh beer. See if they're so eager to scrap when it's five on three instead of five on one.

But the caballeros didn't like those odds, apparently, because despite Hankie's goading they eventually saddled up and clattered down the street.

Pussies, Hankie said.

I had a feeling that I'd end up paying for his impudence, but I didn't want him to feel bad about that, so I said nothing.

By his own count Hankie had almost died six separate times, owing to the fact that he was narcoleptic. All these near-fatalities were ignoble, including the latest: he was at home late, the kids and Lisa long since in bed. He had smoked a bit of hash earlier in the night, which he'd followed with a vodka tonic and a few beers in front of the television after Lisa retired. He found himself watching something called *Barbecue U.* on public television, and he got hungry and went into the kitchen to heat a pair of Hot Pockets. Sat back down on the sofa, got through the first one okay. A bite or two into the second he fell asleep, an unchewed slab of pastry and marinara lodged between his molars. When it slid back into his trachea he woke with a start. After a moment his brain came fully awake, and a sudden awful clarity descended. He tried to call to Lisa but couldn't make a sound. He had maybe a minute before he blacked out and it would be over and his son would come downstairs in the morning for school and find his father stiff and outstretched on the carpet. This thought got Hankie moving. He stood and staggered into the kitchen and slammed himself down on the back of a wooden dining chair half a dozen times, bruising his sternum and diaphragm.

That sounds painful, I said.

I wanted to live, goddammit, Hankie said.

I don't know, I told him. I think I may have just sat there and suffocated. I mean, if it's a choice between that and skewering myself on the back of a chair.

You need to get real, Hankie said. You need to have a fucking family, for starters.

On the beach the next day, I asked Hankie if he'd ever passed out in the midst of coitus.

He rolled his eyes. Have I ever passed out having sex? Think about who you're asking. I *constantly* pass out having sex.

Ask a stupid question, I said.

So listen to this. Back in like 1992 I was in the middle of nowhere in upstate New York, across the border from Vermont, shooting a movie.

Before he and Lisa got married, Hankie had worked for a while as an actor.

We finished the shoot, he said, and we're all just hanging around for the night before we head back to wherever we came from. The art director on the film was this older woman named Frankie. That was actually her name. Wasn't like short for Frances or anything. Hankie and Frankie, no shit. But so we all sat around and got drunk to celebrate the end of the shoot, and I end up in bed with Frankie. And we're being friendly and fooling around, and I actually pass out with my fingers inside her. And then I come to who knows how much later, and she's still there in bed, all snuggled up as if she hadn't had to pull my fingers out of her after I fell asleep. The kicker is, after that she *still* wanted to go with me to Boston the next day. By the way don't talk to my wife about this or I'll kill you.

Lisa is aware that you had sex before the two of you met, right? Dwayne said.

She'd be mad that I was talking to you about it.

Don't worry, I said. I won't say a word to her. But it's going in the book.

What *book*? Hankie asked.

That night we drank shots of Old Grand-Dad, toasting, in order: all the women we'd slept with in the past, my dead father, Hankie's family, and the bright shining day in the near future when we would find ourselves together again.

We didn't realize Hankie had had one of his narcoleptic episodes until he went backwards off his stool and hit the wood floor head-first.

But he was energized, apparently, by the catnap and attendant head contusion, because when we piled into the Jeep after the bartender threw us out, he insisted on driving. We veered wildly through the streets, laughing like we were in high school again, like we'd invented drinking and driving, and Hankie took the turn onto my road too wide and slammed the grill of the Jeep into a palm stump on the corner. Water sprayed from the radiator, soaking the dirt, and blood ran in a trickle from my scalp and down my face. Hankie and Dwayne laughed even harder when they saw I was bleeding, and I laughed along with them, though by that point, mildly concussed, I didn't have any idea what we were laughing at.

On Monday morning I dropped them off at the ferry terminal. I didn't know it then, but the bright shining day in the near future when we'd find ourselves together again would not ever come to pass.

After Dwayne and Hankie's departure, after Roberto's wisdom, I reached out to Emma anew. But she continued to elude me, offering the occasional brief brusque message and little more, always only in response to a message I sent her. What she did not seem to understand—or what she understood just fine but was unable to rise to—was that when I told her I was going to the beach and wished she were there to accompany me, I wasn't reporting the facts of my day to her like some news ticker. I was trying to rivet her to my moments, and myself to hers, insofar as was possible from half a world away.

But her response, when it came at all, would read something like: Sounds nice. Enjoy the sun.

There are those who believe that after the Singularity, machines will not just be perfect lovers to one another, but to human beings as well. In fact, if the machines allow us to go on existing, and if we don't succumb to the terminating effect of our own uselessness, people may never have relationships with one another again.

You scoff, but listen: we develop emotional attachments to inanimate objects as a matter of course—and these things offer only the clunkiest, most transparent facsimiles of companionship. Yet already we often prefer them over people.

A man passes time in the garage, tinkering idly with his vintage Camaro, rather than play cribbage with his wife.

A child simulates feeding and caring for an electronic key-chain pet, rather than pay attention to the very real and oft-neglected family dog.

A teenager spends hours communing with two-dimensional images on a television screen without speaking a word to the family camped out on furniture all around him.

We do these things, make these choices, every day.

Given this, don't you think a man would prefer the machine that pretends to love him, rather than the woman who pretends she doesn't?

Or, in turn, don't you think that this same woman, while pretending not to love the man, would prefer the machine that offers unconditional and flawless middle-aged maternal affection, rather than the flesh-and-blood mother who tries over and over to kill her?

The answer, of course, is an easy yes. If you're being honest.

Emma, of course, being the woman who pretended not to love the man. Which in turn makes her own personal mother the flesh-and-blood mother trying over and over to kill her.

This is not, as you'll see, an exaggeration.

Emma often talked about having to raise herself, and from what I saw this was a fair assessment. Her father was a weekends-and-holidays ghost before she even graduated from a stroller, and through her childhood her mother descended into a slow burn of alcoholism and manic depression, with fierce laser-beam rage aimed directly at her only daughter.

By the time I came on the scene in high school, trouble could occur between them violently and without preamble, like a tornado touching down out of cloudless skies. The usual sad litany: bruises and cuts no one talked about, fleeing to a girlfriend's in the middle of the night, walking tense circles around her mother for days after an episode.

Usually the worst of it occurred when no one else was around. One time, though, it happened right in front of me.

Years later, Emma and I were having brunch, and she said, Sometimes I think it really wasn't as bad as I make it out to be in my mind. Like maybe there were one or two things that happened, really bad things, but beyond that it wasn't remarkable at all. Just your garden variety mother-daughter stuff.

I sipped my Bloody Mary. That's sort of classic, though, right? I said.

What do you mean?

Just that it seems like often when people are abused, especially by people they love, they end up having selective memories about it, to protect both themselves and the people who hurt them. End up making excuses, or else just omitting memories wholesale.

Maybe, Emma said. It's all pretty jumbled, and I have a shitty memory besides.

Maybe that's precisely why you have a shitty memory, I thought but did not say.

Instead I said, Let me tell you something I remember. This is back in high school. You and I were sitting at the kitchen table in your house. Your mother was on the phone, on your behalf in some capacity, like maybe she was talking to a teacher, or your soccer coach, or whatever. And you tried to get her attention—you wanted to tell her something to relay to the person on the other end. When you tried to get her attention she held up one finger to silence you, like this.

I held my own index finger up, put it right in Emma's face, two inches from her eyes, hanging over her plate of poached eggs and hash, over the ramekins of butter and syrup, a black memory casting shadows on the detritus of our happy Sunday afternoon.

And then, I told her, a few moments later, you tried to get her attention again. And this time there was no warning. I don't even think the words were completely out of your mouth before she slapped you. Full-on, digging back and swinging from the hips. Turned your head around. You put your face down, stared at your lap, and you didn't cry and it seemed like you didn't dare to even put a hand to your face to feel at the damage. It was like you were trying to be still enough that you disappeared. But the worst part was, I did nothing. I just sat there and clenched my jaw. I wanted to put my fist through your mother's face. But I did nothing.

Emma stared at me. Really?

Really, what?

That really happened?

Yes.

Are you sure?

Emma. I'm not the only one who remembers her doing things like that to you.

She looked down at the tabletop, much as she did on that day fifteen years previous, and stirred her Bloody Mary. Finally she said, It's really embarrassing, you know, to realize you're walking around with a memory like that in your head.

Around that same time, Emma received a Christmas card from her mother, with whom she hadn't spoken since the summer. She gave it to me, and I struggled to read the messy script, written in the unsteady hand of a woman who had drunk herself into a host of physical disabilities:

> *My Dear Emma,*
> *Wishing you all the best in your life and career this Christmas,*
> *and in the new year. I'm sorry I wasn't a better mother when*
> *you needed a mother the most. I married a Scorpio. I knew*
> *something was wrong but I couldn't get out. You know him and*
> *how he was. Anyway I hope you are well and happy. Have a*
> *happy holiday season and please don't forget me.*
> >   *Love, your Mother*

The week before Christmas, before I left for the island, Emma was rummaging through a storage unit, separating her things from her soon-to-be-ex-husband's, and she came across several of his journals and made the mistake of reading them. She called me halfway through the third notebook, and I could hear she'd been crying.

She said, Sometimes I feel like I'm doomed.

You're not *doomed*, I told her. That's ridiculous.

I mean yes Matty left me, but it's not as though I was blameless in all this. Far from it.

Okay, I said.

Because listen we know I didn't exactly have a great model, growing up, for how to take care of people. And there were plenty of times with him that I was hateful, or indifferent, or plain mean. There were times when he needed me to carry more of the load, and I didn't manage it.

Alright, I said.

So when I say I feel like I'm doomed, what I mean is I worry that I'm turning into my mother.

I thought about this a minute, and it felt like nothing so much as a warning.

You're not doomed, I said. Are not. You don't even live in the same neighborhood as doomed.

Two days before Christmas I drove to Emma through a sudden snowfall. Every ten miles or so I hit a pocket of whiteout, and had to pull into the breakdown lane and wait. The car drifted and shimmied, and I held the steering wheel as though it were a life preserver. Plow trucks bombed past, pelting me with slush and road salt through the driver's window, which I'd opened to vent cigarette smoke. I'd left early in the morning to beat the worst of the storm, and when I got to her place she was still in bed. The shades were drawn. In the half-light I could see her smiling with her cheek pressed against the mattress, and I said cheerfully, Mind if I join you?, and she said, Of course not, and I stripped down to my drawers and climbed under the covers, happy and stupid. She didn't slide across the mattress to meet me, and this was the first indication that something was wrong. The next and clearer indication was when I heard her sniffling.

Hey, I said. What's the matter?

She made an exasperated sound, then was silent for a few moments, then said, Thinking about last Christmas.

When Matty was still here.

Yeah. But it wasn't a great time. It was a disaster, in fact. He told me he didn't love me, and hadn't for quite a while.

That's some Swiss-type timing, there.

We lay quietly side by side under the covers, careful not to touch.

Then she said, I was glad when I heard you come in. I'm glad you're here. I wanted to tell you that when you first came upstairs, but I couldn't get the words to come out of my mouth.

Good, I said. That's good, that you're glad I'm here.

Listen, it's not because I miss him. It's not that at all. Days when I wake up feeling this way, I just don't have anything to give. And that's not fair to you.

I understand, I said. It's like the Berryman poem: 'I must start to sit with a blind brow above an empty heart.'

That's perfect, she said. That's it exactly.

We had a good day despite her upset. Big greasy brunch, after which she walked with me to the Old Port to assist with some emergency Christmas shopping. With her help I found two gifts for my mother in no time, and I goofed around and made her smile in spite of herself. Then to dinner, and a few drinks, and back home, where I showered while she read in bed. I climbed in next to her and she tried, she plumbed herself to find something to give me, and she climbed on top of me and kissed my face, my eyes, and my lips, but the whole time she kept making these sad little sounds I didn't understand, and then she said I'm sorry, I just can't, and I took her under the arms and lifted her off me and set her down on the mattress. It's okay, I said, and meant it. I stroked her hair for quite a while, until her breathing evened out and grew deep, and no other parts of our bodies touched except for my hand, her head.

But other times her grief would recede, and in those moments we often fell together like the teenagers we'd been. The last Sunday before Christmas I got up early, walked out in the cold with my head bent to the wind, in search of the paper and coffee for her. I was always happy to run morning errands, because I liked the idea of her warm under the covers while I strode around, and also because it gave me a chance to have a cigarette. I returned with the *Times* and a medium breakfast blend with cream, got undressed again, washed the smoke off my face and hands, crawled back under the covers with her. She opened the front section; I grabbed the Book Review. It wasn't long, though, before the paper's component parts fell unfurled to the carpet and we got tangled up in each other. I kissed the length of her left leg, let my tongue loiter in the hollow where thigh met hip, close enough to tease, then up the left side of her torso, lingered again at her breast, then on to her neck, ear, throat, across her jawline, to the other ear, then back down the right side of her. Her skin hot, almost burning, from being so long under the comforter. I tugged her panties down over her knees, and she flicked them off her toes. She was ready to come the moment I touched her, but she fought it for four, maybe five minutes, and when she finally gave in she pulled away from me and clamped down on the meat beneath her thumb to keep from screaming, and she went from flat on her back to sitting up straight against the headboard, bite-marked hand now splayed over her face. Behind that hand she was laughing.

We talked and joked, adrift in warm pheromonal ease, the newspaper scattered about the floor, forgotten, and then I went after her again. When it was over she struggled to catch her breath. In between gasps she said, Jesus I need to get out of this *bed*, and we both laughed long and loud, peering at each other, eyes squinted and welling, sharing our mirth like a meal.

If this were one of the novels I used to write, I would portray Emma's mother as a monochromatic villain, because that would be her sole function within the narrative. But this world does not produce monochromes, of course. Hitler loved animals, and passed a law requiring citizens of the Reich to use humane methods when killing lobsters. Pol Pot was, by all accounts, gentle and kind as a boy. Slobodan Milošević married his high school sweetheart. Even Mike Tyson reserved an alcove, in his otherwise murderous heart, for the gentle care of homing pigeons. By the same token, Emma's mother is evil and sad and ill, but she is not a monster. She is, at times, possessed of love, both for her daughter and others.

She apparently even has a soft spot for me, which I learned one night before Emma sent me away to the island. We were at my place making chili. I diced the onions at Emma's request, and she laughed at me as I sniffled and grinned and tears rolled down my face. Somehow we got to talking about how her mother had kept the eight-by-ten of me and Emma at the prom, had left the thing hanging on the wall in her living room for years, which to me seemed hilarious and strange and more than a little improbable.

It's true, Emma said, laughing. I don't know why . . . I think she really loved the dress I wore.

It was red, right? I asked, and she nodded.

I remember that dress, I said. I poked her with my index finger, and she leaned away and cast a mock-scolding glance in my direction.

Then she said, But so you know what's really funny about that. Here's my mother, of all people, holding onto this ridiculous photo all these years, right?

Not ridiculous, I said. We made a handsome couple.

We did, she said. And we've made good-looking couples with other people, too. Because we're good-looking people. Anyway she's got this picture, and then the night before my wedding, in the slide show at the rehearsal dinner . . .

You've got to be fucking kidding me, I said.

Swear to god, she said. I'm sitting there watching the slide show that she and Erica put together, both our families there, Matty sitting right next to me, everybody's smiling and happy, right, and that fucking prom picture comes up on the screen. I nearly choked to death on a canapé.

I slid onions into the pot to sauté and said, Who put it in there?

Had to be my mother.

Jesus. She could have at least cropped me out, for God's sake.

Oh no, Emma said, still laughing. That wouldn't do. Not at all.

I thought a minute while I stirred the onions. Should have taken it as a sign, I guess.

Of what?

Maybe your mother knew something we didn't. Maybe she knew that the goofy guy in the tuxedo next to you would never really be out of your life.

At this Emma rolled her eyes. What*ever*, she said.

Listen, again, a reiteration: this is me talking to you. This is me telling you the truth. As evidence of my forthrightness, I offer these embarrassing facts, which I obviously would not reveal if not for my dedication to comprehensive honesty:

One: this morning I masturbated—this is nothing unusual—then realized I was out of cigarettes and so went immediately to the nearest gas station without washing, and as I gave the clerk my debit card I realized my hand would probably light up like a Mannheim Steamroller concert if someone passed a black light over it. I should also mention that I used a visual aid for my masturbation session, and the theme of that visual aid was an older woman, mid-forties maybe, seducing a boy who appeared to be no older than twenty; this is not necessarily a fetish of mine, simply what I found myself in the mood for on waking.

Two: I have, in the last week, shed sincere unashamed tears while listening to 'Separate Lives' by Phil Collins, and twice while viewing a television commercial currently in heavy rotation featuring a sick boy whom United Airlines flew gratis to a renowned children's hospital for treatment. It was impossible not to be aware of the obvious cold corporate intent to paint United as a benevolent and socially engaged entity rather than a monolithic conglomerate whose sole fealty lies with its shareholders, and despite my awareness of this intent I still cried, and felt weird and silly about that, but have since decided that my emotional reaction was, you know, what it was.

Three: since meeting her in my thirteenth year I have been willing, even eager, to turn myself over to Emma, to let her decide what I should think and how I should behave at any moment—i.e., despite the appearance of a strong will and firm boundaries, I'm all too eager to make myself her automaton. I would do it even now, if she'd have me.

So with Emma's disappearance my frustration spiked there in the heat and the dust on the island, and I saw everything through the lens of this frustration. Bartenders and store clerks seemed un-friendly, even hostile. The few vacationers—giddy with the isolation of the place and the faux adventure it implied, the virgin beaches they had almost to themselves, the guilt-free A.M. cocktails—baffled me with their smiles, with the joyous sounds they made in the street outside my windows.

Nothing was a comfort. I started to feel loose, lethal. In my more rational moments I worried, as the caballeros continued to pick fights, that on the wrong night I might kill someone. And then, right on cue, there occurred a circumstantial confluence that sent the whole thing corkscrewing wildly off into thoughtlessness, and petty re-venge, and regret, with barely a moment to look around and make an attempt to understand what was happening.

Life, I have found, is often only too willing to provide that little push. The butterfly flaps its wings, and lo.

In this case the butterfly came disguised as a text message from a friend named Rick, a bar acquaintance back home who, after a long stint in the Marines, after getting divorced from his wife of ten years, had enrolled in college on the GI Bill, and now was on spring break and happened to be traveling around the archipelago Emma had exiled me to.

Rick was interesting to me insofar as he was pure Id, nothing more or less than the sum of his appetites, of which the three stron-gest were for dope, rugby, and young women. In other words, a good guy to drink with, and little else.

I hadn't heard from Emma in a week—she'd dematerialized into work, meetings, lunches and dinners, political fund-raisers—and that morning I sat at the beach, scribbling in a notebook and sipping a pint of Palo Viejo, trying to calm myself by watching pelicans as they dive-bombed the surf over and over.

This was the state of things when my phone chimed with Rick's message. Pissed off. Tipsy at eleven in the morning. Suggestible. It's no excuse, but still.

The text read, in part, that Rick had 'some serious specimenz from the opposite sex' in tow. Presumably, these were coeds of a more traditional age for undergraduate students than Rick himself, and while I wasn't at all interested in that, I figured what the hell. It wasn't like I was doing much else of consequence. I was watching pelicans eat, for Christ's sake.

I picked Rick and his three specimenz up at the ferry dock, and we drove to the *malecón* and started in with Bloody Marys before the sun reached its apex. By the time the sun had set we were all drunk, and bent sideways on some unidentified pills Rick had distributed. One of the specimenz, a thin, pretty blonde named Charlotte who kept her oversized Jackie O sunglasses on well after dark, attached herself to me.

Charlotte informed me that she was a comparative literature major, and she'd seen me lecture at U Maine twice. She pressed her thigh against mine in the open-air booth. She smelled like booze and aloe, and under that hovered the sharp fecundity of a bottle of multivitamins. She talked about Saul Bellow, and yoga. I listened, mostly, as the second unidentified pill, plucked from Rick's hand in the bathroom and washed down with tap water from the sink, started to turn on me. I thought I felt Charlotte grip my knee under the table, but I couldn't be sure.

Though my senses were leaving me I suggested we drive out to Playa Navio for some night swimming. Navio had the roughest surf of all the island's beaches, and with a southern swell roaring up from Venezuela it would be rougher than normal. I was trying to save myself from Charlotte, but I can't tell you how I imagined going to the beach would accomplish that. Maybe I planned to just swim until I reached South America.

We piled into the Jeep, a boozy mess. On the center console my phone flashed its LED, a green beacon informing me I had messages. I let it sit untouched.

Stars glittered wildly above the water at Navio. In the moonlight, breakers curled into black barrels and pounded the sand. Two of the specimenz saw this and balked, but Charlotte stripped down to just her bikini bottom and joined me and Rick in the surf.

We fought our way past the break, to where the water was calm enough to swim comfortably. I was counting on Rick's indiscriminate lechery to save me from Charlotte, and he didn't disappoint, paddling over to her and speaking in hushed tones as she laughed, his hands presumably on her flesh under the water. Fine enough. I flipped over and floated on the swells with only my nose above the surface. The claustrophobic hush beneath sounded like the womb to me.

The next thing I knew, Rick was pulling me through sea foam up onto the beach while the specimenz fussed and worried above, their three faces framing the moon.

If you asked me now whether I'd simply passed out and gone under, or if I'd intended to drown myself, I wouldn't be able to answer you with anything resembling certainty. But I do remember thinking, as they all four stood gazing down while I lay on my back in the wet sand, that I wished Rick had been too preoccupied with Charlotte to notice that I'd disappeared under the swells. I do remember that, if I'm being honest.

And apparently my near-drowning renewed Charlotte's interest— or perhaps she'd never lost interest and had only been using Rick to try and stir me from my indifference—because when we left she insisted on driving, and she dropped Rick and the specimenz off at the Crow's Nest, and then, and only then, drove me back to the pink stucco casita.

The butterfly flapped its wings. Charlotte helped me up the back steps, unlocked the door, and pushed me onto the bed. When she started taking my clothes off I responded with all the vigor of a quadriplegic. She did what she wanted, and while I didn't exactly participate, I didn't stop her, either.

And for the first time in nearly twenty years I genuinely, if temporarily, did not care about Emma. I didn't care about anything, in fact. Charlotte and I could have burst into flames, for all the difference it would have made to me. We could have fallen instantly and irrevocably in love. The Earth's poles could have reversed. My father could have stumbled in, trailing dirt from the grave.

Of course, none of those things happened. Charlotte made do with my limp indifference, moaning and crying out in ways I remember thinking seemed like a put-on, and the next morning, while she lay sleeping it off in my bed, I smoked on the porch with my head down, and the sun didn't shine on the island so much as beat on it, it seemed.

There was a moment that next day, somewhere between my sixth and tenth beers, when I realized it was possible, likely even, that the reason I didn't trust Emma had nothing to do with her and everything to do with me.

Like the song says, it's no secret that a liar won't believe anyone else.

Because even before Charlotte happened on the scene, I knew the treacherousness that resided in me, and in a deep place beyond words and reason I believed that this same duplicity existed in everyone—Mother Teresa, Gandhi, the Pillsbury Doughboy, and, yes, even Emma, especially Emma.

These are all my imaginings, understand. Me being the template for the universe, as we all are in our little skull-size fiefdoms, it made a certain kind of sense.

That previous Christmas eve, before attending a cocktail party, Emma brought over champagne and two flutes, and we sat on the love seat and chatted, and she talked about how she hosted parties sometimes with a guy she'd had a brief thing with down in Washington where she worked, and that in turn led to her telling me about yet another guy who was always trying to date every woman in their social circle there, and how this guy had tried to kiss her at one of these parties.

Again, this is the way it was with Emma—men swirling about her even while she was married, men steering ships into the rocks over and over. There was a strange comfort in the knowledge that I was anything but alone in my obsession with her. Still, it was dizzying, and troubling, to know that others danced and preened in the hopes of winning her affection, and especially troubling to hear about it in her calm, matter-of-fact tone, as if she were discussing nothing of more significance than what she'd eaten for breakfast that morning.

If you want to be happy for the rest of your life, never make a pretty woman your wife.

But anyway on Christmas eve I didn't think much of it, really, and we went to the cocktail party, where I knew everyone and Emma knew no one, and she drank red wine and made friends and sort of lit up the room, quickly and efficiently gathering the attention of the men there, as she always did. Watching her I started to wonder suddenly about the guy who had tried to kiss her in Washington, wondered how complicit she'd been in the whole thing, though she'd characterized it as being completely on him.

After, we went back to my place and stayed up late drinking. We woke after just a few hours' sleep and exchanged gifts. I gave her a pair of earrings from Tiffany; she gave me a photo, in a beautiful custom frame, of the two of us on a trip to Ireland from a few months before. We made breakfast, drank more champagne. It was nice. But now my mind had fixated on the abortive kiss in

Washington—the guy must have believed he had a green light for a reason, I thought. I wondered if she had, at first, returned the kiss, maybe even let him put his hands on her, and then thought better of it.

This thought blossomed and grew great black thorns, loomed over our breakfast like a floral centerpiece out of Lovecraft, and finally I asked Emma if she had, in fact, kissed the guy back.

She gazed at me evenly. For a moment, she said. He kissed me. I'd been drinking. He's not unattractive. But then the moment passed.

It was her nonchalance, you can understand, that really made my mouth go dry.

After breakfast we fell into bed again—no matter the upset or offense, all it took was one decent look at her in profile, one whiff of her essence underneath the previous evening's perfume, one look at her from behind as she walked away from me, and even if I found it impossible to forgive there was nothing I could not forget.

And in forgetting I regained myself. Pushed her face-first onto the mattress, flat on her belly. Grabbed her wrists and yanked them up, pressing them against the headboard in a way that made clear they were to stay there even after I let them go and set my hands to other things. She squirmed under my weight in faux protest, her legs coming open a bit. Here, in the bed, was the only place where she gave herself over to me, relinquishing control with a sigh as I checked her with one hand, found her inner thighs slick. With the other hand I grabbed a fistful of her hair and pulled hard, and she made muffled noises against the pillow as I pushed into her.

And then, afterward, she said that she loved me.

I couldn't think of anything that seemed like an appropriate response, so I asked her why she would say that.

She told me: Because it's true. I love you. I've loved you again, ever since I read the book.

When she got really turned on Emma sometimes grew angry. My mouth on her nipple, and she'd flail, growl at me a bit. My hand between her thighs, and her hands would clench into fists. It was an obvious effort for her to keep them pressed to the mattress at her sides instead of raising and wielding them.

It's not that I really want to hit you, she said once. Not at all.

I think you should.

Think I should *what*?

Hit me. When the impulse happens. See where it goes.

No.

You're afraid.

Of course I'm afraid.

Which is precisely why you should hit me. See what's lurking behind that impulse. You might be surprised at what you find.

Listen, she said, I know what you're getting at, okay. I just think these are things better investigated with my therapist.

You're going to punch your therapist?

Smiling: Fuck off.

And besides, I said, who said anything about therapy? I'm thinking if you actually hit me you'd probably find yourself as turned on as you've ever been in your life.

But to what end? she asked, her smile melting. To what end, Ron?

So Emma demurred at first, but what I said sank in, intrigued her as much as it frightened her, I think, because after that conversation the sex grew, by turns, more and more violent, and more and more compelling. Her hands used to trace gentle paths along my sides, but now they hooked into claws, raked the corridor between my shoulder blades. She'd close her eyes and let her mouth form a delicate, gorgeous sneer that I wanted more than anything to jam all manner of appendages into, roughly, without regard; I was willing to slough skin against her teeth so long as I could hurt her in kind. She'd grab my cock and squeeze it in her fist, and I'd respond by flipping her off of me and onto her back, putting my hand around her throat and easing my weight down onto it while she snarled defiance.

Our talk turned brutal, too—I've said nicer things in bar fights than in bed with her.

We upped the ante every time we took our clothes off, until, on a still frigid night in January just before I left for the island, she straddled me, rubbing my pubis against herself and moaning, and then she reached back from above and punched me on the jaw, a clean, solid shot, her rings on, easily one of the five hardest punches I've ever taken.

The moment her fist made contact she drew her hands back to her face and said, from behind them, Oh my God I'm sorry!

But I didn't give her regret time to take hold. Still reeling, operating on instinct, I reached up and grabbed her hair and pulled it, hard enough to take a dozen strands away on my hand.

Charlotte stayed on for a while, and I let her—out of stasis, out of loneliness, out of a desire for someone other than me to make breakfast. Rick and the other two specimenz flew back to the mainland. Charlotte told me that, before they left, one of the specimenz had asked her what on Earth she was doing, what she was thinking.

I wondered the same thing myself, but wasn't interested enough in the answer to actually ask.

In fact, I wasn't interested in anything at all, during those first two weeks. My state of mind could best be described as one of pure indifference. I didn't care if Charlotte was taking up space in my casita, or in my bed, and I didn't care if she wasn't. She was there, so I slept with her, but if I'd woken up the next day and found myself alone I wouldn't have given half a thought to where she'd gone, or why.

For her part Charlotte maintained a calm, detached air, which didn't seem to mesh with the fact that she'd blown off school, her friends and family—her entire life, really—to shack up with a complete stranger, albeit one who'd written a book and carried himself with the messy, tragic bent that a certain kind of woman seems to find appealing, at least until she approaches thirty or so, after which she recognizes it as self-indulgent nonsense and steers clear with the same zeal with which she used to pursue.

Maybe it wasn't fair to generalize about Charlotte, an actual individual person, in this way, but she didn't give me anything else to go on at first. I passed hours without speaking and she rarely tried to penetrate my silence, opting instead to read (she'd started with *The Corrections*, but put it aside and began sifting through the copy of my novel that I'd brought, which annoyed me in a distant way), to scribble in a notebook, to deepen her tan in the porch hammock. While I stared through windows at the Caribbean she moved casually around the casita, washing dishes, combing her hair, paying no attention to me at all. For whatever reason she'd decided to behave as if we enjoyed the intimacy of a longtime couple, as though we were a younger version of David and Penny—the sort of domestic arrangement people gradually and inevitably melt into, in which they only truly notice the other person in his or her absence. She saw a space next to me and tried to convince herself that she belonged there by rights. And when I thought about her at all, which was rare, I came to feel as though she deserved my indifference, because if she'd paid any attention to the few words I offered, or had even just given me a good long look, it would have been obvious to her that the space beside me was already occupied, and that if she placed herself next to the rightful occupant of that space, Charlotte herself was the one who disappeared.

From the outside it probably appeared to Charlotte, and maybe others, that I was in a foul mood, but really I'd come to occupy a place of apparent imperviousness—I was as comfortable as I'd been since the day before Emma and I had gotten together again all those months ago.

Or so I'd convinced myself. But of course my longing for her still ran in the background, buzzing like an air conditioner in high summer, easy to ignore and forget but nonetheless powered on.

Even so, I stopped waiting on tenterhooks for contact from Emma, and stopped sending messages and calling her myself. The ironic if predictable result of this was that she started reaching out with more frequency, wondering where I was, what I was doing, if I was alright.

'I know I'll always bear the responsibility of having sent you down there,' one message read, apropos of seemingly nothing. She intuited that I was in trouble, and this made me glad. I didn't respond.

Emma called one night when Charlotte and I were having dinner at El Quenepo and ignoring one another. While I talked on the phone right there at the dinner table, Charlotte continued to read.

You sound sort of . . . happy, Emma said, perplexed and a little worried at the combination of my sudden distance and concurrent high spirits, and I took some bitter, drunken pleasure in her discomfort, her confusion at being, for once, the person who got the slip, instead of the person who gave it.

I'm embarrassed beyond words to recount this pettiness. She'd gotten the biggest slip of them all, for God's sake: her husband had left.

Anyway, I probably did sound happy. There was something brittle in me masquerading as good cheer. I was talking through clenched teeth, but smiling at the same time.

So I told Emma as much: I'm smiling this very moment, I said.

Charlotte flipped a page in her book, then used the same hand to tuck a lock of hair slowly behind one ear, feigning absolute absorption, pretending not to care who I was talking to, pretending not to eavesdrop. I wanted, suddenly, to grab her by the shoulders and shake her, force her to stop acting like she didn't give a shit about anything.

It would turn out that the only way to get her to do that was to tell her she had to leave. But more on that in a minute.

Where are you? Emma asked. I hear music. I hear people laughing.

On the *malecón*. Having dinner.

By yourself?

No. You just said you heard people, right?

There was a pause. Listen, is there something wrong, Ron? Between us? There's very little I can't handle hearing—you know that. So if something's up you should say so. Because I have to tell you, right now I don't feel like we're on the same team.

Everything's fine, I told her. You just got done saying I sounded happy.

You can also just tell me you don't want to talk about it right now. I'll accept that, too. But I don't like being made to feel like I'm imagining things. You barely get in touch anymore. You've stopped calling. And when I call, you tell me you're smiling, and you talk in monosyllables. And you're cold as hell. Icy, even.

Listen, nothing's wrong. I just sort of figured it out. How to be apart from you and be okay with it. I thought you'd be happy.

You've got a strange idea, she said, of what makes me happy.

I sighed, then hated myself for sighing, such an impotent and ultimately dishonest thing to do, the refuge of those lacking the courage to articulate their displeasure. I glanced at Charlotte though I had no real interest in her; she was merely an object in front of me, something to fix my gaze on. She busied herself feigning interest in an open-air salsa place across the street, and I fought the urge to scoop a few cubes of ice out of my drink and toss them at her.

So listen, I said to Emma, gathering myself, what's going on up there? Anything you want to talk about?

She didn't respond right away, and then she said, with almost no inflection at all, The police have shelved the investigation.

I wasn't expecting this. Shelved? What does that mean?

Apparently it means it's not closed, but they're not wasting any time or resources on it, either. I guess because no one's tried to burn me alive for a while they've decided that no one tried to burn me alive in the first place. The detective says he's convinced whoever it was has moved on. Or that it was totally random in the first place and had nothing to do with me. Not that one of his hunches has ever been correct.

For the first time in days I felt something: concern, just the slightest needle point piercing my apathy. I didn't like this, didn't like how vulnerable it left Emma, especially in my absence. Because she was right—not one of the detective's hunches or suppositions had been correct. And further, he didn't understand what I knew intuitively, which was that it had obviously been a man who'd set fire to Emma's house, and men did not just move on from her.

I think he just doesn't want to deal with me anymore, Emma said of the detective. I think he wants to forget that I exist. Because as long as he's forced to acknowledge my existence, he has to remember how wrong he was to drag me in there over and over, to treat me like I'd burned my own house down. He's tired of feeling ashamed, is what's going on.

Maybe, I said. Could be.

When I hung up I asked Charlotte, Don't you want to know who that was?

She was reading again. Who who was? she asked, still not looking up from the book.

The next morning I awoke to my phone ringing. I reached across Charlotte, taking no care to avoid jostling her (not out of meanness, but because the fact of her presence registered so faintly with me that there seemed little need to take any care with it) and lifted the phone from the nightstand. I didn't recognize the number but answered anyway, and was surprised to hear the detective with the curly hair and predatory manner on the other end, the detective Emma had shamed into shelving her case.

We'd like you to come in for a few questions, he said.

I'm out of the country right now, I told him.

I know. This is no big deal, he said.

I was not inclined to believe him, and I'm not sure he intended for me to.

Don't go changing your travel plans or anything, he said. Really we should have brought you in at the beginning, since you were with Ms. Zielinski the night of the fire. Just whenever you get back, give me a call. You have my number on your phone, I presume.

I do now.

That's a direct line. Be in touch, please. And enjoy the sunshine.

The night that the detective wanted to question me about had taken place almost a year before, when Emma and I were still blinking hard at finding ourselves sharing a bed again. We managed to keep our clothes on long enough to go out and eat high-end pizza at a busy place on the waterfront. According to the menu the pizza dough was made from organic wheat. The mozzarella was organic, too, and the sausage nitrate-free.

I cracked wise about the eco-earnestness. Emma smiled politely.

Later we went to a pub where an acoustic two-piece alternated between traditional Irish folk songs and John Denver tunes. 'Whiskey in the Jar,' followed by 'Rocky Mountain High,' and so on. The place was jammed with a mix of yuppies and backward-ball-capped college types, but we lucked in to two seats at the bar. We talked and laughed and drank. After a while I suggested I was ready to switch from beer to scotch, and Emma decided to join me, somewhat reluctantly, but when she ordered a glass of Macallan I changed tack without really knowing why, and asked for a Guinness.

She punched me on the arm.

Near closing Emma got a text from a friend saying there was a fire in her neighborhood, very near her house, even possibly—the friend hated to say it because she didn't want to freak her out for no reason—*at* her house. The friend couldn't be sure; they had the block cordoned off, but damned if it wasn't awfully close.

We paid our tab and started to walk back. Emma always strode with purpose, but now I had a hard time keeping up with her. It was cold, and she blew into her hands while I assured her, from half a pace behind, that these sorts of anecdotal reports were always overblown. As we got closer we saw a great horizontal column of white smoke drifting westward against the night sky, and she walked yet faster.

I moved to grasp her hand, but she shook me off.

I really wasn't worried at all, even though I'd dropped my overnight bag at her house, and in that bag was my Mac, and on my Mac was every word I'd written for the last three years, including the novel I was six months late in delivering. I wasn't worried, even though I'd always been too lazy to back up my files. I wasn't worried, because I quite simply didn't believe her house was on fire. I still suffered from the common delusion that big bad things didn't happen to me or those I cared about, even though my father's death was recent enough that some nights I woke with the smell of his diseased body in my nostrils.

But that night Emma's house was actually on fire. We turned the corner onto her street, and half a block up, three ladder trucks were raining hydrant water on the A-frame she'd bought with her husband back when they still believed in one another, the little A-frame where more recently I'd passed out reading Chekhov on the love seat in the sunny nook of the bedroom they'd shared, and she'd arrived home and woken me with a cool palm to my face, and I'd made her come right there on the floor, within sight of no fewer than five photographs from her wedding day, photographs she could not yet bring herself to box and closet. Beautiful prints, expensively framed in museum glass, meant to endure and pass through the houses of children and grandchildren, meant to last so long that the people who ended up possessing them would have little idea who Emma and her husband were. Now in the process of becoming ash.

I had to grab her wrist to keep her from bolting up the street. There was nothing to be done, and even if she'd gotten past the cops standing guard at the end of the block the only thing it would have availed her was a better view of her life going up in flames. She fought me for a minute, but I gathered her in, and eventually she stopped struggling. She leaned against me and cried while I weathered a few moments of distant regret over my unfinished novel, now extremely unfinished. But then I found myself more interested in why Emma was crying: did she cry for the house itself, or for what it represented? And did it represent anything at all, really, except in its sudden absence?

Arson, according to the fire marshal's office. A window on the ground floor had been pried open, the frame splintered and the lock snapped off. The investigator mentioned something about charring patterns underneath the carpet in the living room which indicated beyond a doubt that the fire had been set. The insurance company was eager to conduct an investigation of its own. Meanwhile, Emma moved into a hotel. She was in the stretch run of a campaign and didn't have time to look for a new house. Plus there was the insurance company to deal with. Plus her husband was dragging his heels on their divorce even though he'd been the one who left. Plus she hadn't found time to buy enough clothes to keep herself in clean blouses for a full workweek. Plus she'd maybe started drinking a bit too much at night in the hotel lounge and found it difficult, some days, to get up for doing much of anything besides her job, which was part of the reason she hadn't yet bought enough clothes. Plus she still averaged two nights a week when she would break down out of nowhere, usually after washing her face and brushing her teeth and applying cream to her elbows and knees and getting in under the covers. She never wanted to talk during these jags, but she would send me text messages, and I would debate whether or not to just call her, try to divine from her words if that was what she wanted but couldn't ask for, and then I would call, and she wouldn't answer, and then eventually we'd both go to sleep, alone, in silence.

The police brought her husband in for questioning twice, but quickly lost enthusiasm when they perceived, correctly, that he was equally hapless and harmless, so they turned their attention to Emma. Of course I corroborated her whereabouts at the time of the fire, but the lead investigator, the man who had called me on the island, the short guy with a patient predatory manner like a leopard in repose, remained hungry for Emma—just like all the other men she knew.

The investigator questioned Emma five times. He could not have known at first how straight her spine was, but he found out quickly enough. She was indignant about being suspected, and in her indignation she grew fierce. She could have hired a lawyer to get the guy off her back, but she chose to take him on herself. She sat for, at first, as long as he wanted, and later, as long as he could take before wilting. She cried afterward, every time, but it would have been the second coming before she broke down in front of him. And when he finally was forced to release her the last time, it was with an apology that she waved away as if shooing a particularly persistent fly.

Then he turned his eye on easier prey. Namely, me.

After two weeks of Charlotte's apathy I decided, over beers at Duffy's, that it had to end. I drove home, performed a cockeyed parking job on the curb in front of the casita, and took the stairs to find her swinging languidly in the hammock. Her smooth, tanned calf drooped from the side of the netting, hanging by the fulcrum of one lovely knee. Her toes, capped by bright red nails, brushed the concrete floor as she swung back and forth. Her face was turned toward me but utterly blank; for all I could tell she was asleep, eyes closed behind the mirrored lenses of her Jackie O glasses. My novel rested unopened on her belly. In the last few days I'd had a growing sense that she was only pretending to read it; that in fact she only ever pretended to read anything. If I'd cared enough I might have quizzed her to test this hunch.

I gazed down at her, a little unsteady on my feet from an afternoon of Medalla and Don Q. She was the very picture of studied apathy, limbs limply askew and face expressive as a chunk of marble, and that was all I needed to realize the impulse that sent me screaming back to the casita had been the right one.

Okay, I said, listen, you have to go.

No visible reaction. Go where? she asked absently.

It doesn't matter to me at all, I told her. I'd say you should go home, resume classes, get your life in order. But I've got nothing—and I mean nothing—invested in whether or not you actually do that. You just have to leave. At least leave the island. Beyond that, you're free to do whatever you like, as far as I'm concerned.

Charlotte sat up and swung her legs over the side of the hammock; the equivalent, from her, of an outburst. What if I don't want to go? she asked, her tone still mild despite this sudden agitation.

Now I allowed my annoyance with her, roiling slowly under the surface for two weeks, to emerge. I want to ask you a very simple question, Charlotte, I said, and I want you to try to answer it honestly.

Finally, finally, she took off those sunglasses, and I was surprised to see that behind them her eyes had gone dark and guarded. She held her mouth in a rictus of anticipated damage. It was the first time I'd seen an expression on her face that did not have a studied intent, and for a moment I almost managed to feel something for her.

Then the moment passed, and I said, Should I take your outward attitude toward me—your utter indifference, I mean, in case it's not clear—as at all indicative of how you actually feel?

Charlotte looked at her feet. No, she said.

Thank you for being honest, I said. And so a follow-up question: let's put aside the fact that you barely know me, and so could not care as much about this arrangement as you probably imagine you do. Let's say for sake of argument that what you think you feel is, in fact, genuine. Why then, for the love of God, would you act as though you didn't care at all?

I waited a beat, two, and she offered nothing, so I prodded her.

I really want to know, I told her. I am sincere. I am trying to understand what motivates you. What you want. I am trying to understand what you *need*. God help me I am trying but I am also beginning to wonder if men and women could enjoy every advantage the future has to offer, lifetimes as infinite as the universe itself, the integration of human and artificial intelligence, and still never have even a basic understanding of each other.

At this Charlotte didn't cry, but she brushed up against it. Her eyes had grown wet, and now her mouth pulled thin and turned down at the corners, one step from devolving into a conduit for sobs, as she tried and failed to answer me.

Or maybe, I said, it's got nothing to do with cats and dogs. Maybe you're just really young, is the problem.

She wiped at her eyes, sniffling in a wet, open, crackling way that made clear she really needed to sniffle and wasn't just putting on a show. I seriously haven't got any idea what you're talking about, she said.

I looked down at her, and suddenly I saw her rawness, her sorrow, all on open display now, and for the first time in a long time I felt that comfortable, noncommittal tenderness I'd felt for every woman I'd been with since Emma dismantled me all those years before. In her sudden vulnerability, Charlotte somehow had opened that room inside me again.

We stripped the bed down to the fitted sheet and made love, and I was careful, putting one hand on her lower back and lifting her hips gently to meet me. She cried at one point, quietly, like water seeping through rock, and she did not punch me or carve gouges in my skin with her fingernails. For my part, I did not pull her hair, or leave any bruises on her. It was all very nice and calm and safe, and later, when we sat on the porch sipping Medalla and watching the sun set, she asked if it would be alright with me if she read my novel.

I had a feeling, I told her, that you were only pretending to read it before.

That's true, she said. That's what I was doing. I would look at the words and daydream and every once in a while when it seemed like I should turn a page, I'd turn a page. I didn't read any of it.

We were both quiet for a minute.

I don't even know why I was pretending, she concluded.

It's no problem, I said, leaning back against the stucco with my fingers laced behind my head. You're firmly in the majority, not having read it, if that makes you feel any better.

But I'd like to read it now. I mean, really read it.

Of course, I said.

Later, when the nocturnal insects and coqui frogs had set about their nightly call-and-response, Charlotte asked me, So who is the girl?

She'd read the first fifty pages or so of the book at this point.

Which girl? I asked.

The one you wrote about in here.

That's a character. Fictional. Made-up.

But not entirely, Charlotte said. There's someone real, for sure. A flesh-and-blood girl walking around out there somewhere. She's smart, and pretty, and she won't let you have her.

All three of those things, I said, are true.

And I could never replace her.

Also correct, I said.

That doesn't make any sense, Charlotte said. I'm right here. I could offer you everything. But you keep yourself for her.

I may be perennially reserved. But you see from this afternoon that I could be very, very nice to you regardless.

Still doesn't make any sense, she said.

I am inclined to agree with you, I told her.

Eventually the cancer in my father's lungs moved into his brain. He wasn't thinking right all the time, and his hands grew weak and he couldn't feel his feet and so he had to give up driving. He and my mother arranged to trade in his truck, along with the old Mercury Grand Marquis she drove, in exchange for a new SUV that would suit her after he was dead.

My father, present at that moment, was planning quite calmly for when he would, in the near future, no longer be present.

He had always been actual to himself. There had never been a time in his experience when he hadn't existed, and now he was being forced to consider and act upon the impending fact of his nonexistence. Something about that still strikes me as intensely strange and sad, though it's the sort of thing that has to be done, obviously, from a practical standpoint.

But so the day came to trade in their vehicles, and before driving to the dealership my mother and I cleaned the bed of the truck out in the driveway. My father, who was by then too weak to help, sat on a lawn chair in his checked hunting coat, buffeted by an autumn wind that swirled leaves at his feet. It felt like he was watching us clean him out of our lives. Which was in fact what we were doing—kindly, perhaps, regretfully, perhaps, but nevertheless. When we finished, he wanted to take the truck for one last drive. My mother didn't like that idea at all, and frankly neither did I, but the whole affair was sad enough without punctuating that sadness by telling him no, so I helped him into the driver's seat and got in on the other side, belted myself in.

An inauspicious start: he took out the mailbox with the passenger-side mirror before we even got out of the driveway. I would have laughed if he hadn't been dying. We got on the road and he settled down, even stopped for a phalanx of turkeys crossing 201, but all the same it was a lot like being sober in a car driven by a drunk—he weaved and drifted, crossed the center line several times, couldn't maintain speed. For about twenty minutes I tried to make myself tell him to pull over. Problem was, I'd never *told* my father anything. No one did. But I was starting to worry he would kill us, or someone else.

Finally I said it. He looked across the cabin at me, but didn't respond for a minute. He kept driving. Then he said, She treats me like a child now, you know. Your mother.

I didn't know what to say to that, so I just nodded.

He hit the steering wheel weakly with the heel of one hand. I'm not a goddamn child, he said, breathless in his sudden frustration.

I nodded some more.

And then, after another minute or so, he pulled over to the shoulder and put the truck in park. He was no longer angry, just resigned and pensive. I helped him get into the passenger side and arranged his oxygen bottle for him and drove back home, then to the dealership. And while my father admitted to the salesman, by way of signing paperwork, that he was not much longer for this world, I walked laps around a brand-new Mustang in the showroom, and thought of when my father had told me about the Mustang he'd dreamed of buying during the two years he spent getting shot at in Vietnam, the Mustang he'd not, after all, ever been able to afford, and now here he sat at the salesman's sad little desk with his back to this beauty, a Shelby GT, supercharged V8, and even if he'd had all the money in the world he couldn't have driven it even once.

One day while my father was sick, toward the end, I was supposed to be keeping an eye on him at the house while my mother ran errands, and there had been a gap of maybe an hour between when my sister had dropped him off from lunch and when I showed up to take over, an hour during which my father was alone, a casual and honest and heartbreaking mistake on my sister's and my part. When I arrived I looked down the hallway into the bedroom and saw my father asleep on top of the covers. I didn't want to disturb him because sleep came hard or not at all at that point, so I set up my laptop at the dining room table, in a spot where I had a line of sight to the bedroom. I noticed him stir a few times, but he never moved to get up, so I let him be and worked on my first novel. I was there for an hour before my mother arrived home and went to him and discovered what had happened. An hour. That was what I kept thinking about then, and what I think about now. A full hour I let him lie there. An hour, was what I thought, all I thought, as I used an old toothbrush and a bowl of warm soapy water to scrub the shit out of his toenails, shit that had run down his pant legs and settled into his socks when he couldn't get to the bathroom by himself after my sister dropped him off. And then when I arrived I left him like that. For an hour. An hour, an hour, an hour, was what I kept thinking about.

The week before my father died he tried to write me a note. I didn't find out about this until after he was gone and my mother showed the paper to me. A single page. Scrawled at the top of the page were the first five letters of my family nickname. That's how we knew he meant it for me. He didn't have enough energy to write the last letter, and gave up in what I imagine was a fit of frustration. He was frustrated by just about everything at that point. His handwriting had always been a bit messy, but now it looked like a kindergartener's first efforts. The lines on the 'R' didn't quite connect, and the 'o' was a big bumpy loop, outsized when compared with the rest of the script. That was it: five letters, followed by the silence of blank ruled lines. And so it goes without saying, probably, that whatever he wanted to communicate died with him. All he left behind was five-sixths of my name.

On the island, the day after I found it in myself to be tender with Charlotte, I discovered a note of a different kind from Emma in my email. A catalog of data from what had been a very happy trip to Ireland:

> *I have been meaning to send this to you for a while . . . You may recall that I was making notes on the plane ride home. For me, details like this are better than a narrative for capturing and aiding memories (my poor memory . . .), though I certainly wouldn't call it comprehensive.*

9/5
2 matching bruises
1 minor car accident
3 very expensive meals
3 (?) bottles of whiskey
1 bottle of Bailey's
4 (?) nights of hot-tubbing
5 days of driving (or was it 6?)
2 pairs of shoes
2 bus rides, 4 flights, 2 boat rides
very little email
2 dreams about Matty; 1 dream about Mr. Harvey
   [from The Lovely Bones*]*
no naps; 2 very good nights of sleep
2 nights of difficult conversation
crepes for breakfast
carton+ of cigarettes
3 showers together
1 extra day
lots of laughter

So needless to say, both the timing and the content of this . . .

what do you say about any of it, really? Comings and goings, the way we all drift into and out of each other. There are times when I feel I can't take these inevitabilities, though I always manage it, with the emotional equivalent of bubble gum and chicken wire.

After that email, I drank and drank. I did away with the pretense of ice and mixers, and shortly thereafter with even the rocks glasses, eliminating all mediation between myself and the lip of the bottle. The local garbagemen, unreliable as any other service on the island, could not keep up with my Medalla consumption; trash bags full of empty cans piled up at the foot of the stairs outside, baking sour in the heat and attracting flies. I swept the rum shelf clean at the supermarket, literally swept it with one arm, as though my life were a movie, consequence-free, nothing but entertainment, and two or three pints detonated in my cart and coated the floor with distilled sugarcane. Gringos shot me frightened glances, then looked quickly away when I met their gazes, and even the locals stared.

Charlotte tried to keep up, to her detriment. She was twenty-two but could have passed for thirty after just a couple of weeks. Reversible damage, but damage nonetheless, and when on most afternoons she retired to the bathroom to vomit, I sat on the tile with my back against the door frame and asked her, not unkindly, to consider what she was doing to herself.

You should be at school, I told her. You should be finishing your degree, breaking boys' hearts, vomiting only on the weekends.

She tried to respond, but retched instead.

This is advanced drinking, Charlotte, I said. It looks a lot like what you saw at college, but it's different. You have to work your way up to it. It takes years. Drinking this way at your age is like plucking a toddler off her big wheel and giving her the keys to a bulldozer.

Whatever she was trying to say before, she apparently thought better of it. She flushed the toilet, let her head hang for a minute while water and vomitus swirled in the bowl, then crawled across the bathroom floor and put her arms around my neck. I let her hold me, and rubbed my hand up and down her back, and thought about Emma, far north in her wool toggle coat, bent to the wind, an angled slash of green and auburn against a white-gray landscape.

With my heart squashed again like a kitten in a crush video, and my head on the briny, I began to notice small strange inexplicable things around the casita. Usually in the mornings. I'd wake with a head like a toothache and emerge from the bedroom into unbearable sunlight and find something not just strange and inexplicable but also *sinister* in some exquisite way.

First I discovered a dead cat on the porch just outside the back door. Its insides had liquefied and run out of both ends, forming gray-orange pools that had, in the cool of the overnight, grown skins like cups of pudding.

The very next day I walked into the bathroom and found the sink painted with drips and drabs and fingered smears of blood. I had a terrible thought and went to check on Charlotte, found her unmarked and snoring softly in the bed, just as I'd left her.

Later that week I noticed that the picture frame Emma gave me for Christmas had moved from the end table to the coffee table, and the picture of us on the Cliffs of Moher, which had come with the frame, was missing. I knew I hadn't moved the frame, or removed the picture. I drink a lot but I'm not like your average drunk—my recall is pretty ironclad.

I asked Charlotte if she'd done it. She said no, and I believed her. By now she'd read my book, really read it, and loved me because of how I loved Emma. This came as no surprise; it had always been this way, with each of the hundreds of women I'd fucked and been kind to. They loved me for the way in which I loved, despite the fact that my love was not directed at them. It made no sense. It made perfect sense. It simply was, sense or no.

I love you, Charlotte said to me, her breath redolent of Bacardi and bile, and when I smiled kindly and nodded and did not respond she said, I know you don't love me. I know you never will.

And I was reminded of the many times I'd told Emma I loved her, and how she'd smile kindly and nod and not respond.

I would have believed Charlotte about the picture even if she didn't love me, because she was one of those people for whom liquor is like sodium pentothal. Get her drunk, and she'd make immediately clear why as a species we're hardwired to avoid absolute, comprehensive truthfulness. She'd told me many things about herself, in the few weeks since abandoning her act of nonchalance, that I could have happily spent the rest of my life not knowing. I learned, for example, that often her menstrual blood issued as a sort of gritty sludge. I learned that when she was eleven and her brother ten, they had, on several occasions, in the provocative quiet that followed bedtime, 'touched' their genitals together, and that while this repeated act fell short of full coitus it nonetheless produced such a riot of Catholic shame within her that to this day she often flashed back to it when she had sex, felt herself transported to that time and place, and sometimes even saw her brother's face in those of her lovers. I learned that she once slept for three straight days, waking only long enough to gobble handfuls of Halcion, after suffering the sudden and immutable realization that she had the desire to create art, but not the ability. I learned that riding the bus in junior high had been a daily ordeal, because she'd suffered from chronic and apparently incurable foot odor that would fill the bus's interior and become the subject of loud speculation among the other students, while she sat there tense and silent, hoping no one would trace the smell back to her Topsiders.

And so, knowing all this and more, I also knew that when Charlotte was twelve fingers into a bottle of Don Q and said she had no idea what had happened to the picture, she was telling the truth.

I tried for two weeks to locate the photo—Emma and me arm in arm, smiling at the camera, our faces shadowed by the hoods on our rain slickers—and never did find it.

People often dismiss the idea of the Singularity as science fiction, of course. A wild fantasy that could never make the leap from drugstore paperbacks to their everyday lives. They smile indulgently at talk of reverse engineering the human brain, shake their heads in a pitying way. People believe that what makes them uncomfortable about the concept of the Singularity is that we will lose something essential and ineffable that makes us human. But they're wrong. What makes them uncomfortable, whether they recognize it or not, is that we will lose our gods irretrievably, and that we will do so by becoming them ourselves.

In the beginning, the child's play stuff: neurological implants will circumvent all manner of damage and malfunction, and like Jesus before them, doctors will tell the crippled to rise, the blind to see, the mad to be still.

Eventually they will move beyond this, and tell the dead to come forth. If my mother chooses and can afford it, they will be able to remake my father out of the same dirt from whence he came originally.

Soon after that, there will be no more dead, for the rest of time. No one will die, and no one will grieve, ever again, until the universe collapses upon itself.

Sometimes I wonder if I could have saved my relationship with Emma if I'd been able to shit when she was around.

Don't laugh. I am serious, here.

Because I am shy about it. And with reason. I stink. I make a lot of noise. I am able, on my worst days, to clear out entire public restrooms, make them as uninhabitable as Chernobyl.

Not that I often use public restrooms. Only as a matter of absolute last resort, when the one thing standing between me and soiled underwear is the industrial neutrality of a public bathroom stall. And even then I'll fight it, as long as the fight seems winnable. A lot of people don't realize one can battle most any bowel movement into stasis. As with many things, it's a mental game. There's almost never any real danger of shitting yourself; there is only the question of how much discomfort you can tolerate. And I can tolerate a lot.

If I found myself searching for Emma even as we sat side by side at a bar, if I found myself missing her, somehow, even in the midst of coitus, then part of that was her fault, certainly, part of that was her peculiar way of hiding in plain sight, the way her face set itself in neutral, an impenetrable expression of absolute containment, a vault of self.

But might that distance also be my fault, in part? Did I lie by omission to avoid her displeasure? Did I censor and groom myself out of desperation to have her, and did she intuit that the me I presented was an ill-fitting flesh suit, a character from one of my books who defied the laws of both his own nature and nature at large, a character who, for example, seemed never to need to take a dump?

Before the island we spent weeks together, rarely leaving each other's sight; thus few or no opportunities for me to use the bathroom. Add to this the fact that eating, and eating well, was among her favorite ways to pass time and satisfy a multitude of appetites: for sustenance, for ambience, for companionship, for aesthetics. We ate pâtés and terrines and galantines, great steaming bowls of mussels, duck confit dripping salty globules of fat, rare hanger steaks plump with warm blood, spit-roasted pork loins. Preceded by whiskies and bourbons, accompanied by wines red and white, followed with cordials. And the desserts: chocolate peanut butter tortes, champagne-infused sorbets, stomach-rupturing blocks of bread pudding.

All this, and me too shy to use the toilet.

I agonized. I cramped and bloated and hobbled about with a body so full of intestinal gas—gas that I could rarely vent, even on the sly, because the irony of course was that the longer I held a shit, and the more it built up after every expensive fat-laden meal, the worse it smelled—that I worried, a couple of times, that I might actually burst somewhere inside myself. I lay awake at night, staring at the ceiling while she slept beside me, and suppressed groans while violent cramps rippled through my gut.

So really when I stop to think about it, I realize that my not taking a shit when I needed to, when you unpack that and extrapolate it, is really a kind of betrayal of self. Do you follow? No less than, say, pretending to like a movie because you think it will please a person you want desperately to please. Or else sitting calmly and smiling at a dinner party when someone's acted in a way that makes you want to flip tables and throw glassware. To smile through a movie you loathe, or to refrain from breaking things, is a betrayal of self.

And when you try to *live* there, to live in a place where you're betraying yourself over and over, not only do you grow to resent the hell out of it, and resent the hell out of whomever you're betraying and censoring yourself for, but the very idea of your self begins slowly and inexorably to erode. Until you realize one day out of the clear blue that you have no idea who your self is, anymore.

This was what I was doing every time I had to take a shit around Emma and chose not to. Chipping away at myself, assuming a persona that looked like me but was not. I know it sounds ridiculous. I know. But it's the truth. And every time she went to work or yoga and I would steal upstairs, secure in the knowledge that she'd be gone long enough both for me to shit and for the stink to dissipate before she returned, there was a shame in my relief. At first I thought it was just some weird infantile Freudian thing, like the shame we all supposedly learn to feel very early in life about our shit itself, over the very fact of it. But I came gradually to understand that that was not the nature of my particular shame. No. The shame I felt was deeper and broader and more complex and, frankly, more grown-up. It was the shame of one who has betrayed himself repeatedly, and knows he has, even if he won't admit it to himself. But how could he admit it to himself, with no self to confess to?

And so because I did not recognize the source and nature of my shame, I couldn't talk about it, and certainly not with Emma. But neither could she talk to me about what she no doubt realized, at least subconsciously, and was affected by: a strong if ineffable sense that the me she dealt with on a daily basis, went to sleep with at night, wrapped her arms around and allowed to penetrate her, was not the authentic me.

No doubt it sounds silly. But these things have consequences. And I think, sometimes, that one could draw a straight causal line between my reluctance to shit when Emma was around and the fact that today she is married, once more, to a man other than me.

Eventually the caballeros grew weary of fighting me. Not because I was any good at it, really—I lost more fights than I won, though no one walked away unbloodied—but because I was dogged, and probably, in their view, a little crazy. I bit and scratched and wasn't above a nut-punch or two, and the caballeros eventually wanted no more of it. So they proposed one last fight with their biggest guy, a hulking, home-tatted *cabron* who, because he was gigantic, and because I never found out his name, and because our fight had all the elements of a champions' duel straight out of Homer, I came to think of as Ajax.

Which, I suppose, made me Hector by default.

The challenge came one hot morning when the local drunk (a genuine distinction on an island full of drinkers) pounded on the door of my casita. I left Charlotte in bed and went down the stairs, found the drunk grinning at me through the aluminum bars of the security gate. He was a whip-thin, anemic man with the features of a Latino weasel and a pint of Palo Viejo always jutting out of his back pocket. I thought I recognized his scheming eyes and crooked smile, the teeth like rusted, broken knife blades. Then I placed him in a specific memory, beyond his ambient, rambling presence on the *malecón*: I'd once seen him tumble off the pier fully clothed, so drunk at nine in the morning that he couldn't swim the twenty-five yards to shore and had to be fished out by a gringo bartender setting up for lunch at Duffy's.

Bueno día, the drunk said, grinning, grinning. He hooked his fingers around the bars. Give me rum, and I give you a message.

I don't have any rum, I lied.

I smell it on you.

It's not the rotgut you like. *Muy caro,* my friend.

This is not a problem, he said, pulling the empty pint from his pocket and tossing it in the dirt. I didn't always drink this *gasolina.* I had money when I was young. *Mi padre* the car dealer. *Mucho dinero.* All the Bacardi I wanted.

He grinned wider, revealing black gaps in his mouth where molars had gone missing.

I eyed him a moment longer, then went back up the stairs and returned with a near-empty bottle of Don Q. That's all I have, I lied again, handing it through the bars.

He twisted the cap off and downed the two fingers or so. I waited.

They say you like to fight, he said finally, his grin disappearing and reappearing in intervals as he licked rum from the corners of his mouth.

There was a pause. So? I said.

So maybe you like to fight tonight. At *la gallera.*

La gallera? I asked. You must be mistaking me for a rooster.

No no, he said. A special fight. Man-fight. Just two of you. No funny business.

I laughed. 'Funny business?' Where did you learn English?

They say to tell you, the man continued, that you fight tonight, and there be no more after that. They leave you alone, no matter who win.

I thought for a minute. It was intriguing, I had to admit. Not because I wanted the fighting to stop—I was indifferent to that. No, I was intrigued because *they* obviously wanted the fighting to stop, and they imagined this proposal an acceptably macho way to end it and save face at the same time.

The *gallera* was a large corrugated aluminum building set beside the main drag in Isabel, like the world's biggest garden shed. The ring in the center, a ten-foot-diameter scrap of Astroturf hemmed by a short concrete wall, was surrounded by concentric circles of theatre-style seats rising up to the rafters. Big Medalla banner on the wall. A small window through which beer and roasted chicken *pinchos* were sold. Cumulus zeppelins of cigar smoke and chlorinated fluorescent light and crowds of men who never bothered to use the seats provided. This was where I found myself that evening, nine sharp, the hour when the actual cockfights always started.

Ajax stood across from me, stripped to the waist, three hundred pounds if a pound and streaming sweat just standing there. He sneered at the comparatively insignificant amount of air I displaced, and here was my chance, if I had any: hubris always makes one vulnerable, no matter how strong.

His arrogance was the only stroke in my favor, though. Everything else worked against me: the crowd; my poor physical shape after so much heroic drinking; the tiny ring, designed to house the clash of angry fowl, not a no-holds-barred match between grown men. I was giving up over a hundred pounds and had nowhere to run, let alone hide.

But things were even worse than they appeared at first blush. Because I realized quickly, after the buzzer screeched to begin the bout, that not only was Ajax massive and fierce, but he also knew how to fight. He had training. He slipped my berserker rush out of the corner, intended to surprise and intimidate, with a deft, practiced side step, and as I passed he cuffed me with a left jab, then landed a blinding right cross to the nerve center just below my ear.

I staggered, tripped over my own feet, nearly went down. The crowd, as smug as Ajax himself, and as certain of his victory, murmured approval. Ajax waited for me to clear my head and made a show of looking bored, letting his hands drop a bit.

Of course he knew how to fight. Half the island's men had spent more net time in the boxing gym than in school. While I'd been busy playing JV basketball and getting into the occasional undisciplined scrape in the neighborhood, conflicts that usually looked more like an awkward slow dance between two dudes than an actual fight, Ajax had passed his days cutting class and working the speed bag and sparring without a head guard.

I went after him again. He tried the same side step, but I anticipated it and met him at the spot. I lowered my head into his belly, felt him cough up the air in his lungs. The crowd grumbled, but as far as I was concerned the fact that no one had outlined rules meant that there were none. This wasn't a boxing match, it was a street fight.

But though Ajax was winded, I couldn't press any advantage. He was too big. I tried to wrap him up and pin him against the wall, but my arms weren't long enough to circumscribe his girth. Then I put my forearms against his hips and tried to push him backwards, but the physics wouldn't cooperate, and as I shoved at him in vain he sucked air and landed kidney and rabbit punches with impunity.

The third shot to the back of the skull dazzled me, and when I felt his arm wrap under mine to hold me in place I knew he'd recovered from the head butt to his belly, and I knew I was in trouble, and so, in desperation, I bit the loose flesh where his hip met his upper thigh.

Ajax moaned and let go of my arm. He stumbled back against the concrete barrier, looking down at his shorts to check for blood. I realized I had maybe five seconds before he got over his shock, and then it wouldn't be enough for him to simply win—he would want to levy punishment, to break parts of me, to make sure I had a limp or detached retina or some such physical reminder of him for the rest of my life.

I squared up, drew back, and threw a mighty kick at his balls, but too slow, too slow. He sidestepped once more, shockingly nimble for such a huge man. My foot caught nothing but air, and I ended up on the ground. The crowd rewarded my effort with a jeer, and as Ajax shuffle-stepped forward with murder in his eyes, it occurred to me, inanely, that with feet like those he could have been a good heavy-weight prizefighter, instead of a two-bit thug on this two-bit island.

I clambered up just in time to meet his right cross again. The feeling was not unlike being hit in the side of the head with a good-sized chunk of feldspar. I went down and now Ajax had no interest in showboating. He set on me with kicks to the gut and ribs, cursing me in Spanish. Blood smeared my vision. I tried to regain my feet as the crowd, sensing the endgame, began screaming in earnest. If

Ajax had been on my now-blind right side that would have been it, but I could still see out of my left eye, and managed to time a kick well enough to trap his size-14 boxing shoe in my hands. He was badly overextended, and went down easily with a strong upward thrust on his heel.

A groan of disappointment from those assembled, followed by a sudden hush. Ajax, breathless again from the impact with the turf, now lay prone and momentarily helpless, like a huge June bug stuck on its back. I straddled his chest, thought about hitting him in the throat, considered the possibility that this could kill him, then slammed an elbow into his face instead. He sputtered and raised his hands between us, weak, vain warding. I hit him again, and the bridge of his nose zagged half an inch off center.

A crushed Medalla can bounced off the back of my head. Then, between my shoulder blades, I was stung by what felt like a D battery. This last provided enough of a distraction for Ajax to gather himself and flip me over. Both of us were exhausted, and his heaving mass pinned me so tight against the turf that I could feel individual blades of plastic grass abrading my back.

And he was truly, truly angry now. He and I were the same in that regard: fatigue could not mitigate our gall. He propped himself up on one elbow and dropped a fist into my face over and over. Where his tired muscles failed to provide force, gravity compensated. Somehow my teeth were spared, but most every other feature north of my throat wound up some degree of mangled.

I'd never given up in a fight before. That's what had landed me here—the caballeros didn't want to deal with my tenacity any longer. I had what real fighters call heart. And real fighters talk about heart all the time—who has it, who doesn't, how it's more important than a snappy jab or solid footwork or good cardio. Heart. If a fighter takes a genuine beating, if he gives up in, say, round 2, and just sort of hangs on for the rest of the match, absorbing shot after shot and refusing to fight back in earnest, as though he deserves to be punished for some transgression he knows he's committed but cannot admit to, they say the other guy took his heart. The fighter himself will say this. He took my heart, he'll say, usually from the humiliating comfort of a slightly inclined hospital bed. The discussion will not touch on physical fatigue, or painful calcium deposits in the hands that hindered his punching, or a slight cold that made breathing through his nostrils difficult and necessitated opening his mouth, thereby leaving him vulnerable to a knockout punch. The conversation will start and end with that all-important intangible: heart. He just took the heart right out of me, the fighter will say, sounding awed, as though the other man had not just handed him a sound beating, but performed a genuine miracle for which there would never be a satisfying explanation.

And this is what Ajax did that night. Whatever heart Emma had left me with, Ajax beat it out of me there on the Astroturf. If I'd been able to stand, or speak, I would have thanked him and shaken his hand. He'd earned my gratitude. He'd done more to shape me, in just under ten minutes, than my own father had in thirty years, and I owed him a tremendous, unpayable debt. I consider myself in his debt to this day, although his share of the book from the fight must have been pretty substantial, judging by the money I saw exchanging hands in the crowd as I lay there and choked on my own blood.

And the caballeros were good to their word. Not a single fight found me after that, for the rest of my time on the island.

In twenty years Emma's life will look like this: she lives outside San Francisco, clear across the fruited plains, on the flip side of the mountains' majesty. Had a kid with Peter Cash. He's in college now—the kid, not Peter Cash. She left politics and went into policy work on behalf of former professional football players, of all things. We won't have talked for ages, but every year I'll send her a birthday card with a longish letter folded inside. I'll do this because I like to believe it makes her feel good, to know that at least one of the promises I made—to love her for the rest of my life—I actually followed through on.

She rises in the morning and makes herself tea. Her hair is now mostly white. She puts it up in a loose bun, looks herself over in the mirror, presses her hands to her neck, turns this way and that, frowns, wonders, like the rest of us, where the time went. The mug of tea sits untouched on the back of the toilet tank, next to the sink, an ignored ritual. Peter Cash comes into the bathroom, showers while she plucks her eyebrows, shaves quickly at the sink while she showers. They move around the small space with the synchronicity of a water ballet, each of their bits of personal grooming timed perfectly to make room for the other's. She brushes her teeth and puts in her earrings with NPR in the background, slings her work bag over her shoulder, says good-bye to Peter Cash. Some mornings she kisses him; most mornings she does not. He's fine either way. She drives her car to the office without appearing to think too much about anything. Face stuck in a kindly neutral. Great and painful and passionate things roiling below, forever below, like the molten rock beneath Yellowstone. A walking manifestation of Hemingway's iceberg, a cypher with eyes that startle you to attention one moment, break your heart the next when she turns them away from you. The eyes are the same. The eyes never change.

I don't know who brought my carcass to *la emergencia*. Presumably someone in the crowd took pity on me, or maybe the owner of the *gallera* realized how bad off I was and worried it'd be his ass if I died. Regardless, someone dropped me without ceremony or explanation on the pavement by the entrance to the clinic, and the next day I woke up to find the doctors making plans to transport me to the hospital on the main island.

I pulled the IV out of my hand and hobbled out, glimpsed in passing lives suspended by the pain and debility of bodies prone to failure: door no. 1, a plump girl, fifteen maybe, face wan and vacant, a tube up her nose and, presumably, snaking down into her stomach; door no. 2, a fortyish woman alternately vomiting into a large emesis basin and moaning in a way and at a volume that I had a tough time thinking of as anything other than melodramatic; door no. 3, a quiet bloodbath—stabbing, looked like—the patient silent and still and the professionals in lab coats and pastel scrubs milling about with an alarming lack of urgency; door no. 4, a young tow-headed boy enduring a spinal tap, the physician murmuring reassurances while himself appearing quite nervous, the boy screaming, his limbs held down on the bed by well-meaning adults I hoped he would grow old enough to hate.

I stumbled through the rush of automatic doors, went down to the main road, and hitched a ride back to the casita.

Charlotte, looking drawn and tired and very old from three days of drinking and worrying, fussed over me. I told her I was fine, that I just wanted to rest on the porch with a Medalla, and she was welcome to join me. We sat in silence as the afternoon sun blasted us. Sweat sprung up all over my body, stinging cuts and contusions. Charlotte wanted to caretake, but really the only thing to do was spare me painful hobbling trips to the refrigerator, and she retrieved beers for us both with great doting kindness until early evening.

Roberto's work truck pulled to the curb in front of the casita around seven. He removed his bulk from the cab and looked up at the porch, shielding his eyes against the slanting sun. I waved to him, and he came around and took the stairs.

I am sorry for what they did to you, he said.

What who did? Charlotte wanted to know.

I did not ask them for this, Roberto said.

I thought he might cry.

Roberto, it's fine, I told him. For God's sake, man, I know it wasn't you.

Why did you go? he asked.

I thought for a minute. It was a good question. I don't know, I said. I guess I was intrigued. You know 'intrigued'? Curious?

Roberto, understanding now, nodded. Yes, I know curious. It killed *el gato*, my friend.

I laughed, then grimaced at the pain.

You should go home, Roberto said. To your woman. Go home and no come back.

It's no problem now, I said. There won't be any more fighting.

Fights will not be your problem, Roberto said, if you do not go back to her. You will have other problems.

Which woman? Charlotte asked. Which woman is he talking about?

Another theory I find appealing is that the Singularity could and likely will render the body, and therefore sex, and therefore by extension romantic love, as obsolete as a Walkman personal stereo.

The fact that you don't know what a Walkman personal stereo is only serves to illustrate my point, of course: after the Singularity, it's likely that the sight of two people kissing on a sidewalk will seem as strange and anachronistic as a man going out into the world with a cassette player clipped to the waist of his pants.

In any event, the point is that our bodies will be rendered obsolete through any of a number of potential processes. One such process is called mind uploading, in which what we think of as our selves can, if we choose, exist and function perpetually as software on a computer system. In a virtual-reality simulation, or something akin to one.

The nearest current analog I can think of is the movie *Tron*, although the reality and circumstances of mind uploading, when it happens, will no doubt bear only the slightest resemblance to the film.

Think of it: existing free of a physical body, and therefore free of its frailties, its requirements and desires. No disease, no death, no pain. No need to eat, or brush one's teeth, or worry about body odor. And the macro-picture: overpopulation becomes effectively moot. Shortages of any kind of resource no longer a concern. I could go on, but you get the point, and the aspect of mind uploading that concerns us here is, as I said: without a body, there is no impetus for, and indeed no possibility of, sex.

Because with Emma and me our problems started, or at least were made most manifest, in the bedroom. We punched and clawed at each other, fought like animals. I've told you a little about this, but you don't yet understand the scope of it. I took beatings from her that rivaled anything the caballeros did to me. The sheets were almost always spotted with blood. On more than one occasion she stood before the bathroom mirror, fingers parsing her hair, and complained that I was leaving bald patches on her scalp. Neither of us seemed to know why we did it. We couldn't stop hurting each other, and we couldn't leave one another alone.

But take away our bodies, make us both purely digital manifestations of our consciousness, and what happens? Uncertain. Maybe we live calmly together in an accelerated virtual reality, loving one another until the end of all existence, our brains operating at a speed that necessitates that the virtual sun rise and set 260 times in 24 hours in order for the day/night cycle to seem normal to us. Or maybe without the brutal clash of our bodies Emma and I lose interest in one another and spend forever comfortably productive, cultivating endless stores of knowledge and attendant deduction, making connections of logic and cognition we never would have otherwise, because although we wouldn't be any smarter than our former selves we would think much faster, and therefore could understand things we never would have had the time to glean understanding of before. Like maybe why we were compelled to punch and claw, to bare our teeth at each other, why our lusts were never satisfied until someone was bleeding.

Although as a novelist I could have spent most of my days darning socks or playing solitaire and no one would have noticed or cared, I did occasionally have an obligation that required I be somewhere at a certain time on a certain date, and also that I be capable of standing for at least an hour and speaking in complete sentences. One of these obligations surfaced not long after Ajax beat the heart out of me. A small liberal arts college in Pennsylvania had asked me to read, the invitation coming many months before, when it had seemed like a much better idea. Now I wanted nothing to do with it, but being my father's son I packed a decent pair of pants and a pressed shirt in my garment bag, got on the Cessna that took me to the mainland, boarded a much larger plane for a flight to Philly, then took the train west through hills and valleys where people sat mourning the loss of steel and wondering what came next.

The reading was well attended, and I didn't shake too badly, and the audience seemed to appreciate the material from the novel I was working on about Emma, though neither they nor I had any idea what a phenomenon that novel would become. In the front row sat a willowy redheaded undergrad, quiet but attentive, achingly beautiful. Beautiful and sexy in equal measure, and you understand that the two aren't necessarily synonymous. Skin like 2 percent milk, this girl. When the reading broke up I thought about her a little bit over a beer—her features, fragile as a Fabergé egg, and her black leggings, and those boots, and the way she listened and gazed as though not just taking in the words but sort of calmly absorbing something essential about me. Somehow this quiet watchful girl found the hotel where the school put me up, and she had the front desk page me just after one in the morning. I came downstairs, perplexed and with a head full of whiskey, and found her in the lobby, arms crossed over her chest, collarbones standing out above the scooped neck of her blouse. Now all her calm watchfulness had abandoned her, and there was something desperate on her face.

And I said, Hi.

Do you remember me? she asked.

From the reading, I said.

Yes.

There was a long pause, during which I considered that she might be drunk.

I said to her, Is there something that you want?

She was trying to smile, trying to appear cheerful, but still just looking desperate in a way that made me feel bad, even though I wasn't responsible for her desperation. She shrugged at my question, more out of frustration than perplexity, and looked away quickly as her eyes began to shimmer.

It seemed like maybe I should put a hand on her shoulder, but I didn't want to commit to that.

Finally she looked at me, and she was genuinely close to tears, and she said: I don't know *what* I want. Her voice broke a little, as she said this.

Later, after she stopped crying and I shook her hand and sent her home, I had another glass of whiskey in my room as regret flowed through me: regret that she was so sad and vulnerable, regret that, even if my mind hadn't been on someone else, and even if the willowy redhead had not been so young and sad and vulnerable, I still could not have given her what she thought she wanted from me.

That same night, after the reading but before the waif showed up at the hotel, I turned on my phone and found I had a text from Emma: 'Thinking of you.' That was it.

The next morning I had a brief but friendly conversation with a railroad police officer as he swabbed my garment bag for traces of explosives. While he waited for a machine to tell him whether or not I was a terrorist, he asked why I'd been in Pennsylvania, and where I was headed. For whatever reason, I neglected to mention I was spending the winter in the Caribbean, and simply told him I lived in Maine. He said he imagined the seafood was good there. I assured him that it was. He pointed to the fading bruises on my face and asked what had happened. I told him I'd gotten into a fight, which news he accepted with a bare nod, the Yankee sensibility to mind one's business trumping the police officer's innate suspicion. We stood there in silence for a moment, looking at each other. Then the machine beeped, exonerating me, and the officer said I was free to go.

Down on the train platform the sun was too bright, and the wind bared its teeth, and I tried without luck to find a place to hide from the cold. Guys in sweatshirts and hard hats ground old paint away from steel I-beams. The sound was like robots screaming. A paint chip flew into my eye right out of a Plath poem, and I had to turn away from the train as it pulled in because I was afraid I might have the urge to jump in front of it.

When I got back to the island Charlotte hadn't had a drink for four days. Her eyes were bright and clear, her hair tied in a neat, gleaming French braid. She smelled good in a hippy kind of way, like lavender and fresh sweat, and she seemed very calm. I was impressed with her lucidity; intimidated by it, in fact. She'd cleaned and organized the fridge, for God's sake, and lined our footwear up neatly just inside the door.

I don't care why you stopped drinking, I told her. Just don't start again. I'm going to set a bad example, but don't follow it.

I probably won't. At least not at first, Charlotte said.

I opened a Medalla. You were fine with being sober while I was gone. There's no reason why it should be different with me here.

You don't really understand how alcoholics work, do you? Charlotte asked. Which is weird, considering.

You're not an alcoholic.

Maybe not. But I know how they work. My father is a drunk.

I'm sorry to hear that, I said, and meant it.

Don't be. He quit. I was just talking with him about it the other day. I called him after you left.

I swigged from the Medalla. So how'd he manage it?

Well he went to rehab a dozen times. Tune-ups, he called them. You wake up in a locked ward and aren't really sure how you got there, leave after a couple of days. Other times he would just start going to AA meetings at the church. He'd be good for a couple of weeks, a month maybe, and then he'd start up again. This was pretty much the whole time I was a kid. He even went to a hypnotist. Nothing took.

Here Charlotte paused. She seemed to be waiting for me to contribute in some way, so I said, It can be a tough thing to quit, for sure.

Well, yeah. But the thing that ended up working for him was this not really deep realization he had one day. It was a normal morning, for him. His head hurt and he was confused and didn't remember much from the night before. There was no reason to think that this day would be different from any other—he'd get up, spend some time in the shower pulling himself together, then go off to paint houses and stop at Calucci's on the way for a sandwich and a twelve-pack of Bud Heavies, which was what he called regular Budweiser. You know, as a counterpart to Bud Light. Bud Heavy. Get it?

I get it. Very clever.

But anyway, on the day he quit drinking for real, instead of his usual routine he lay in bed for a while, and all he could think about was that he hadn't been *born* drinking. That when he was a kid not only did he not need alcohol but had never even tasted it once, and was perfectly happy and didn't feel like crap all the time. And somehow that was all it took, after years in and out of the hospital and dragging himself all hungover and embarrassed to AA meetings. After ruining his marriage with my mother and disappointing my brother and me God knows how many times. Just this one thought: that he'd been able at one point in his life to exist happily without booze. And he hasn't touched it since. It's been six years.

Charlotte looked at me, not expectant, really, just radiating this new calmness of hers.

So that's why you stopped drinking? I asked. Because of the talk with your old man?

No, Charlotte said. I'd already stopped, and I mentioned it to him, because he was asking why I'd dropped out of school and when I was coming home and all that. I told him it was kind of a confusing time but that I'd stopped drinking so much and things were getting clearer to me.

They are?

Sure.

And so what about this clarity? I asked.

Well for one thing, Charlotte said, I know now that I really am in love with you. That it's not just, you know, boozy disorientation.

Once, shortly before I left for the island, Emma and I were stretched out on the sofa in her new house, and I said to her, You are equal parts utter self-reliance and tremendous vulnerability.

And she said, The inevitable consequence of having to basically raise myself.

I said, There's a lot of 'Come closer, get away from me' going on, here.

And she offered a sad, wry smile and said, Yeah you've probably noticed some of that.

The night Charlotte told me she really loved me I waited until she'd gone to bed, then broke out the bottle of Macallan twelve-year I'd stashed for special occasions. I drank half of it while considering how to respond to the text Emma had sent while I was in Pennsylvania. I wasn't angry anymore—Ajax had relieved me of my anger, along with every other discernible emotion—but I was still dedicated to the truth, and so finally I wrote: 'Don't repackage your fear and try to sell it to me as indifference.' And she went silent for two full weeks after that.

Emma was thirty-four and childless and rolling downhill without brakes toward a divorce, and when she couldn't sleep sometimes she'd concentrate on the gentle mechanisms in her belly and wonder when they would call closing time.

Wet as she got when I touched her, I imagined she'd be fertile as Kansas's inclined plains for years to come. But I didn't say that to her, of course. And besides, I'm no doctor.

As I mentioned before, I did toss around the idea in my mind, back before the island, that maybe with Emma I would want to have a child myself. Maybe I could give her what she wanted. Maybe I could want it. Maybe I'd even be good at it, and make her and this theoretical child wildly happy. Maybe I could understand, finally, what everyone else seemed to ken instinctively without having to think about it at all.

But now, with her silent in the snow and me sweating and feckless a world away, bestowing kind indifference upon Charlotte, it didn't seem at all likely I'd have the chance to find out. And one morning at the beach, while I watched birds playing on the cliffs, it came to me that if Emma ever did have a child it would be with another man, and soon, as we were both, in our thirties, feeling the actuality of growing older. Aging was no longer the abstraction it had been a decade before. It was now a fact made concrete by every gray hair discovered in the mirror, every randomly sore knee and forgotten factoid and irregular, spotty period, every unbidden thought of where our parents were at our age and, moreover, how old they had seemed to us then. Advances in fertility science notwithstanding, Emma was approaching forty and wanted kids and if she were to have them it would not be with me. She did not believe in the future I believed in. I knew this as surely as I knew my own name.

After that revelation, I spent a week staring at my navel and waiting in vain for it to blink. Charlotte traced wide barefooted parabolas around me in the casita, and drove the Jeep to the *colmado* to replenish my rum stores, though she didn't touch a drop of it herself. Kept the ice trays filled, a good and loyal partner. She read book after book, I remember that. Sometimes two a day. When she finished the small library I'd brought with me—*The Corrections*, along with a couple of slender, wry little volumes by Sergei Dovlatov, a pop psych book on the parallels between Vietnam veterans and Achilles, and last but by no means least, *The Sot-Weed Factor*—she extended her daily forays for rum to include a stop at the bookstore in Isabel, where she bought used English-language paperbacks for a quarter apiece.

Her getting smarter, me getting dumber, concurrently, exponentially.

On the fourth day of the contretemps between me and my navel, I spied, from the hammock on the porch, a skinny, shirtless local beating up his horse.

I remember this less like an actual event, and more like a vivid dream. The horse was mostly white, with yellowish splotches, and well-muscled. The man was so thin I could see the knobs of his vertebrae, and he wore only a pair of denim shorts, slung halfway down his ass in the style of no-account hoods everywhere. While I watched, he very casually smacked the shit out of the horse. The horse wouldn't let him throw a saddle blanket over its back. Every time the man raised the blanket, the horse angled its hind end away, shoes clattering staccato on the pavement, and every time the horse shied, it got hit. First the man punched it on the snout; sharp, snappy blows I could hear from a hundred feet away. Then he grabbed the braided rope that served as reins and whipped the horse across the eyes. I sat up in the hammock, my blood rising, and watched. With each blow the horse bowed its head, capitulated utterly, struggled against the bit to move out of range. I kept hoping the horse would realize it was much bigger and more powerful than its tormentor, hoping it would turn and give him both hind hooves square in the chest. But thousands of years of domestication won out, and the horse cowered and did not fight back.

Then the man merely raised his fist without hitting, and the horse flinched, and suddenly I'd had enough. I could tolerate him beating the horse with purpose, but I could not accept him bullying it for sport.

I hollered at him in Spanish. He looked over, grinned evil, invited me to come down for a taste of what the horse was getting. I got to my feet, muttering as I strode across the porch, but Charlotte intercepted me on the landing.

No way, she said. You're not fighting anymore. That's all over.

Nothing is over! I yelled in her face. Nothing! You just don't turn it off!

I didn't realize it at the time, but of course I was quoting Stallone's final monologue from *First Blood*, complete with the nonsensical transposition of 'just' and 'don't'.

I pushed past Charlotte, went down the stairs and into the street, crossing toward the man without words, without any hesitation. As I drew closer, it registered distantly that he was in fact a boy, maybe sixteen or so. He took in my expression, realized he'd made a mistake, and fled, holding the waistband of his shorts to keep them from falling.

When he was gone I looked at the horse. Its eyes were wild, showing white at the edges as it watched me warily. I put a hand out; the horse flattened its ears but let me stroke its muzzle. I worked my fingers carefully around the raised red slashes from the rope. Then a strange and powerful grief welled in me, and I put my arms around the horse's neck. I laced my fingers together through its mane, and clung there.

I'm not sure how long we stood together. Not long, I don't think. Soon the horse tired of our embrace, and it bit my ear, then clattered off in search of its master.

After the horse some time passed quietly, until on the sixth night I started yammering about sentient, evil appliances. Or so Charlotte told me later; I had and have no recollection. Apparently I was flailing through some sort of waking nightmare in which I imagined the oven was trying to set the casita on fire, and the refrigerator was spoiling food deliberately in an effort to poison us. At some point, while Charlotte watched, I shoved the vacuum cleaner down the stairs and threw the toaster off the porch and into the street. She recovered the vacuum, but the toaster disappeared pretty much the moment it hit the pavement, salvaged, no doubt, by one of the neighborhood kids.

When I snapped out of it on the morning of the seventh day, I told Charlotte she was a regular angel, or else a saint, for abiding this madness.

It's not what most people would imagine, she said. Dating a writer.

You ever read Kerouac? I asked. Or Fitzgerald? Or Poe? Or Bukowski? Or Dorothy Parker, for that matter?

Some, she said. Still, it's different when you see it in person, rather than reading about it.

Fair point. But if it bothers you, maybe you shouldn't be, you know, running out to buy more booze for me every day. Not that I don't appreciate it, I added.

Who said it was bothering me? she asked. Maybe the thing is that I want you dead. Maybe I want to see you drink until your heart gives out. Did that occur to you? That maybe I want to be here to watch you choke on your own vomit? And maybe that's why I go to the store? Because every time I go I've got my fingers crossed, that I'm hoping today will be the day?

She looked me in the eye, paused a beat. Then she smiled. Just kidding, she said.

That afternoon, when I'd managed to eat some oatmeal and, later, a banana, Charlotte admitted that she hadn't been kidding entirely.

I don't want you dead at all, she said. Don't get me wrong. I am angry at you, though, sometimes, because you can't see me. All you see is that other woman.

What other woman? I asked.

You know who I'm talking about.

Yes. But you don't.

What do the details matter to me? Charlotte asked. Blonde, brunette, redhead. Big tits, no tits. Tall or short. It doesn't matter what she looks like, or when she was born, or what her name is. She's all you can see. That's what matters. Still, I keep hanging around here because I hope that might change, though I feel like I know better. I feel like all I'll get out of this is a good chunk of time spent reading. But I can't bring myself to leave.

So you go to the store for me because you're angry? You want to punish me with booze?

No, she said. That's got nothing to do with how angry I am at you. I go to the store because I love you.

Before I left for the island, every once in a while, after all the punching and scratching and growling, after she had a particularly strong orgasm, Emma would start to cry, and she would clutch my shoulders with frightening strength and plead, Please don't leave me.

Out in the larger world, in the daylight, when she would treat me like a bare acquaintance or else disappear altogether, I wondered if these moments had really happened. In the face of her apathy I doubted myself, though I knew damn well that this same woman who now appeared indifferent to my existence had recently begged me to never go away.

The term 'singularity' comes from physics. It means a spot in space and time where gravity becomes infinite and nothing can escape its pull.

I will repeat that: nothing—not even light—can escape the pull of a gravitational singularity.

Just before leaving on spring break with the specimenz and Rick, Charlotte told me, she'd made a pornographic film at a Theta Chi kegger, a film that could now be found on porn websites all over the Internet.

We lay in bed after midnight, watching the ceiling fan funnel up smoke from our cigarettes. This was after the long week of suicide drinking, and I'd recovered well enough to be able to listen with my customary attentiveness. It was hot. The sheets were lumped in a damp mass at the foot of the bed, and with the windows open we could hear dogs bawling at a gibbous moon.

So maybe that's why I haven't gone back, she said. Maybe it's got nothing to do with you at all. Or very little to do with you.

You're too embarrassed to go back, you're saying?

That's not it. I'm not embarrassed in the least. Notorious, probably. But not embarrassed.

Good for you. Don't let the bastards get you down.

Do you want to watch it? Charlotte asked. I could find it online in about three seconds.

I guess I don't, I said. And I really didn't. Maybe describe it to me, I told her.

She shrugged. Pretty stupid, she said. I was at this party, and a group of guys were asking every girl in the place to go upstairs with them. We're making a movie, they said. Making a movie. They said it over and over again. They were afraid to be more specific and say We're making a porn, or We're shooting a stag film, though it was obvious to anyone with half a brain that that's what they meant.

Charlotte took a long drag on her cigarette. The first time they came to me I told them no, she said. The second time I asked what the details were. Just head, they told me. Maybe some titty-fucking. This was their term. But no actual intercourse, they said. 'Intercourse' is my term. The way they put it was: No real fucking or anything. I told them, Not all five of you. And they said, No, just Brian.

They pointed to this one tall kid who was staring at the floor. The rest of us are going to watch, they said.

So I said, Sure. And they just stood there for a minute, staring at me. They couldn't believe it. I think part of the reason they were shocked was because they realized suddenly that they had to actually do this. It wasn't just a crazy idea they'd come up with, anymore. It was real. They had a taker.

They didn't realize that it wasn't about the thousand dollars. I sure as hell took the money, but money wasn't why I did it. Not to sound too much like exactly the sort of fantasy they were trying to create, but I just decided I wanted Brian's cock in my mouth. It had been a while since I'd given head. I like it. I liked the idea of taping it, and I liked the idea of them watching while I did it.

Charlotte must have thought she saw something in my expression then. Everyone wants to be bad sometimes, you know, she said. Not just you boys. And Brian was cute enough. He looked like he had a nice cock. Sometimes you can tell.

She paused again, looking at me. I made what I hoped was a noncommittal face: not shocked, not judging.

Anyway there I am, kneeling in somebody's bedroom, a towel on the floor underneath me—one of the guys had put it down so my knees wouldn't get sore. Almost a sweet gesture. Shirt off, bra off. Brian's standing in front of me, his cock bobbing up and down in my face, and now that it was actually happening I knew for sure that it was *me* using *him*. That their little plan had turned all the way around, started eating its own tail. And he knew it, too. You know what it was? As soon as he realized that I actually wanted to be there, and that I was not compliant, that I knew just how to stroke and suck him and would not take instructions, that if I put the lube they offered on my tits it would be in my own time and of my own volition, he got scared. Because this was not the way it was supposed to be. I wasn't scared, and that scared the shit out of him. I could see it when I first took his cock in my hand and looked up. He was petrified. I felt calm, and when I saw his fear I also felt very, very powerful.

Anyway, Brian's friends egged him on, so he made a good show of it. He grabbed my hair, slapped my tits around a little. But it was all bluster. There was a point when he started to lose it, started to go soft, and I actually felt bad for him. I wondered if maybe his buddies had put him up to it, if they'd hatched the idea but none of them had the guts to do it themselves. And if you watch the film you can see, you can actually see how scared he is, and how I am totally in control. His pale little butt, pinching as he thrusted. His trying to talk dirty, and the way his voice cracks. I ended up coaching him through it. Worked him like I was in love, until he had no choice but to get hard again. Then when he got ready to come I told him, very sweetly, and you can hear this on the tape, I told him, 'Don't even think about coming in my mouth, kid.' And he didn't. He came on the towel, mostly. And his buddies cheered and slapped five. They still thought it was their good time, not mine. And then I put my clothes on and went back to the party. I stayed for a while, and when they came down none of them even looked at me. I had another couple of beers, went home. Slept pretty good that night.

Anyway, it paid for my trip here, Charlotte said, tapping her cigarette in the ashtray on the nightstand.

After the initial radiation and chemotherapy treatments, the offending lung was removed from my father's body during an eight-hour procedure at Brigham and Women's Hospital in Boston.

We sat in a lounge for families of surgery patients. Nauseating green carpet, the eggshell walls one always finds in hospitals. My mother and oldest sister played cribbage and flipped through back issues of *Ladies' Home Journal*. I reread *Cat's Cradle*, Vonnegut having long been a sort of literary comfort food for me. In between pages I thought about my father's lung, and how as I sat there people were carving it out and placing it in a bag and sending it to the basement to be incinerated. This was back when I still had a reverential sense about our bodies, and I couldn't shake the conviction that something as critical as a lung deserved a better send-off. That lung had gone to seminary with him, had breathed the sodden air of Vietnam for two tours, had kept him supplied with oxygen at every one of his children's births. Sure, now it was trying to kill him, but like any faithful companion that suddenly goes rogue, it deserved some regard before being dispatched. It was owed some note for its fifty-five years of service. It had earned a little ceremony. What it got, instead, was dropped into a biohazard bag like so much offal.

Night had fallen by the time my father was moved from surgery to the intensive care ward on the eighteenth floor. We made the slow trip up in the elevator, visited him in shifts. I stroked his head, much as I would in the moments after his death. Above the oxygen mask that covered his mouth and nose, his eyes blazed at the world. He looked surprised, more than anything. He kept blinking rapidly, as if trying to figure something out. I wondered in a distant way if he was simply reeling from the trauma thrumming through his body, or if he was trying to reconcile somehow the fact of his continuing existence.

For lack of anything better I asked, How are you feeling? The recovery-room version of small talk.

He bounced the question back at me. How am I *feeling*? he said, incredulous even through the lingering fog of anesthesia. And then, once more: How am I *feeling*?

Did you know that Ray Kurzweil, the man who borrowed the word 'singularity' from physics to coin the phrase Technological Singularity, appeared on the Steve Allen game show *I've Got a Secret* when he was only seventeen?

Actually, it's the author Vernor Vinge who is credited with first using 'singularity' in reference to artificial superintelligence. But Kurzweil has become the celebrity face of the theory, the one who gets interviewed in mainstream media like *Time*, while Vinge has remained, for the most part, a peripheral figure.

In any event, the point is that Kurzweil's slot on *I've Got a Secret*, like Watson's triumph on *Jeopardy* and Deep Blue's dismantling of Kasparov, was a seminal moment in the march toward artificial intelligence. Because the reason Kurzweil appeared on *I've Got a Secret* in the first place was because he'd invented a computer that wrote music for the piano. A machine that created art, in other words.

But people missed the point altogether. No one on the show found it all that noteworthy, let alone arresting, that a nonorganic entity had composed a melody. They were more impressed with Kurzweil having invented anything at all at such a young age. They got it completely backwards. A bright young man building a computer in 1965, while impressive, was nothing compared to what the computer itself could accomplish.

But in fairness, I doubt that at the time even Kurzweil understood the significance of what he'd done. He was just a boy, after all.

A few months after his diagnosis my father went to Boston for radiation and chemotherapy treatments, the idea being to shrink the tumor in his lung and then remove the lung itself in the hope that this would leave him cancer-free. It was beyond a long shot; all the other doctors he'd seen had told him he was finished, and no surgeon would touch him for fear of pointlessly swelling their mortality stats. But the team in Boston was working at the outer edge of treatment, where medicine and cruelty meet and mingle, and they were the only people offering even a whiff of hope. So Boston it was, where for two months my parents stayed at a Hampton Inn while smart, kind people poisoned and irradiated my father.

I spent some time there with them. I went to appointments and treatment sessions because I wanted to hear firsthand what the doctors were saying, and not receive this information through the sieve of desperate hope my mother had become, filtering out all information that pointed to anything but a positive conclusion. We had a lot of downtime between hospital visits, which we filled with shopping and eating and trips to the aquarium and the natural history museum and most of all Fenway Park, where we took in more games in that brief period than we'd seen together in the thirty years previous.

After one of these games I was standing outside Fenway with my mother, waiting for my father, who'd peeled off to buy a sausage toward the end of the ninth. We waited outside gate C while a couple of street kids who'd committed the great offense of sitting on the sidewalk against the park wall were being rousted by half a dozen police officers.

Boston cops being the Mick thugs that they've always been, even if they happen to be black, or Portuguese, or whatever.

I watched the cops surround and holler at the street kids, who to their credit kept their heads down, eyes trained on the pavement, faces locked in expressions of calm disdain, not pretending that the cops weren't there, merely letting the cops know they didn't *care* that they were there.

And into this, from the far side of the confrontation, strolled my father, his own head down, munching on the second half of a messy sausage, dropping bits of sautéed onion and dribs of mustard on the sidewalk as he went. Oblivious, he stepped between the Boston PD and the street kids, and made it three-quarters of the way through a gauntlet he wasn't aware existed before one of the cops, a hulking white dude with a baby face that was nothing short of shocking attached to such a huge body, seized him by the arm.

I stiffened and stepped forward, my hand cocked in a fist at my side.

What the hell's the matter with you? the cop screamed at my father. Can't you see there's something going on, here?

There were so many things wrong with this one moment that my mind seized up at the sheer incongruity of it—which was fortunate, because otherwise I probably would have hit the guy. Here was a man easily five years younger than me, little more than a child himself, no matter how big, who had my father by the upper arm and was scolding him—not instructing, not issuing directives, but *scolding*. Add to this the fact that the cop was obviously a bully, maybe even a sadist, his reaction to my father's modest and unintentional violation of his work space hideously overblown.

But the worst thing, the unforgivable thing, was my father's own reaction.

Because in his illness, in his sudden debility, weakened by poisons meant to cure him, he stood playing the part of the chastised schoolboy: head down, shoulders sloped, arms extended pleadingly, one hand still holding the soggy remnants of the sausage.

And he was *apologizing* to this cocksucker. Even now, I can't believe it. Apologizing over and over, not meeting the cop's gaze. I'm sorry, he said. I'm sorry, okay? I didn't know. I'm sorry.

In my momentary paralysis, looking at my father, I could think only of Mercutio, hissing through clenched teeth, on seeing Romeo plead with Tybalt: O calm, dishonorable, vile submission!

But then I snapped out of it and stepped forward and yelled at the cop, a move both reflexive, the product of rage, and calculated, a gambit to transfer the cop's attention off of my father and onto myself. Which worked.

It was the first time I'd ever had to protect him from anything. Turns out, though, that all it takes is once. Nothing is the same after that.

Ray Kurzweil's dearest hope, incidentally, is that on a bright and cheerful morning shortly after the Singularity, while overhead, obscured by a cobalt summer sky, the heavens spin invisibly, he will collect DNA from his father's grave and use it to resurrect the man he'd called Aba.

His father's real name? Fredric. My father's name? Frederick.

One of the things Emma wanted to start putting in order, with me gone to the island, aside from finalizing her divorce and finding traction at work, was figuring out a way to have some semblance of a relationship with her mother, who was now mostly housebound. But despite the long episode of silent treatment Emma had subjected her to, and despite the penitent Christmas card, despite years of apologies and promises to be better, to be a mother, to stop being the only person on Earth who could really break Emma down, the woman, nothing if not consistent, tried to kill her again.

It started when Emma, against her better judgment, drove north two hours to pick her up and take her to lunch. Things began well enough—talk of Emma's work, discussion of her mother's myriad medications, including one that she blamed for an assault at an AA meeting that had earned her a weekend in jail.

And this was the thing with her mother. It was never her fault. *She* didn't knock the lady into the coffee urns at the AA meeting— the medication made her do it.

But so anon the nice stuff came to a close, and her mother began asking questions about what had happened to Emma's marriage, and implying that it was all Emma's fault, going so far in fact as to suggest that the reason Matty left her was because she'd been unfaithful, though this was not the case and her mother had no reason, outside the delusion factory of her own skull, to think that it was.

Her mother's getting worked up, angry now as if it were her own marriage Emma had sabotaged—and here's a detail worth noting, that there was and remains a decided lack of boundaries when it comes to where Emma's life ends and her mother's begins, in the woman's mind—and Emma's growing more and more nervous as she drives and her mother's ire rises, remembering the last time she had her mother in the car and she got pissed off and tried to steer them into a gulley at fifty miles an hour.

Emma's gripping the wheel hard, to keep from shaking, and her eyes are welling up, and her mother sees her weakness and goes for the kill, tells her only daughter that that which she fears most will in fact be Emma's fate: she will be alone for the rest of her life, and she will grow old and angry and bitter and hateful and eventually go crazy. That in other words, she will become her mother.

And then the bitch goes for the steering wheel again.

I was sitting at Duffy's when I got the call.

I asked Emma why she'd let her mother steer them into the tree. Emma was much stronger, after all, and could have overpowered her easily.

She was lying on a bed in the ER, and she said, But I wasn't stronger than her. I was ten years old again. I wasn't even old enough to have a license, all of a sudden. I had no business driving that car, with her screaming at me like that.

I told her I knew exactly how she felt. I was my father's son, after all.

And then, after a pause, Emma asked if it was okay for her to come to me pretty much the moment they let her out of the hospital. No questions, and no discussion. The first flight she could find.

Six months after my father's diagnosis, after the lungectomy, after a good amount of time during which the cancer had been polite and stayed put in the neighborhood in which it had started, one of the lymph nodes under his jaw started to swell with the stuff.

We didn't know yet that the cancer had spread—the last set of scans had come back clean—and despite what we'd been told about my father's prospects we had all, I think, settled into the comfortable delusion that perhaps he would be given a respite, perhaps he would defy the laws governing malignancy and the cancer would halt where it was and he would live for many more years and die comfortably in his sleep at a proper age, a medical miracle. These things happened; one heard about them from time to time. But then one night I noticed my father worrying something on his neck while we watched television. I could see a mass rolling under his fingertips, stretching the skin as it moved back and forth, and in that moment I felt the distance between what I suddenly knew, looking at that evil lump, and what I wanted to believe, a distance I could not reconcile. And of course he must have known, too, at the moment his fingers brushed against the offending node and then paused, doubled back, palpated more carefully. Here was proof that his proverbial goose was cooked, just as the doctors had been telling him this whole time.

During the few months remaining he played with the lymph node compulsively, kneading it between his fingers while he stared out the window or listened to the Beatles. As it grew to a grotesque and disfiguring size and made the left side of his mouth look like it was full of jawbreakers, I could see the tumor become a sort of talisman in his mind. Maybe he thought if he touched it enough, learned its contours by heart, he would gain some understanding of what was happening to him. But I don't think it worked. Its contours kept changing, moving outward, consuming all. I think in the end that murderous node didn't help him comprehend anything. I think like most of us, he didn't understand much more than he had in the beginning, at the moment they'd spanked and swaddled and lowered him, screaming, into my grandmother's arms.

After I hung up with Emma, knowing that Charlotte would not seek me out at the bar, I finished my Medalla at a pull, got up off the stool, and sought her out instead.

Drunk, and in shock at Emma's imminent arrival, I slalomed across the island, drifting over the center line once and again, accelerating into blind turns, scattering roosters and dogs and the occasional bicyclist before me. I came to a full stop only once, waiting while a group of wild horses made their languid way across the main road. I practically leapt from the driver's seat when I got to the casita.

Charlotte looked up from her book—a leather-bound copy of *Don Quixote* discovered at the used-book store—and before I'd even opened my mouth she said, Well I guess that's it, huh?

Taken aback, and drunk besides, I was silent.

She continued: Because I'm guessing there aren't too many things that could have you screeching down the road like that, and running up the stairs two at a time.

She dog-eared her page and stood up, set about gathering her things. Won't take long for me to clear out of here, she said. There was no obvious anger or resentment in her voice. She stuffed several T-shirts and a bikini into her tote bag. Maybe an hour to pack, she said. Is there another plane off the island today? Can you pay for it, by the way? I'm pretty broke.

There's a 5:20, usually. I hesitated, then said, Don't you want to talk about this?

Charlotte stopped packing and looked up at me. No, she said. I don't want to talk about this. What I want is to see her picture.

Her picture?

Yes. I want to see her picture.

I looked at her a minute, then fished my phone out of my hip pocket. There are a few on here, I said.

Okay. She resumed packing. Balled-up jeans and T-shirts joined the signed copy of my book in her knapsack. Find a good one, she said. Make it count.

What I found was a shot, from the previous summer, of Emma in the garden of her old house. This was before the place burned down, of course. She had her back to the camera. You could tell from the angle of the light that it was early morning. Emma's shoulders, clad in black, slumped forward sleepily. She'd just become aware that I was taking her picture, and she'd turned her head toward me in profile, an indulgent smile playing on her lips. In front of her, in the picture's background, was a rosebush in full bloom.

It was a favorite of mine. I'd consulted it many times, there on the island.

I handed it over to Charlotte. She dropped her knapsack and took the phone in both hands. She ran one finger down the side of the screen, slowly.

She's beautiful, Charlotte said, then added: Older, obviously.

I nearly laughed at this. Everyone's 'older,' of course, when you're twenty-two.

But beautiful, Charlotte reiterated. There's something about her eyes.

There is, I agreed.

Charlotte handed the phone back to me. Still, she said, she's no Helen of Troy. But I suppose it's like Jay McInerney said: taste is a matter of taste.

He didn't say that, I told her. One of his characters did.

What's the difference? she asked.

But I was tired, and thrilled beyond language, and explaining the difference didn't seem important enough to warrant the effort, right then.

Later, at the airstrip, I sat with Charlotte while we waited for her plane to arrive.

She wasn't angry at all. I was happy for this, of course. But right before her plane left she did give me a version of a speech that I'd heard probably twenty times before, from twenty different women.

It goes like this: Tell yourself whatever you like, they say. Tell yourself there were a thousand reasons why we could never have worked. But even if you don't realize it now, there will definitely be a time when it dawns on you that we could have worked just fine. That 'working' is a choice people make every day, and that the use of the present participle of 'work' is no accident, because that's exactly what it is—work. Not fate, not true love. Just work. You've chosen otherwise. And that's okay. But just remember that it was a choice, after all. That you don't *have* to love that woman. And remember I said all this when the light finally dawns on your thick head. If it ever does.

When she finished with her version of this speech Charlotte thanked me, somewhat inanely I thought, for helping her get sober, and for encouraging her to start reading widely again. She kissed the top of my head and hoisted her bags and walked out through the double doors onto the tarmac. Her plane hadn't touched down yet, and I didn't understand at first why she would choose to wait in the sun. I sat there for a few minutes, staring at her back, and then I understood, and that's when I left, finally.

Somewhere in there, before Emma's accident, and before Rick showed up with the specimenz but after the caballeros whipped me senseless, I got an email from my editor saying my first novel had been picked up by a large Midwestern university for its incoming freshman reading program, and that this was great news, and they'd need me there in late August to speak to four thousand newly minted undergrads, and congratulations, my editor wrote, and then at the end he added, in a brief casual way meant to seem almost an afterthought, no big deal at all, that he was looking forward to seeing the book I was long overdue with, the book that had burned in the fire, the book he thought I was still working on when in fact I was working on a new book unknown to him, on Emma's book, which I'd become convinced was the literary equivalent of a thalidomide baby.

At the beach that same afternoon I sat in the driver's seat and watched the Caribbean roll in and out, and gave serious thought to driving the Jeep up over the dunes and straight into the warm water, into all that gently rolling green.

When I looked at Emma and my heart leapt into my throat, as it always did, I sometimes realized that if I could figure out a way to see her as other people no doubt must—as human, in other words, pretty, certainly, but flawed, real, *actual*, doomed to expire like the rest of us—then I would be free, finally. But there seemed to be only one way that I could see her.

And certainly that was how I saw her, after not laying eyes on her for months, the afternoon she flew in to the island's small airstrip. This was four days after her mother steered her car into the tree. An angry bruise ran down her left cheek, bleeding into her jaw and throat, but this did nothing to dim her beauty. And that unmistakable gait as she came across the tarmac toward the little terminal, in faded jeans and, I hoped, no underwear . . .

I knew I had an obligation to tell her about Charlotte. But I couldn't do that. Not then. Because I could see, from the moment she stepped through the doors and favored me with a wide smile, that everything had changed.

She had her hands on me before I could get the door to the pink stucco casita unlocked, and by the time I closed the door behind us she had my T-shirt off and was at work on my belt.

Several minutes later she punched me on the temple, a dazzling shot that put me immediately in mind of the whip-wielding caballeros, and then she came, spectacularly by the sound of it, while I watched tiny meteorites blaze around the edges of my vision.

That night we slept tangled up in each other, our bodies exchanging sweat in the heat even with the ceiling fan raising a small tornado, and with the windows open the omnipresent night sound of dogs barking woke me again and again.

The first time I woke, when I saw Emma in the bed next to me instead of Charlotte, I started as though she were a specter.

The third time I woke, Emma lay on her side, gazing at me, the bruise on her cheek darkened to black in the dim glow of the streetlamp outside my window, and when she saw my eyes come open and fix on her she said, without affect: I love you.

The fourth time I woke she was still gazing at me, and I felt her hand on my face and realized that her touch, and not the dogs, had interrupted my sleep. She traced the fading bruises on my cheeks and jaw, the scar in front of my left ear, and the half-healed laceration above my eye where Ajax's knuckle had split the skin.

What's been happening to you down here? she asked.

You sure you didn't do that? I joked.

She cocked her hand back into a fist, a mock threat, then dropped it to the mattress again and said, Seriously, though. Who did this to you?

Doesn't matter, I told her, tracing the bruise on her own face with my fingers. It's all over now.

And we went back to sleep.

The seventh time I woke, it was the dogs again.

I did sometimes wonder what those dogs imagined they were accomplishing when they barked and barked and barked and barked and barked and barked and barked and barked and barked and barked and barked and barked and barked and barked and barked and barked while I was trying to write, or sleep.

I mean, at a certain point it had to become clear, even to a dog, that whatever's pissing you off isn't backing down, or going away, or otherwise changing, and so you'd think the dogs would accept that and pack it in, conserve their energy.

But no.

They just keep barking.

When Emma noticed the missing teeth the next morning she again demanded an explanation, but I refused, guilt weighing on me like the gravity on Jupiter, and this was a strange transference of that guilt, as the manner in which I lost my teeth was pretty much the last thing I felt guilty for.

We laughed, furtively, about people at the beach encroaching on our space. We laughed when Emma moved toward me in the water, then dog-paddled frantically away when she caught my expression and realized I was pissing. We laughed in the fancy restaurant of the island's one resort when I did three laps around the mammoth dining room, trying and failing to find egress to the toilet, finally coming to a stop and catching her gaze across the room and shrugging my shoulders in utter perplexity. We laughed when, on the beach, I inhaled a swatch of her hair, gagging and flailing my arms in genuine distress. We laughed when I convinced her to try escargots and she remarked, with a grimace, that all she had to say was it seemed clear to her that she'd just eaten something that spent its entire life in dirt. We laughed when, while we beat one another on the bed, John Coltrane's *Ballads* wrapped and, in its wisdom, my iTunes decided to play 'I Just Called to Say I Love You,' bringing a swift if mirthful end to our odd brand of lovemaking.

For a while I was able to carry on without my conscience getting the better of me. My guilt was eclipsed by the pleasure of Emma's presence—and she was truly present now, for the first time, a pure and unprecedented *thereness* that sometimes left me blinking in disbelief.

After she'd been on the island for a week, while we sipped Medallas on the beach at sunset, she took my hand and apologized for her distance, for her many disappearing acts, for offering nothing in return but a smile when I told her I loved her.

We were sitting in beach chairs. Squinting at the setting sun.

I feel a lot, she said, that I'm just really, really bad at expressing. That's no excuse, of course. But I think you know me well enough to understand that for whatever reason the outside doesn't match the inside, sometimes.

Of course I do, I said—the very picture of empathy and acceptance, as if all along I'd abided comfortably with this deep understanding of her, as if I'd never doubted her for a moment, as if I hadn't yielded to petty frustration, like a spoiled child, in yielding to Charlotte.

But other than that brief moment we were simply getting it right, finally, finally, without forethought or effort, and there were times, I won't lie, when I was convinced that the Singularity had happened without my noticing. Which of course was impossible—no one knows what form the Singularity will take, exactly, but one thing that's certain is it will be noticed. Nevertheless, I had a few moments, there on the island with Emma, when it seemed perfection had been achieved.

I don't know when it happened but all of a sudden the guys wearing VIETNAM VETERAN ball caps look just like the paper-skinned old men from my childhood wearing WWII VETERAN ball caps. All those who remembered Guadalcanal and the French hedgerows died quietly and out of sight, and the men of my father's generation slipped into their spots on the age continuum when I wasn't paying attention. They use canes now, and oxygen tanks. Their bottom eyelids droop, revealing wet red interiors. They rely on machines even more than the rest of us: supermarket scooters, electric wheelchairs, stair lifts, therapeutic vibrating shoes, hearing aids the size of pinkie nails.

None of it makes sense to my eye. There's an incongruity I can't reconcile when I see a man in a black POW/MIA shirt who needs help getting out of his Oldsmobile. To me those men are frozen in time, somewhere around my eleventh year, the mid-1980s, which would place most of them forever in early middle age, a good season in the life of a man, when his callowness has melted away but he remains vigorous and sharp-minded and can still reasonably expect his life to go on forever.

My father always looked like a Vietnam veteran is, in my mind, supposed to. His hair never turned white, and his skin never wore thin and ashy. His arms and shoulders were tanned and thick with muscle, what's usually called work strong. He was that way until almost the end, when seemingly overnight he traded Tonkin and Tet for Normandy and El-Alamein, and then he died.

When my father was alive and still healthy you couldn't take his photograph with a flash camera. Or rather, you could, but it was ill-advised. Everyone in our family knew better and never used flashes at Christmas or birthday parties, so I only saw it happen twice before he got sick. The first time was at my oldest sister's high school graduation, when her friend wanted a shot of my father and my mother flanking her. They stood arm in arm in the gymnasium post-commencement, with graduates and their families milling around, and when the flash went off my father hit the deck, belly-down on the polished wood of the basketball court. Everyone stared while he gazed about wild-eyed. Finally my mother crouched and whispered until, gradually, she convinced him to stand up and walk out of the gym. The rest of us stood there, silent, our hands in our pockets, left with the strange sense of having witnessed something that would have been funny if it hadn't so obviously come from a place of great and, to us, unfathomable horror.

The second time was at a Brownwater Navy reunion in Chicago, where my father posed for pictures with a dozen guys he'd patrolled Mekong tributaries with four decades earlier. I'd gone on the invite of my father's friend Chappy. It's telling that the invitation came from him, and not my father. But I thought it might be fun, not to mention enlightening—thought I might even write something about it, though I never did—and so I found myself in the Marriott ballroom, marveling while my father stood with his buddies and hardly blinked as flashes popped over and over again. I asked my mother about it later, and she told me this was the only time she'd ever seen him sit still for a flash photograph. Somehow he was healed, among those men, however temporarily.

But it was temporary. After he became really sick, when he was too weak to turn over furniture or run away, people seemed to forget that flashes weren't just forbidden, but that they traumatized the guy. And the irony was that now, with him dying, these people wanted to take his picture all the time—by himself, with my mother, with just me, with just my sisters, with the whole family. And it seemed like they always used a flash, and more than once I had my arm around his thin shoulders and felt him wince, over and over, as the flash went off. But he was too wasted to leave the room and, so near to death, too meek to tell them to stop.

During the time we spent together, both in high school and during the more recent stretch, I had to be careful not to raise my hands to Emma's face too quickly. Say I was reaching out to stroke her cheek, or tuck an errant swatch of hair behind her ear—if I moved my hand toward her too fast, she would flinch, and sometimes even turn away. She never hit the deck like my old man—really, she was the greatest paragon of apparent calm I've ever known, even greater than my namesake, who if dispassion were money would have been a wealthy man indeed—but the essence of her reaction was the same as his. Casualties both, stamped by trauma, they ruled like despots over their everyday to make up for the moments when they had no control, when they were most vulnerable, when all they could do was duck and tremble. Or at least that's how I understand them now, at this great remove, with him long-buried, and her gone from me.

On the beach one day I found a woman hiding topless behind a lean-to built of driftwood and dried palm fronds. She was in her late forties. I walked by, jumped a bit when she suddenly came into view, then stared at her breasts a moment, on reflex. They hung loose and heavy, looking like they'd never once enjoyed the support of a bra, but the nipples, well, unless there's something seriously amiss I always respond to nipples, and in that moment, for just a moment, I wanted one of hers between my teeth. I stood there. The woman eyed me back, cool appraisal, a smile playing on her lips. The palm fronds chattered in the breeze, sounding like a squadron of prehistoric insects. Then my senses came to me, and I returned the woman's smile, awkwardly, and turned back in the other direction.

Emma sat in the sand a quarter of a mile back, and when I returned and told her about the woman's sagging breasts—leaving out, of course, the part where I'd briefly wanted to gnaw on her nipple—she smiled behind her sunglasses and patted my shoulder and said, That's what they all end up looking like, you know.

Not yours, I said. Those little Hottentots will still be standing up when you're in your eighties.

But what if I have kids? she asked.

And sidestepping her choice of the singular personal pronoun over the plural, I held my hands out, palms up, as if hoisting some invisible weight, and I said, Then they'll just get big. That's a win-win.

And, again, she laughed.

My father only ever cried three times in my presence, all when he was sick, and I have no doubt that if he'd been given to talking about his thoughts and feelings, he would have said that this was the worst thing about a slow, lingering death—not the pain, nor the creeping debility, but the ways in which it honeycombed your personality, made you weak of mind and spirit.

The second time he cried was when he'd shit his pants and I left him sitting in it for an hour. He slumped in his La-Z-Boy after I scrubbed his toenails with the old toothbrush, and I was standing behind the chair for some reason I don't remember, sort of hovering over him, and I saw his shoulders start to hitch so I leaned over the back of the chair and put my arms around him. This did not come easy, this simple act of compassion. I did not ever hug my father, and hugging him now felt like the sort of thing you do because circumstances dictate it—*the guy's dying and just shit himself besides, give him a hug for Christ's sake*—rather than because either of you wants it to happen.

The first time he cried was a few months before that, at his last birthday party. He knew it would be his last birthday party. Everyone did. And because of this he tried to explain how he loved and valued us all, and sort of managed it but not quite, and it was difficult to tell if he was crying because of how he felt, or because even with his own death looming he still couldn't articulate it.

I would rather not talk about the third time my father cried.

For nine days after his lungectomy, my father was not allowed to drink any fluids.

In removing his lung, the surgeons had cut one of the nerves that controlled his vocal chords, rendering him unable to swallow properly. They worried that if given fluids, he would aspirate them into his one remaining lung. They worried that in his weakened state this'd be all it would take for him to succumb to pneumonia. They had reams of statistics, presumably, upon which to base these concerns. They tried for more than a week to find an open slot in an operating room to repair the damaged nerve. In the meantime I and others swabbed my father's lips with moist sponges, and told him to be patient. When no one was paying attention mercy got the better of us, and we slipped him illicit chips of ice.

After a week I was running low on patience. I began to suspect that getting my father back into the operating room was a low priority for everyone at Brigham and Women's. I had a hunch that his suffering was allowed to continue in order to make way for a cataract surgery, or so some kid's tonsillectomy didn't get bumped. And I began to grow angry.

I told the charge nurse how uncomfortable he was, how his throat was so dry that the NG tube had stuck to the inside of it and as a result he kept trying with greater and greater violence to cough it up. I told her I was worried that his flesh would tear away from the staples holding the left side of his chest together. I asked if they couldn't give him some sort of mild sedative, at least. She leveled her gaze at me, an expression equal parts impatience and condescension, and said: He needs to learn how to manage his discomfort.

I stared at the nurse for a moment, and then I knocked a stack of files off the half-wall between us, showering her and her desk with papers. I told her that she needed to find a new line of work, since it was clear she'd become so well acquainted with pain that it bored her. She called security, and the surgeon in charge. The surgeon arrived first, and I told him that, for his part, he had the bedside manner of a mechanic gutting a wrecked Volvo. I spat the words at him. Two security guards arrived on cue after that. I was invited to leave the intensive care ward. And during the elevator ride down, flanked on either side by a guard, I chastised myself for the outburst, not because it had been inappropriate, but because after the incident with the cops at Fenway I'd realized that my father needed my protection, and I could not protect him from the sidewalk eighteen floors below his room.

By the way, don't ever let someone convince you there's anything—and I mean anything—good about dying. There is nothing redemptive in decline and decay. The hard candy of necrosis has no nougaty center where the human spirit prevails over all. Death is not a 'journey,' a 'part of life,' a 'release from suffering,' or any other such bullshit euphemism we employ to comfort and delude ourselves. And while we're on the subject, no one 'passes on' or 'passes away,' either, and they sure as fuck don't 'cross over.' They die, and then they start to swell and stink in the very next moment. When I knelt in front of my grandmother's casket at the funeral home at age twelve, I snuck a look at her face and saw—under the grotesque makeup job, the screaming circles of rouge and the bloody lipstick—what I saw was the aspect of a piece of roadkill, her mouth caked dry and her eyes sunk under their lids, like a squirrel in the gutter with its legs up in the air and its entrails drying under the sun. The flies would have been on her, if not for the formaldehyde, is what I'm saying. And then when my friend Ronnie died at boot camp in Parris Island and the Marines shipped him home, the stories we heard were of Ronnie begging not to die on the table in the infirmary, and as far as I know he didn't say anything profound or affirming, just pleaded with strangers to save his life, then died when they failed. And then when my father died I kissed his corpse on the forehead, over and over, and ran my palm along the side of his face, stroked the short sparse hair that remained, and all I could feel was how cold and vacant he already was, how every thought and aspiration and heartache he'd ever experienced was now and forever negated by his sudden nothingness. Later, when I helped move him onto the undertaker's stretcher, there was a warm stench when his body left the mattress, and I realized he'd shit himself when he died, and this fact evoked in me the sudden understanding that in life we can fool ourselves into believing we are something more, and more permanent, than our constituent parts, but in death the truth becomes impossible to deny: we are nothing more than meat, bones, fingernails, and hair. Broken down further: proteins, mostly. Further still: carbon, hydrogen, phosphorus, and so on. Molecules on loan for our brief lives and times, reclaimed eventually, with grief as interest, by the creditor.

I tried to explain to Emma once that what men think they want from women, and what they actually want, are two different things. We think we want sex, or a friend, or someone to birth and raise our children, or some combination of these and other things. But here's the truth that we keep hidden even from ourselves: men's appetites and preoccupations tend to be simple, obvious; whereas women, at least from the simple perspective of a man, are complex and mysterious creatures.

And when a man sees a beautiful woman and thinks he wants to fuck her, what he's actually after is that mystery. It's the mystery that makes his heart pick up the cadence, makes his pupils dilate, makes the words catch in his throat. The pussy is a fulcrum, a mechanism, a mere mode of entrance into the mystery. A man wants to hold the mystery, turn it over in his hands and examine it close-up, even if he has no chance of ever understanding what he's looking at.

And I said all this to Emma, and she listened quietly, and offered nothing by way of response, just gazed at me and smiled for long moments after I'd finished, and as was usually the case I had no idea what she thought—about me, or my ideas, or really anything. And those unknowable eyes, and the desire they aroused in me to reach across the table and take her face in my hands and kiss her hard, to plumb her body when she refused to let me plumb her mind, only served, of course, to prove my point.

Good as things were with Emma on the island, I still stayed up nights. Something still screamed inside of me. Guilt over Charlotte, sure, but something else, something abiding, fundamental, entrenched. I spent a lot of early mornings watching movies while Emma slept. One of those movies was *Solaris*, with George Clooney. In the film he plays a psychiatrist who is asked to investigate strange goings-on at a space station, and like the people he's been sent to rescue, he begins to have bizarre experiences. He is visited by his dead wife, or actually a doppelgänger who in every way replicates his dead wife but is not in fact her, and this understandably causes him more than a bit of anxiety and confusion. The doppelgänger claims to be happy to see him again, and asks if he still loves her, and he doesn't know what to think or say or feel, and he paces around the room and slaps himself in the face and claps his hands, trying to reassert, or reaffirm, reality. But of course reality is shifting and liquid and subjective, especially when it comes to who and why we love, and really that's the whole point of the film, and so the comfort or reassurance he seeks to find by slapping himself is not on offer. The film is also about physics and how it informs emotion and perception. At a certain point the physicist onboard the space station says to Clooney's character, regarding the doppelgänger, 'It's a mistake to become emotionally involved with them. You're being manipulated.' We learn, eventually, that the doppelgänger is nothing more than a physical manifestation of Clooney's character's memory of his wife. And this is the irony of him trying to reclaim the reality he thought existed, the reality wherein his wife is dead, because it's his own brain that brought his wife back into existence in the first place. And the movie is sort of beautifully shot and ruminative and has an understated, almost nonexistent score, and raises basic and unnerving questions about time and memory and delusion and the nature of existence on this plane and others, and I was tired, exhausted actually, and though I watched the film from beginning to end I was sort of determined to not feel much. When it was over I went to bed and tried to wrap myself around Emma, but she was deep asleep, her limbs arranged so that it was impossible for me to lie close to her. Clooney's character at one point in the movie tells his wife that he can handle all of their problems except one: 'What I can't deal with is you hiding from me,' he says. After a long time lying next to Emma but not being able to touch her, I finally slept, and as you can tell none of this really makes for anything resembling a coherent narrative but anyway it seemed significant in a manner I hoped to figure out but have never quite been able to, obviously, because here I am still going on about it. But that one line, 'What I can't deal with is you hiding from me,' well I'd be violating my promise to tell the truth if I said it didn't immediately make me think of Emma. Because she hides. She doesn't realize it, I don't think, but she hides. Sometimes right in front of you. She can be sitting across from you at a table in a nice dining room somewhere and the expression on her face changes suddenly and she disappears, is in a very real and unmistakable way no longer there. You always find yourself reaching for her an instant too late, and grasping at smoke.

Often I used my index finger to trace constellations among the tiny moles on Emma's back while she slept. Andromeda. Aries. Aquarius. In my mind it was as though she had not just invented moles but imbued them somehow with an aching romantic significance. Canes Major and Minor. Cassiopeia. As though she were the only woman on Earth whose waist blossomed into her hips quite like that. Hercules. Horologium. Hydra. When the muscles in my shoulder started to ache, I'd shift my weight and switch hands. Leo. Libra. Lyra. She'd stir a bit, murmur, press her feet against mine under the covers, settle again. Sagittarius. Scorpio. Serpens. I'd let myself ruminate, briefly, on how simple it would be to replace the photos that had burned in her old house—the photos of her and Matty on their wedding day, the photos meant to last generations—with new ones. Taurus. Triangulum Australe. Tucana.

It's the way she moves, too, that men find maddening. I can't do it justice with words; you'd need to see it for yourself, and then when she approached and those eyes fell on you, you too would get as tongue-tied as a schoolboy, and wonder what she did with your self-assurance—it was just here a minute ago—and then you would understand. Her feline saunter, I call it. But don't get the wrong idea, it's not overtly seductive in the least. It's not contrived, it's just the way she locomotes, born in her as surely as the color of her hair or the galaxies of moles on her body. And like the rest of her qualities it's at once distinct and elusive, so that as I sit here and close my eyes and try to picture her for the purpose of describing her gait to you, no image comes, nothing rises at all, in fact, except the stew of emotions always inspired in me by the mere sight of her walking across, say, a kitchen: lust and fear and wonder and gratitude and more than anything a great, dazzling yen that thrummed and ached like infection.

The pit in my stomach when she entered the room. Her hips rising and falling in languid sine waves.

If you continue to doubt that we are all drawing air at the beginning of the end of the human era, I refer you to May 6, 2010, the day on which what became known as the Flash Crash of 2010 occurred.

You remember this, surely. Between 2:42 and 2:47 P.M. the Dow shed 600 points. In less time than it takes to smoke a cigarette, a trillion dollars in market value vanished.

Initially, nobody knew what had happened. Over the next few months investigations revealed that, in large part, the crash had been caused by bots, automated trading algorithms that went into an orgy of selling at 2:42 P.M. It had little to do with, and could not be controlled by, the human beings whose money was disappearing before their eyes.

One morning we were making breakfast at the casita and I don't remember how it came up but Emma wanted to know how many women I'd had sex with. I hesitated, hemmed and hawed, did some math, then told her. Her eyes went a little wide and her lips formed an oval of disbelief, and I knew it was a mistake not to have lied. I thought about explaining to Emma that with every one of these women I'd been alternately looking for her and looking to fuck her away, but then I decided not to explain, because it wouldn't make a difference or she wouldn't understand or maybe it was just bullshit, I couldn't decide, but anyway there has never been a time in my life when keeping my mouth shut turned out to be a bad idea and so I didn't say anything else after that.

That same day we spent the afternoon at the small private beach of an older man, a friend I'd met drinking at the bars. Jerry lived in the ruins of a sugar mill, sketching and painting and assembling kinetic sculpture. He was a widower, and his artwork featured a preponderance of the female form that was hard to miss. He and I sat at a low-slung table in the sand, drinking rum and talking about Robert Lowell and Dr. Seuss, while down the beach Emma lay on a towel reading. After a while the conversation dried up and we set about our respective work, he with his sketchbook, me with my Mac, alone together, until Emma rose, used two fingers to pull her black bikini bottom out of the mild wedgie it had settled into, and moved in her feline saunter toward the water. Both Jerry and I looked up from our work and followed her with our eyes. We watched as she bobbed among the blue swells and floated on her back with her toes poking up out of the water, watched still more intently as she emerged and came back toward us, her shoulders and midriff shimmering with saline droplets. When she settled back down onto her towel our eyes lingered for a beat, two, and then we got back to work. I looked up a few minutes later and saw that Jerry had flipped to a fresh page in his notebook, where he'd started a somewhat abstract sketch of a chestnut-haired beauty in a black bathing suit walking forever away, toward the water.

Incidentally, there are innumerable trading bots operating in the stock market which no actual person has created. No one knows what they are, or how or why they function the way they do. The only thing we know is that they exist, and that the activity they engage in has discernible patterns. And where there is a pattern, there is usually intent. And where there is intent . . . well, you see where I'm going with this.

Over glasses of straight rum, sitting at the high-top table on the porch, I told Emma I'd started a new book, and that it was all about her. I said I didn't know if it would ever be publishable, but I was going to write it anyway.

I'm worried, she said, that your version of me will come across as sad. I don't want people thinking I'm as sad as you make me out to be.

And so I'm telling you now that she was right about this. She is not as sad as I make her out to be. Emma is happy, the very picture of resilience. She wakes up in the morning and contemplates how much she loves her bed. She's friendly and open with strangers who sit next to her at bars, and when the Patriots beat the Jets she jumps up from her seat and claps wildly. She smiles when no one is watching. She hopes for better things, even expects them. She is not like me. I doubt she's ever once considered jumping in front of a train, or pointing her car at a concrete bridge support and flooring the accelerator. She is not sad.

A month or so before my father died, by which time his end had announced itself unequivocally, I found myself at the grocery store contemplating a small plastic container of salsa. Medium spice, all-natural ingredients, no preservatives so keep refrigerated and consume or discard within seven days of opening. Because the salsa contained no preservatives it seemed more important to check the expiration date than it would have been otherwise, and I turned the container around, flipped it upside down, searching for the tiny print. I examined the lid a second time and found the date, partly obscured by a graphic of a goofy cartoon donkey who may or may not have been drunk. And I read the date, and thought about it a minute, and realized suddenly that in all likelihood this container of salsa had a longer shelf life than my own personal father.

Apropos of nothing, at the beach, while a mackerel sky dimmed the midday sun, Emma asked me, Did you ever notice the orange towel on the back of the bathroom door? In the old house? Before the fire?

I thought for a minute. Shook my head.

You didn't see it? It was hanging there forever.

No. Never noticed it.

It was Matty's, she said. He put it up after the last shower he took, and I couldn't take it down. So I just let it hang there. Eight months. Until the place burned.

How did you know it was his towel? I asked. There were three or four hanging up there all the time.

It was the only one there when I got home, she said. The maid had done the laundry right before he split.

Wait. When you got home?

Yeah, she said. I was in D.C. when he left. Didn't I tell you that?

I paused. No. What? No. He left while you were away?

She stared at me. He sent me a fucking email, she said.

Later that day, after driving the narrow switchback roads from beach to beach, standing knee-deep in azure bathwater drinking Presidente, and coming home to the casita with pink ears and noses and shoulders, we went to the porch as the sun set, and Emma started to cry.

I asked what was wrong.

Nothing worth talking about, she said.

I tried a few jokes without luck. We sat quietly in the awkward wake of those duds, watching ramshackle fishing boats return to port in the half-light. I glanced at her a few times, and her eyes remained wet and red-rimmed.

After a while she looked at me and said, I may need a few minutes.

As I stood to walk inside I tried to make an agreeable sound, a sound that conveyed understanding and empathy, but it came out choked and lame, gave me away. I went into the casita and resolved, in sudden frustration, that if things would always be this way, I would at least write about it and make a lot of money.

I had no idea how right I was. Things would always be this way, and I would make a lot of money.

And though she cried for someone else, someone long gone, someone who'd seen nothing wrong with ending an eight-year marriage
via email, I was the one who comforted her, once she finally came in
off the porch. I was the one who stroked her hair and held her hand.
Kissed the top of her head once and again. That was me. God knows
where the hell he was.

Emma took a long shower, emerged from the bathroom smiling. She asked if I wanted to go out to dinner. By now I'd had a couple of drinks—her favorite, the Emma Original, rum and tonic with a splash of orange juice—and I smiled back, my gratitude at her improved mood magnified by the booze.

I drove us into town. Emma talked and laughed the whole way. We parked the Jeep in a small dirt lot on the *malecón* and worked our way, in the gathering dark, through a mixed crowd of locals and sunburned gringos. We sat down at a tapas place. Emma smiled at me, and nothing else in creation mattered a bit other than that little streetside table, a glass of whiskey for me and an Emma Original for her, distant steel drums, and her laughing at my jokes now, chin down, shoulders shaking, eyes shut tight against her mirth.

The earliest known mention of a person enhanced with a prosthesis, believe it or not, comes from the Vedas. We're talking 1500 B.C., or thereabouts. A female warrior loses her leg, and is given an iron replacement. We've had 3,500 years to get used to the idea, yet when I talk about the Singularity people still get an indulgent look on their faces, like they're humoring me and my absurd notions of human beings with brain/computer interfaces and titanium exoskeletons. I mean, they're polite about it, usually, which I appreciate. But, you know, 1500 B.C. The first time a person was joined with a machine, however primitive. Consider that, I tell them, and then ask yourself: who's being naïve, do you think?

On our return from Ireland, before the island, before she asked me to leave, Emma and I flew back to Maine and were set to go our separate ways, but shortly after hitting the tarmac we learned that a young man barely out of his teens had taken a Glock to a political meet-and-greet at an Arizona Safeway. It was a sunny day in the desert. People were supposed to be smiling and having their picture taken with a congresswoman, asking her questions about Medicare, but instead twenty people had been shot, including the congresswoman, who'd had a bullet go clean through her head. The FBI had descended and the parking lot was polka-dotted with blood and a girl who'd been born on 9/11 had died with a hole in her chest the diameter of a plum.

At first Emma seemed okay. She handed me her phone as we emerged from the plane, and I read the bulletin. We carried our bags up to the gate in silence and strode through the waiting area and out into the cold. I stopped on the sidewalk to light a cigarette, and we stood there in silence, gazing at nothing of any particular interest: security guards, baggage handlers, a ticket agent sneaking a smoke, people who would always be inconsequential to us except insofar as they kept a tiny part of our world operating so that we could get to where we were going.

After a while I looked at Emma. I wondered what was going on behind her eyes, and then she gave me a clue.

Can you come to my place tonight?

I said Yes, of course.

We loaded our bags into the car, and Emma drove us to her home. Along the way she told me she'd met the congresswoman back in 2005, when she'd worked on a campaign in New Mexico, before the job she had now. She told me she and the congresswoman were neighbors in her apartment building in D.C., had parking spaces next to each other.

We listened to radio reports: The congresswoman was in surgery. The congresswoman was dead. Earlier reports claiming the congresswoman had died were erroneous. Six others were dead for sure, though, including two members of the congresswoman's staff.

Later that night we stood on Emma's porch smoking cigarettes and not talking, when I noticed her flinch visibly at some thought.

I asked her what was the matter.

After a pause she said, I was just thinking. About what it would be like to get shot in the head. About what it would look like.

We didn't talk much after that. We drank until four in the morning, poured bourbon into coffee cups and bundled ourselves in down and Thinsulate and walked to the promenade, the same place where six months before she'd set the whole thing spinning with the simple, lethal act of resting her head on my shoulder. This time, in the bracing cold, we shivered past the scorched foundation of her old home, and we sat on a different bench and she put her head on my shoulder again. Snow wafted down through the orange glow of streetlamps, and we might have been the only two people on Earth, maybe even the only two who had ever existed. Later, in bed, with our fingers and toes stinging as they thawed and a reluctant winter sun beginning to rise outside, Emma lay on top of me and kissed my neck, my chest, let her lips and teeth linger over my nipples, and she fell asleep this way, still lying on top of me with her knees pulled up along my sides, her face buried in my neck, like a child.

On the beach, her feet resting in my lap, the tiny brown hairs on her toes: three on the big, two on the next, one on the next, and the two smallest toes bare and capped with tiny unpainted nails.

On a rare rainy morning on the island, over coffee mixed with scotch, Emma contended that happiness was the ultimate aim of all human undertaking, ordained in us by nature, written into our very genes.

I bristled at this notion. She smiled at my bristling, unmoved, calmly resolute.

We're happiness ciphers, she said, as if it should be obvious. All of us.

But why? I asked. Why is that automatically our goal? Because it's comfortable?

It's hard, she said, and then, after gauging my expression, more serious: Happiness is hard.

You mean hard to achieve. Not hard to occupy.

Right.

No argument there. But it is also, by definition, comfortable.

A palm frond scraped the window, and she looked over at the sound, thought a moment, shrugged almost imperceptibly, nodded. Sure, she said. This was not a concession of any kind regarding happiness and its merits.

I mean, you've read my novel, I said. Do you think that book ever gets written if I'm happy?

Emma made a show of considering this, moving her head in a manner that was neither yea nor nay.

I tried another tack. Baudelaire said . . . I want to make sure I get this right . . . he said, 'I can barely conceive of a type of beauty in which there is no melancholy.'

Emma smirked at me, lifted her mug, and said, Too bad there aren't any dead French poets here to help me through my day, huh?

And then she took a long, pointed drink of adulterated coffee, her eyes on mine, daring me to offer a response.

That night, after watching movies on the sofa all afternoon while rain pelted the metal roof, we sat at the same table in the kitchen. Over my rum and her bourbon, I put my chin in my hands and said, Don't get me wrong. On my worst days, happiness? Contentment? Hell yes. Give me some of that. Forget the books. I'll go sell fucking insurance. But then those worst days pass. And I want my sadness back.

True to form, she gave no indication of being moved by this in any way. She offered a bare nod. She might have been deeply touched. She might have thought I was silly. There was no way to know.

That night I woke terrified from some nightmare, the details of which were lost the moment it ended. Upright in bed, stiff as raw ore, I felt not merely that I didn't know where I was, but that I was actually nowhere. Like I'd come to in a vacuum, and neither I nor anything else existed any longer. For a while I thought maybe I was dead. As I stared around the void, warm hands reached out. One rested on my waist, the other on my ribs on my left side, pulling me back down, and Emma's voice, drowsy and kind, asked what was the matter, but I couldn't tell her because I didn't know. I followed the hands and found her body, and I lay down again, and her warm sleep smells brought everything back into existence—the mattress underneath us and the covers above, the rain ticking against the windows, the points of light on the main island across the bay, grappling tirelessly with the dark.

Would my preoccupation with Emma seem more sensible to you, less melodramatic, if the way in which she became absent from me was something more than my inconstancy and her decision not to abide it? Would my grief carry more weight, and would you share in it, if rather than being separated merely by our mistakes, Emma and I were instead separated by the Styx? If she had, for example, died in a plane crash on her way to the island? And if it *would* carry more weight—if you *would* share in it—then why? Why is grief, when inspired by certain types of loss, considered something to surmount, to get over, while when inspired by other types of loss it's given a pass, allowed and even encouraged to go on forever?

My mother's grief, incidentally, seems like it will be forever acute. She sleeps three hours a night, and still wears my father's wedding band on a necklace. She cries while waiting at railroad crossings, or in line at the pharmacy. It's been four years.

It was a night like any other. Emma had been on the island nearly a month. I took her to dinner at the resort. We sat on the deck in a warm northern breeze and traded bites of our dinners and made fun of tourists and went back to the casita and fell into bed. When she climbed on top of me she moved slowly and moaned and whispered that it was better than it ever had been with anyone else, and she punched my chest while I grabbed her by the throat and squeezed, pinched and twisted the flesh on her hips, and all was perfect, there in that moment.

To this day I have no idea why I decided, on that early morning, to tell her about Charlotte.

Emma stood nude at the side of the bed, cutting the air with her hands as she unloaded her grief. Her eyes burned with a wrath I knew and recognized and, yes, I will admit, feared. No doubt she had learned this wrath from her mother—it shimmered too violently in the pools of her irises, was too impervious to reason, to have come from anywhere else—but whether it was transmitted to her by the womb or by the fist is a mystery that, like Emma herself, will never be solved.

Everything is wrong, she said. In the semi-dark the skin of her bare breasts shone pale against the tan on her shoulders, her upper arms, her belly. Nothing ever lasts, she said. Nothing works. I try to believe it will but look at the fucking evidence. Matty and I were in love once. I know we were. Look at us now. Look at my *life*! I lost everything, Ron. Everything. How can I trust this, now? You and me? How can I trust my own judgment? I trusted my judgment before, and here is my reward. Choices, Ron. These things did not just happen to me. I made choices that created these circumstances. How do I account for that, and still trust myself? I can't. My instincts—everyone's instincts, Matty's, yours, my mother's—our instincts, the basis for all our choices, are fucked. Therefore, our choices will be fucked.

I wanted to reassure her, tell her she was mistaken. I knew it was my responsibility, knew that everything between us going forward depended on my ability to convince her that she was mistaken. But then I thought of my own choices—thought of Charlotte—and remained silent.

And now Emma, who stalked happiness so keenly, said: I want to be away from everyone. From you. I want to crawl away and be alone. Like a fucking dying animal. She brushed tears from her cheek with a violent swipe of one hand. I hate it. But that's what I want.

Here's the thing: she was constant, and I was not. She was absent, yes, and she asked me to go away for a while, but only so she could construct a better version of herself to present to me. But I saw what I needed to see to make my victim narrative real: a selfish, insensate woman who cared only for her own feelings, insofar as she had any. I realize now, of course, how wrong I was. Because while she tried to prepare herself, I pulled away by increments. She was constant, and I was not. And that, ultimately, was all that mattered.

I am so reasonable now, so understanding. I see so very, very clearly. All of this is true.

The next morning I pulled on a decent pair of jeans and the one button-down shirt I had, and stayed sober all day, filled with a creeping dread of the empty space Emma would leave in her wake, and in the afternoon I brought her to the airstrip and sat beside her as we watched Cessnas and de Havillands alight on the ground like giant aluminum dragonflies.

Then her plane arrived. We stood, both of us stiff and eager in the way I imagine a man about to be hanged would be stiff and eager. She had a messenger bag slung across her chest, which made it difficult to hug her properly. We shared a brief, awkward embrace, and kissed each other once, lightly, and she told me that she was sorry, and I told her the same thing though I wasn't sure about the particulars of what we were apologizing for; all that seemed certain was there was definitely something to be sorry about. Then she walked out to the tarmac and climbed aboard, ducking her head on the way in so that her hair fell forward and obscured what I believed then would be the last glimpse I'd have of her face, because already I was thinking, see, plotting, and the engines coughed to life and the plane made a short taxi past the little terminal, then turned and whisked by again in the opposite direction, and the pilot banked left the moment the wheels left the ground, drawing a sharp parabola back toward the mainland, taking Emma away to a place where she could be alone, like a dying animal, as she wished.

I'd like to pretend it was a selfless act, but I can't, because I don't believe there's any such thing. And understand I say that not out of some easy, obvious cynicism, but simply because it seems to me that all motivation is internal, no matter how philanthropic or otherwise outwardly directed the act it inspires. The impetus never comes from outside of us. Therefore, by definition, every act is selfish.

All the same, my reasoning when I drove the Jeep off Mosquito Pier was to ease Emma's burden the only way I knew how. I couldn't do anything about her mother, or the cold, sooty remains of her marriage, or the fact that she was in her midthirties and childless and worried to the point of panic, sometimes, that she would share her mother's fate and go insane and grow old alone. I had tried to help with all of those things, and failed. I could, however, do something about the supplement of pressure and sadness I'd brought to her in the guise of love, like a cake laced with arsenic.

But if I'm being honest, that wasn't all of it, and even if I tried to pretend it was, you surely and rightly would not believe me. There is no such thing as a selfless act.

Because I wanted out. For my own sake, my own reasons. One can only have so many fantasies about crashing airplanes into the jungle or leaping in front of trains before one finally takes that tiny step across the threshold between fantasy and reality. And listen, I grappled with these urges when all was well. They came unbidden, even while I had a smile on my face. So imagine their insistence when I was contractually obligated to write a novel, but couldn't find either the motivation or the acumen to finish a grocery list. When I had a detective waiting to ask me questions at home, and my state of mind and relative drunkenness were such that I'd begun to suspect he might actually have reason to be interested in me. When I had become, in Emma's estimation, just another poor choice among thirty-five years' worth of poor choices.

I'm not expecting empathy. Wouldn't want it, in fact, if someone were to offer. Just trying to give you an idea of why I committed an honest and sincere act meant to draw the curtain down, an act that instead set in motion a helix of increasingly bizarre circumstances that bring us right to this very moment, with me trying, and probably failing by increments, to explain everything to you.

As Emma had said, so sage, so beautiful in her sadness and fury: when our instincts are fucked, our choices can't be anything but.

The plan, if it can be called that, was neither very detailed nor complex for all the time I spent thinking about it. The idea itself seems, in retrospect, to have stemmed from the day I parked the Jeep at the beach and sat there for hours thinking about driving into the ocean.

Mosquito Pier, on the island's north side, was straight and true and over a mile long, provided a veritable runway for launching myself at high speed into the water where the Atlantic met the Caribbean. Built by the Navy during WWII, these days it was abandoned except for the occasional tarpon fisherman or dog-walking gringo, but all the same, not wanting to be dragged sputtering out of the surf by a strong-swimming Samaritan, I drove there early in the morning, when even wayward local teens would have finished their six packs of Medalla and slunk home to bed.

When I arrived the pier was dark as crude oil and, as I'd hoped, deserted.

I sat with the engine idling at the spot where the pier met the island. The decision to actually hit the gas, when the time came, was surprisingly easy, almost matter-of-fact. I depressed the pedal steadily, gaining speed until the moist night air roared through the windows and around the cabin. The headlights illuminated cracked pavement, then gobbled it up in an instant. Dark shapes flashed by on either side of me. Overhead the galaxy shimmered with great good cheer: stars winked, a flip sliver of moon shone happily.

There was a lot of noise, I remember that. The wind. The throaty whir of the Jeep's old engine, stupid, reliable machine. The tires snapping over chunks of broken asphalt. The Dopplered chirrup of a thousand coqui frogs. The ocean, inhaling and exhaling at steady intervals. The splintering crack as the Jeep burst through the wooden guardrail at the pier's terminus.

And then: silence, airborne.

This silence persisted, even after the Jeep's grill hit the waves and my face bounced off the steering wheel. Viewed through the suddenly bloody lens of my sight, the last moments of my life were like a television set to mute. Black water flooded the cabin silently, soaking my pants, then the bottom of my T-shirt. As the water rose I felt my breath coming quicker, but could not hear it. I'm sure I moaned once or twice, but that sound failed to register, too.

But my hearing returned, somehow, once the water enveloped me fully: the womb-noises I'd noted the night I went swimming with Rick and Charlotte. A hush that was somehow full of distended, elongated, peaceful sounds.

I felt the water lift me gently out of the driver's seat.

Then I drifted. Both figuratively and, it would turn out, literally.

Ray Kurzweil has pinned his hopes for resurrecting his father on what he calls the Law of Accelerating Returns. He argues that technological progress occurs exponentially, rather than linearly as most people believe. In other words, computing power does not accrue in increments, like forming a snowball and then adding bits of snow to it one at a time. It's more like the proverbial snowball running downhill—it gains size and speed exponentially. It does not add; it multiplies.

This is why Kurzweil believes we will see the Singularity within the next fifty years, rather than at some hazy future time so distant as to remain comfortably fictional in people's minds. This is why Kurzweil eats very few carbohydrates, and takes 150 different health supplements each day. This is why he drinks vats of green tea and alkaline water, and gives himself IV treatments with chemical cocktails. Because he wants to make it long enough to see the Singularity, after which he, and everyone else, will live forever—or at least until the universe spreads itself so thinly across space that it becomes impossible to exist here anymore.

The time between when I drifted up out of the car seat and when I came to on what I'd later realize was Green Beach is an absolute inkblot, a cognitive black hole. No recollection whatsoever, although one has to wonder if perhaps I was swimming in a sort of blackout, as it seems unlikely that I would have survived if I'd been completely unconscious, just limp and drifting.

Emma told me, from time to time, that I talked in the middle of the night. Apparently I would say something to wake her, and we would have whole conversations, and then she would realize at a certain point that though my eyes were open and my mouth formed words, I was actually still asleep. It spooked her.

In any event, it doesn't take a tremendous imaginative leap to figure out how I ended up on Green Beach. I mentioned that the spot where I drove into the water off Mosquito Pier happens to be the convergence of the Atlantic and Caribbean. And you have to understand that these are not separate bodies of water in name only. Most days, standing on the pier, you can easily distinguish where one ends and the other begins—a sharp line dividing deep Atlantic blue from warm Caribbean aquamarine.

I'm not trying to bore you with minutiae. The point is that the Caribbean current runs in a whip from that spot, away from its communion with the Atlantic and around the western tip of the island—precisely the route one would take to get to Green Beach.

So the water lifted me up and out of the Jeep, then carried me around that western point, where the inbound swells pulled me ashore and deposited me on Green Beach—the most remote place on a remote island, a beach unoccupied for weeks at a time in the winter.

I woke half-interred in wet sand, with two things competing for the bulk of my attention: a face that felt shattered, and the most powerful thirst I had ever experienced, a Saharan thirst, the sort of primal dryness one imagines the Israelites hunkered down with after Yahweh told them they'd be sticking around the desert for another forty years.

I would come to understand that my face wasn't shattered; just my nose. And I would come to understand that I'd been on the beach, unconscious, for more than a day, thus explaining my thirst.

At this point I'd actually forgotten about the suicide attempt, and as I struggled to my feet, my skin like an undersized glove from dehydration and sunburn, my thoughts were consumed entirely with the need for water. I almost drank from the Caribbean, such was my desperation and confusion. But then I squeezed my eyes closed for a moment, making an effort to gather myself, and when I opened them again I turned and saw the jungle and realized where I was.

And then realized, immediately after, what I had to do to get out of there.

Waiting for someone to show up, at that time of year, was no good. In the summer, boats from the main island weighed anchor off Green Beach every day, but as I said, this was winter, and I could have been sitting there for days. So, dehydrated to the point of delirium, concussed and horribly sunburned, I staggered off into the jungle. It made as much sense as anything else.

Several hours later I came to the laguna, where once, on a happier day, I'd gone fly-fishing. I drank deep from the muddy, brackish water, tasting shit and swallowing small fauna and not caring at all.

From there it was easy to find my way to the main road. By and by I was able to flag down a *público* driver who, after a long dubious look and some questions in Spanish regarding what had happened to me and whether I wanted to go to *la emergencia,* agreed to drive me back to town. I thought I would have to negotiate an IOU, but then found a waterlogged twenty in my hip pocket. I gave it to him, told him to keep the change.

Inside I drank bottled water until I vomited, then drank some more. I took a cold shower and fell into bed. Some time later I got up long enough to loose a meager stream of what looked like Coca-Cola into the toilet.

When I woke the second time it was dark, and I decided I felt good enough for a drink.

At Duffy's the television over the bar was set, as always, to CNN. I nursed an Emma Original and watched footage of revolts in the Middle East and a segment that made me glad the sound was off, about how the human penis once bore spines but had lost them over the course of millennia. My eyes, in search of something less appalling, wandered to the ticker at the bottom of the screen: *Children forced to work 15-hour days*, it read. *Let it grow: Clapton's guitar on sale.* And then: *American man missing, feared dead in Caribbean.*

The bartender, a big bespectacled gringo named Lyman who never learned my name and always called me buddy or chief, came over and asked me if I needed a refill.

Sure, I said, still staring at the television screen.

He swiped my glass from the bar, rinsed it under the tap, and set about mixing another rum punch. You just get to the island? he asked.

Beg pardon?

He looked up from his work, and no recognition registered in his eyes as they settled on me. I asked if you just got here. Haven't seen you around before.

I hesitated. Something occurred to me, suddenly, and I said, Yeah. Just got in today.

Lyman set the drink in front of me. What happened to your face? he asked. How'd you get the broken beak?

Again, I balked.

After a moment Lyman held up his hands. No problemo, he said. None of my business anyway. There's plenty of gringos on the run from something down here. You'll fit right in.

He rapped his knuckles on the bar, twice, then turned around to wash glasses.

I finished the rum punch quickly. I wanted to go home and get online and find out what this missing American business was all about, so I asked for the check.

Can I settle up? I asked Lyman.

Sure thing, buddy.

He went to the register, punched a few keys, and when he slapped the check on the bar in front of me I automatically pulled my debit card halfway out of my wallet before deciding, after a moment's thought, to pay with cash instead.

It's possible that after the Singularity the machines will see us not as a threat, and not as obsolete, inferior versions of themselves, and not as kindly soft-headed grandparents—but as gods.

Perhaps they will travel out into the universe, far beyond where we could imagine going, and when they inevitably encounter other intelligent life they will spread the gospel, as it were, of humanity, impart their creation myth—which will, of course, not be a myth at all.

It's also possible that, driven by motivations we cannot conceive of—in the same way groundhogs cannot conceive of what motivates humans—the machines will in their travels bring self-replicating strands of RNA to some distant planet they consider suitable for their purposes, and they will seed that planet with the RNA and observe, over eons, as life takes hold, first as bacteria and protozoans and algae, and then, gradually, more and more complex organisms, until, in a slow and inefficient manner it is difficult to believe the machines would have patience with, intelligent life finally emerges. In a very real sense we will be gods to this new form of organic intelligence as well, whether they know it or not.

And then this new intelligence will, much as we did, begin figuring things out. They will learn to make and yoke fire. They will invent the wheel, or something like it. Discovery and invention will continue until, assuming they aren't exterminated (either by one of the myriad dangers in an endlessly hostile universe or by one of their own creations), this version of organic intelligence will experience their own Singularity, thereby becoming gods themselves.

And so on.

I slipped into the casita quietly, leaving the lights off, and found my way in the dark to the kitchen, where my laptop sat on the bar. I punched my name into Google, and an instant later sat staring at a screen full of briefs about my own death.

CNN's piece featured a photo of the island's police force—all three officers—standing aside their cruisers at the end of Mosquito Pier as a crane hoisted the Jeep from the water. According to the article, one of these officers had noticed the broken guardrail the morning after I'd driven off the pier. Something so obvious and glaring that even the Keystone Kops on the island couldn't miss or ignore it—but then, I hadn't been trying to hide anything. I was supposed to be dead.

Now, though, a new possibility, which had taken seed in my mind the moment Lyman failed to recognize me at the bar, began to blossom.

I was presumed a suicide. The police speculated that the current had carried me off, which explained, to their evident satisfaction, the lack of a corpse. Chief Morales told reporters he was waiting for my landlord to arrive from the main island with a key to the house, after which they would inspect my living quarters to try and turn up some explanation of what I'd done and why, so that my friends and family might better understand.

I knew that the real reason they hoped to turn up an easy explanation was so they wouldn't have to do any more work, so the gringo reporters and cameramen would go away, leave them to settle back into their ineptitude.

And it was precisely that ineptitude, I was beginning to think, that might make it possible for me to stay dead.

I would have to leave a note—something, as I mentioned, that I had failed to do when intending to actually kill myself, but something that seemed essential now that I planned to fake doing so.

It gets a little convoluted, I know. Imagine how I felt.

I tore several blank sheets from my notebook, still there where I'd left it next to the laptop, and wrote quickly, my messy script made messier still by fervor and the relative darkness. I wrote to my mother, my sisters, to Dwayne and Hankie, and then, when it came time to write to Emma, my hand paused over the page.

And I wondered, could I really do this? Could I really stay away from her? If one were going to fake being dead, it went without saying that one had to do it consistently. There could be no waffling. And I had demonstrated that, when it came to Emma at least, I was a world-class waffler.

But the alternative—slinking to the police station and announcing my continued existence, confessing what I'd tried to do (there was no way to spin driving off a pier at high speed as an accident, as far as I could see), suffering the attendant fifteen minutes of dubious fame, then returning home and having to explain myself to my mother, my sisters, most of all to Emma, who I knew would be furious in her relief and would not have interest in or time for any explanation—that did not exactly appeal, either.

I considered, as my hand continued to hover over the notebook page, that I had already spent a good chunk of my life—the majority of it, in fact—separated from Emma. Years, while we led entirely discrete lives, seeing each other in passing only once or twice on every trip around the sun, when we might share half a drink at the bar and chat for a few minutes while Matty loomed somewhere in the background with other friends of theirs. I'd become adept at hiding the tumult that occurred inside me at the mere sight of her. I assumed a preternaturally calm, smooth, neutral persona, one so convincing that she'd told me more than once that during those years she was convinced I didn't really care about her one way or the other.

I'd been apart from her, in that way, for almost two decades. Why should this be any different? I'd done it before, I could do it again.

So I wrote to Emma. Stripped away every bit of artifice I'd girded myself with over the years, and fucking wrote. I realized, at a certain point, that I was holding my breath. By far the best piece of scribbling I've ever managed.

I still loved her. There was never any denying that. But it is amazing, isn't it, what we can learn to live with, or in this case without. A simple equation, really: time plus grief, multiplied by base human failure.

I reasoned that I could once again do that math.

I've mentioned that after the Singularity, most people will choose to slough off the limitations and frailties of the physical body. Ray Kurzweil and others believe this will occur by the turn of the twenty-second century. By then the vast majority of us will exist as digital consciousnesses. Without bodies, the only way to die will be to choose to. It follows that suicide, in this new reality, will consist of simply having our selves erased.

There will likely be one important difference between corporeal suicide and digital suicide. Right now, one cannot destroy oneself utterly. We can blow our heads off, get the chatter to stop and cease having to pay bills, but we persist in the minds of those who knew and loved us. We continue to appear to them, unbidden, in myriad ways. They recall our smiles, hear our voices, jolt from frightening dreams and reach for us on reflex before remembering that we are no longer there. Until they themselves are gone, they continue to suffer the chafing pang of our absence.

But when we all exist as pure thought, we can be deleted not just from ourselves, but from the minds of everyone. With a keystroke (or its post-Singularity equivalent) parents will be spared grief, lovers loneliness, friends the pain of having known and knowing no longer. When we choose suicide, we will choose not merely to destroy ourselves, but to never have existed. In this way, the one compelling argument against suicide—the anguish it causes to those left behind—will be eliminated.

And we are already, today, nibbling on the front edge of such a paradigm shift. Consider this recent news: EU legislators have proposed laws granting people the right to erase personal information from social networking sites. If passed, these laws will let people force Facebook, Twitter, and the like to behave as though they never existed.

The sanctioned shorthand for this proposal? 'The Right to be Forgotten.'

Which is as apt and succinct a description of suicide as any I've ever read.

left everything, save the clothes I wore, my watch, and around eighteen hundred dollars in cash. I felt a twinge of regret at abandoning the draft of my novel, malformed failure though it was. It may have been self-involved and plotless and incomplete, but I had labored on it honestly, and aside from Emma it was all I knew. But everything had to go, and not just for the purposes of feigning my death. Some part of me, the part that was steering the ship, recognized that.

There was no way for me to know, at the time, that leaving behind the manuscript would be the best career move I'd ever made.

And it came to be that Roberto, the man who had run me off the bridge, the man whom I'd repaid by beating him badly enough to put him in the hospital, would be the only person on Earth who knew I was actually alive.

I went to him that night, walking clear across the island while dogs howled in the hills all around me. It was nearly dawn by the time I reached Roberto's house. I checked my watch and discovered it had stopped working, the crystal clouded with vapor. I unhooked the strap and tossed it in the bushes, then reconsidered—the watch could be discovered and possibly linked to me—and spent several minutes locating it in the twilight.

Why Roberto? Well, first, who else did I know? But beyond that I reasoned that here was a rare bird, a wholly trustworthy man who, because of what he'd been in a former life, must have known the sorts of untrustworthy people I would need to make my disappearance actual. This was a bare hunch, but I had seen on Roberto's face that drinking wasn't the only thing he'd given up nineteen years ago. He'd been rough. He'd done bad things, had most likely been involved with the island's small circle of organized criminals, a cabal that stole boats and dealt crack and regularly and systematically stripped casitas of everything that wasn't nailed down. If I'd picked a fight with this younger version of Roberto, I probably would have been the one who ended up in the hospital.

I went through the gate on the chain-link fence, wincing as it creaked and rattled in the stillness of the early morning. Several taps on the aluminum security door produced no response, so I made a fist and pounded three times, then stood and waited while roosters began shrieking at one another all over the barrio.

After a long moment came the dull click of tumblers rolling in the lock, and then Roberto stood looking at me through the bars of the security door, half-asleep and incredulous, wearing only boxer shorts. He had one of those enormous bellies that do not hang like flab but rather jut out aggressively, as though he'd swallowed a pony keg.

What is this? he asked, but despite his incredulity, despite the rude hour, he turned the deadbolt and swung the security gate open to let me in before I'd offered any explanation of why I was there.

Roberto listened in silence as he stood at the gas range making coffee for us in the island style—with a saucepan, at a simmer.

When I was finished he said, You want to be someone else. I understand this.

He didn't understand perfectly. I wanted simply to be gone, not to be someone else. But his imperfect understanding was sufficient for my purposes. I guess I shouldn't have been surprised, having intuited the way in which he'd reinvented himself all those years ago, that he had no objection to my disappearing. What he did object to, though, was leaving Emma behind.

You love her, he said simply, slicing the air with one hand as if this were the beginning and the end of the discussion.

It's a hell of a lot more complicated than that, I told him.

Maybe, he said, but his expression, and the way he moved his head back and forth, indicated that he did not believe any complication was sufficient to excuse abandoning her. Maybe.

What about you? I asked. You're such a proponent of love.

What is this?

I mean if you believe in love so much, where is yours?

Roberto turned toward me with the saucepan in hand, poured steaming coffee into two mugs on the table, then settled into his chair and looked straight at me.

She die, he said finally, clapping his hands together lightly and then raising them overhead to indicate the ascension of this departed woman. He looked at me with a sad smile, the expression of a man who long ago came to accept the pain of such a loss as a fixture in his internal landscape.

Can I ask how?

He hooked one thumb toward a closed door opposite the kitchen table, behind which his son lay sleeping. *El parto*, he said, still smiling. Miguelito birth. So I have no choice, see. You, you have a choice.

We didn't say anything after that, just sat looking at one another. I understood his point, of course—life had a nasty habit of stealing things from us irretrievably; we didn't need to rush to get rid of them ourselves—but what I ended up feeling, once again, was the exact opposite of Roberto's intent.

Because I'm sitting there looking at him, right, and that smile is still on his lips, even through our silence, and I'm thinking this man clearly felt for his wife what I felt for Emma, and when his wife died and left him alone with an autistic child who would never be able to care for himself, Roberto not only weathered his grief but let it mold him into the calm, decent, happy person seated across from me, a man who sacrificed himself daily, and through that sacrifice made himself whole.

But I didn't want to be whole. I didn't want to be calm, or decent, or happy. The best I can say for myself, at the time, was that I wanted to want to want all those things. There was a distance between Roberto and I, and his wise, wistful smile, no matter how hard-earned, couldn't bridge it.

Roberto went back to bed. I slipped out to *la tienda* for rum, slugged from the bottle as the sun rose and the island woke up and the dogs and horses made their daily fuss. A few hours later Roberto found me drunk at his kitchen table, and he took the bottle away and dumped what was left in the sink. Then Roberto blessed me. At first I thought he did so in Spanish, but later, sober, remembering, I realized it was Latin, the language from the Masses of my childhood. He placed his hand on my forehead, shook salt on his finger and pressed it into my mouth, as though he were John the Baptist. *Accipe signum Crucis tam in fronte, quam in corde*, Roberto told me. He traced symbols on my face and chest with his thumb, symbols I remembered but could not name. Slumped and insensate, I accepted his blessing. I did not resist.

It turned out Roberto only knew one untrustworthy person, but that man knew the people I needed, being a fixer.

The fixer clearly hadn't seen Roberto for a while, but greeted him warmly, whatever bond they'd shared long ago spanning the years that had passed. Me the fixer was less sure of. Arms crossed, he eyed me with open skepticism while Roberto talked a streak of Spanish. But the fixer's dark, seamed face brightened considerably at what was, for him, a simple enough request to fulfill: one counterfeit passport.

The man extended a hand toward me, rowing his fingers back toward his palm to indicate payment was due at that moment.

I hesitated, looked to Roberto.

Quinientos, he said to me, nodding his approval and assent. Almost a third of my money. But without the passport it didn't matter how much money I had. I counted off five hundred dollars and handed it over.

The fixer held the bills up to the overhead light, one by one. Then, satisfied, he removed a small silver camera from a desk drawer. I stopped him, explaining in Spanish that I needed to look different than I did now. He led me to the bathroom, where he produced clippers and sheared my face and head without asking permission, without a word. He left me with a safety razor and a can of Barbasol to finish the job myself, and when I emerged he took three pictures of me, shook Roberto's hand and clapped him on the shoulder, and bade us fuck off until *mañana*.

At Roberto's I took a long bath while my one set of clothes flapped on a line in the backyard. I sat there, submerged up to my chin, for a long time. As the water cooled around me my hands returned again and again to my face, bearded for so long, now bare, alien to both my touch and, as I stood for a minute gazing into the mirror, my sight. Not to mention the shaved head, lumpy and pale, spotted with blemishes. I realized that if I'd caught a glimpse of myself in a storefront window, I might for a moment see not my own reflection, but the presence of another person entirely on the other side of the glass. Which of course was the whole point.

Before my father took sick, but after he had a heart attack at fifty-two and retired, he and my mother moved from the house where they'd raised me and my sisters and into a prefab double-wide outside of town. The house sat on an acre of grass bordering a dairy farm, with a view of the river half-obscured by a stretch of oaks and white pines. At night, sometimes, they could hear coyotes howling.

This was to be a fresh start for them, after his near-death and long convalescence, and he took to retirement well, if in the usual fashion: spending a lot of time in his new garage, tilling a patch of the yard and planting a garden, joining cribbage and bowling leagues.

But there were unexpected things as well, things that hinted at a complexity to the man, and also a tenderness, that I had never suspected in twenty-five years of knowing him. In addition to the garden, the utility and sensibleness of food plants, he also tended flowers—rosebushes on the side of the house facing the road, rows of violets in front of the deck, a clutch of white turtleheads near the flagpole.

What he favored most, though, were a dozen cherry trees that he planted on either side of the driveway, over three hot summer days during which my mother worried that he would work himself into another heart attack. The trees were very young, far from bearing fruit, but this was a long-term project for my father—or so he imagined—and he shepherded the trees through the seasons for two years, watering and fertilizing, training them with shears and knife, staking them firmly to protect from the winter winds.

But then the doctor told him he had cancer, and the trees went neglected, though I did my best to keep the aphids at bay and prune away signs of blight. The next spring, my father's last, the rosebushes grew wild. The garden never progressed beyond an incongruous patch of dirt surrounded by bluegrass, a glaring vacancy that hardened and split when summer came. Two of the cherry trees died of something called silver leaf, and a third came loose from its stakes in a violent thunderstorm and snapped halfway down its slender, delicate trunk.

After he was gone, my mother spent three years trying to wrest herself away from that house, which they'd come to live in only because he'd had a heart attack, and in which they had experienced little other than his illness and death. One of the reasons she gave for continuing to torture herself by living there was the trees. He loved those trees, she told me. He wanted to watch them mature. He used to talk about making cherry pies, she said.

Understand, again, that when I left the island for the Sinai I was not interested in assuming a different identity. I did not intend to become another person. There was never a moment when the thought even crossed my mind, in fact. Changing my appearance was not a reinvention—it was an erasure.

So when I bought a bus ticket out of Cairo, then sat for eight hours watching the infinite sameness of the desert as it approached and receded all at once, I had no intention of learning Arabic, or doing anything other than subsistence work, or making new friends, or rock climbing, or finding God, or any of the other things people do to cobble together what is usually thought of as a full life. There was no life to fill, and no need to clutter up purgatory with aimless activity or self-improvement.

I knew that I'd made the right decision to disappear when I realized, as the bus inched through a sandstorm so dense the road was obscured almost entirely, that for the first time since faking my death I genuinely had no feelings whatsoever about my unfinished novel. I was blank about it. Utterly so. A corpse, after all, has no use for books, any more than it does for eyes, those unseeing things.

I slouched off the bus in a hamlet halfway down the Red Sea coastline. I'd been there years before, while staying in Cyprus with a friend as I wrote what would become my first book, and I'd fallen in love with the gorgeous desolation of the place. The Holy Land's moonscape and my insides had matched like a pair of socks, and I felt this recognition thrum in me again as the bus pulled away and I stared out beyond the road, where the desert brooded behind red cliffs that rose up out of the sand like titanic sentries.

Not that I was allowed to ruminate on the sense of coming home for long. In short order a dozen men descended, demanding that I buy a soda, henna tattoos, or a ride to the few ramshackle buildings that made up the town, a mile back in the direction I'd come from on the bus.

I pointed to one of the men at random and mimed turning a steering wheel back and forth. He nodded eagerly and hurried away, reappearing a minute later in a battered old Datsun.

We sped off in a burst of combustion and rising dust, and here was something I remembered from my first time in the desert: things didn't move much, but when they did there was always something frantic about it, as though the object in motion were in pursuit of something, or else being pursued.

The driver assumed I was looking for a room, and dropped me at Habiba Village, a loose collection of thatch huts and wooden shacks abutting the languid Red Sea. This place, like everything aside from the bus depot, seemed deserted. I made my way through the huts to the water as the driver went inside the office to negotiate a finder's fee for delivering what he must have thought was an American tourist with bottomless pockets.

On the beach I found a metal cage atop a post. Inside the cage was a small monkey, baring sharp canines as I approached. The cage was full of candy wrappers and cigarette butts. Across the water, a few miles distant, lay the coast of Saudi Arabia. I imagined that someone standing there looking back toward me would see a mirror image of what I stood gazing at: brown, flat, featureless, endless nothing.

A thin Arab in khakis and a cream-colored polo shirt appeared beside me. You need a room, sir? he asked.

I need a job, I told him.

The Singularity, of course, will mark not just the end of death, but the end of suffering as well.

First, we will merge with our technology through a process called wireheading, in which the pleasure centers of the brain are stimulated remotely. This will not merely fabricate pleasure, but more important, eliminate all physical and psychological discomfort.

Alternately, those who still appreciate the analog human experience may opt, at the end of the day, to upload onto a computer any moment that was painful or boring or otherwise not good, in the same manner, and with the same ease, that one uploads a photograph from a camera today.

I mean, imagine it.

Next will come genetic engineering on a scale, and with a precision, that will make Dolly the sheep look like something out of a nerdy kid's science kit. A whole prototypical generation whose genomes are programmed to render unhappiness in any form biologically impossible. And before you dismiss this as some sort of Stepfordian nightmare, consider: If there weren't something fundamentally wrong with the way we're wired by nature, would there be such a tremendous sum of suffering in the world? And if we agree on a fundamental wrongness, what, then, is the objection to correcting it?

You loathe the thought, I know. You tremble and ululate, clutch misery to your chest, guard it tooth and claw. You are as attached to suffering as a child is to its blankie. But not me. Not anymore. Take my memories of Emma and cast them into a pit deep enough to feed the five thousand. Take the image of my father's dead sunken face from my mind's eye, load it onto a flash drive, and watch me crush it under my heel screaming *baruch sheptarani*, because even though I am a gentile I am also a son of the world and of humanity; I belong to every language and so I will speak in whatever language suits the moment.

The thin Arab, whose name was Asif, put me to work in the kitchen of Habiba Village's small restaurant. He couldn't afford to pay me, but in exchange for busing tables (the 'tables' being ground-level platforms surrounded by cushions in beachside cabanas) and washing dishes twice a day, I was fed and given a small thatch hut, complete with bed mat and mosquito netting.

I would have felt guilty for taking a hut that Asif could otherwise be renting, but he always had multiple vacancies. In fact, there were rarely more than three or four guests at a time in the village. Asif told me that until recently business had been good—especially in summer, tourists had flocked to the Red Sea from Cairo and Israel—but then two bombs had detonated in Sharm El-Sheikh, the glimmering tourist mecca at the tip of the peninsula, and the Israelis in particular stayed home in droves after that.

Thus the sense I'd had, on arrival, that the place was deserted. And with the dearth of tourists, a current of desperation ran through those trying to make a living near Habiba Village, a desperation I felt every time I strode through the gauntlet of jewelry tables and kebab stands that ran the length of the beach between my hut and a polished, incongruous Hilton resort at the other end. Almost always on these daily walks I was the only person other than the shopkeepers themselves, and as I passed by they called to me from behind rickety folding tables, waved their arms wildly to get my attention, sometimes walked out onto the pathway and grabbed me by the upper arm in their anxiety to sell me something, anything.

And because I wanted nothing, had interest in nothing, I never stopped to consider the handmade necklaces, never sat for an application of henna, never even spoke a word, in fact. I walked with my eyes on my feet, not turning my head to either side. When the vendors touched me I shrugged their hands off gently, and did not break stride.

And when I reached the gleaming white walls of the Hilton, I turned around and traced the same path back to Habiba Village, and again the shopkeepers hollered and harassed, as though they'd never seen me before.

It turned out, though, that I did register with at least one of the shopkeepers. During one afternoon walk—I had been in the Sinai for at least a month, but certainly less than two—I was confronted by a dark, stringy-muscled Arab, who moved from behind the folding table on which he offered tea and Coca-Cola, stepped directly into my path, and put his hands on my shoulders to halt me.

Every day you walk through here, he said. Twice a day. And not buy anything. You pretend we are not here. But we are here.

I looked him in the eyes and saw a gentle dignity there that was hard not to respond to, especially when he'd been able to preserve that dignity in the face of what had to be a difficult life. But I couldn't bring myself to explain that I was not what he imagined me to be. I was not a rich American (Americans, in the Egyptian mind, always being rich). I was not a tourist. And I was not trying to be rude. I was simply *not there*. But I didn't have the language to convey this to him, and even if I had, I doubt he would have understood.

You don't have to buy, the man continued. But you do have to see we are here.

Without a word I stepped carefully to the side, and when he didn't move to block me again I continued on, head down, watching my feet kick up little clouds of dust.

After my father was diagnosed I didn't do much writing for a while. Instead I spent most of my time driving aimlessly on the country highways that spiderweb the hills around town, smoking and listening to music, with a constant low drawl in my head akin to thinking. I took to fishing the Sebasticook River a lot, carrying an Ugly Stik around in the back of the car and pulling over and walking the banks whenever the urge struck. My father used to take me there when I was a kid, to a spot just below the dam where a huge boulder juts up out of the water, a section of shimmering eddies the smallmouths like to hide in like phantoms. I fished there fruitfully for more than a year, pulling out bass and crappie and the occasional chub, while my father shriveled and became a child again. And then one day a few months before my father died, I snagged an eager smallmouth in the eye with a barbed treble hook. There is no way to gently remove a hook from a fish's eye, but I tried. As I worked the barb out the eye bulged grotesquely, threatening to pull free along with the hook, and I had a moment when I realized that if the fish could scream, it would have. But instead all it did was gape, and I released it back into the river, hurting and silent and probably bound to die. And after that I lost the stomach for fishing, and have hardly done it since.

Every day a lone old Bedouin woman unfurled a blanket full of jewelry on the sidewalk in front of the Hilton. She sat cross-legged and hunched, all but her eyes and desiccated hands hidden under a black *thobe* and matching veil. Normally the women's veils bore strings of coins, the quality and quantity of which indicated their relative level of wealth within the Bedouin community. This old woman's veil, however, had no coins at all.

From what I was able to see on my walks to and from the Hilton, the few people who stayed there rarely strayed beyond its all-inclusive walls, and those who did pass by the woman were usually safely ensconced behind the privacy glass of SUVs that ferried tourists back and forth from the airport and Mount Sinai. Only a handful of times did I ever see anyone examining the woman's wares, and I never witnessed an actual purchase.

I made the mistake of walking past her once. She leaned forward beseechingly at my approach. She held her hands, trembling with age, up over the array of trinkets, a pitiable attempt at salesmanship. She made pleading sounds as tears seeped from her eyes. Her veil fell open, revealing a face ravaged by some ancient injury—it looked as though someone had thrown acid on her, and for all I knew, in this dry and holy place, someone had.

And not even for this woman, as wretched an example of humanity as I have encountered before or since, could I muster anything resembling fellow feeling, or feeling of any kind. I did not stop and at least pretend to consider buying one of her brooches or necklaces. I continued on, even as she reached up to clutch at my hand with her own. I pulled myself away, and I never walked that close to her again.

Asif, to his credit, never asked me who I was, why I'd come there, what I was running from. I sensed that this was not a lack of interest on his part—we talked often, if briefly, throughout the day, as he dirtied pots and I scrubbed them—but more an intuitive understanding that if I'd wanted to discuss who I was, I would have brought it up myself. Thoughtful, kind Asif, doting father of three, devout Sunni, quietly tireless laborer: it never would have occurred to him to pry.

Instead we discussed post-Mubarak Egypt, the barracudas he'd seen while guiding several guests on a snorkeling trip, Zamalek soccer club's chances in the CAF championships (which I knew nothing about, but nodded politely where it seemed indicated, as the topic was one of few about which Asif actually became somewhat animated).

For three years we had these little discussions every day, and not once did Asif ask my real name, though he had to know the name I'd given him, back there on the beach when I'd first arrived, was a counterfeit.

Despite my reticence about who I was, though, Asif considered me a friend. The way I first came to know this, really know it, was through the monkey imprisoned by the water.

Every day on my funereal beach walks, I passed by the monkey in its tiny, refuse-filled cage. And though it had an invariably nasty disposition, baring those yellowed canines, thrashing the side of the cage in a futile attempt to get at me, I actually liked the thing. I *felt* something when I saw it—miracle of miracles—though at first I didn't realize this, mistaking the dull hum of emotion as a stomach soured by Asif's fiery *shakshouka,* maybe, or else just tightness in the muscles between my ribs. After I did recognize the sensation as a feeling, I was still hard-pressed to identify precisely what I felt. I wandered past the shopkeepers, deaf to their pleadings, and grasped at this emotion as it receded, trying to recognize it. Was it regret? Pity? Or just unadorned sadness, plain as the dollops of Greek yogurt Asif spooned onto guests' breakfast plates?

Whatever its name, I did not enjoy the feeling—either the fact of it, or its quality. And so after months of enduring these emotional spasms each day, I went to Asif and asked him to let the monkey go.

It would not survive, he told me. It doesn't belong in the desert.

I considered this. Nodded minutely, a tic I'd absorbed, as through osmosis, from seeing Asif do it countless times.

All the same, I said to him. Better to die in the open air than to live in a cage. Especially a cage people use as a garbage can.

Asif tilted his head to the side and pursed his lips, eyebrows arching, a silent concession to the sensibility of my argument.

I went to my hut. For the first time since arriving in the Sinai I could not sleep, an unpleasant throwback to earlier years, when wakefulness had been a constant companion that I battled with liquor and willful forgetting. I lay under the net with my eyes open, listening to a squadron of mosquitos buzz their frustration at being unable to get to me. I wished for any sort of distraction. I wished I had a book to read, though I hadn't read a word since coming here. I wished, God help me, for a television to stare at.

I thought of Emma for the first time in months, the faint warmth of her breath on my neck, the weight of her leg resting across my thighs as she dozed, the way her presence had banished a lifetime of insomnia.

Eventually I fell into something resembling unconsciousness, more a tense void than restful sleep. I woke bleary the next morning and stumbled to the kitchen, where Asif, always there before me no matter how early I arrived, was busy preparing breakfast. We barely spoke. Habiba Village had enjoyed increased business in the wake of a Hamas cease-fire, and as the Israeli tourists began to reappear in large numbers we often found ourselves with too much work to allow for real conversation.

A couple of hours later, with the tables cleared and the last of the dishes washed and stowed, I stepped through the back door and set out. This portion of my walk, the minute or so before I cleared the huts and set eyes on the cage, had started to instill a tension in me, and of late I'd even considered forgoing the walk altogether. That day I fought through my anxiety. Right foot, left foot, gritting grimly in the sand. I came around the side of the last hut with my head down, reluctant to look at the monkey, but when I didn't hear it growl and spit I glanced up to discover the cage was now vacant— monkey gone, garbage gone.

We never spoke of it, Asif and I. For all I know he took the monkey and, instead of releasing it to suffer a lingering death in the desert, killed it himself with the cleaver he used to rend legs of lamb. In any event, I didn't have to see it anymore. I resumed my days of utter blankness, and at night slept like the dead, as unperturbed again by emotion as on the day I'd arrived.

In my four years in the Sinai, I did not drink even once. This was holy land, and outside the walls of the Hilton, at least, abstention was strictly observed. Even if I'd wanted a drink, and could find it, Asif would not have tolerated this vile habit of Westerners on the grounds of Habiba Village. Not even in me, the friend whose name he did not know.

I engaged in nothing that was not essentially functional. I breathed. I ate with all the enthusiasm of a man filling the gas tank in his car. I drank water each day, more in the summer, when emerging from the kitchen felt like stepping into a blast furnace. I slept when the day ended and the only lights to be seen were a few winking pinpoints across the water in Saudi Arabia. I worked and walked because bodies are built to move, to manipulate objects and mark their environment.

The only indulgence I allowed myself was the occasional Silk Cut cigarette, produced by Asif after particularly grueling shifts, when we found ourselves overrun by tour groups returning from the Colored Canyon. And these I smoked not because I wanted them, not because I took any pleasure in the act, but simply because Asif offered, and the proper thing to do, when given a gift by a friend, is to accept.

It turns out, though, that even the dead grow restless. Vacant as I was, I nevertheless came slowly to resent Sinai's beauty and quiet. In my time outside Asif's kitchen I stared at the cliffs guarding the desert and longed for a 7-Eleven in their place. I drank tea and tasted scotch. I lay on my mat, listening to God's breath rustle the thatch roof, and wished for the rush and fade of passing cars, and the blunt, stupid sounds of drunks arguing in the street. I dreamed of pavement and neon, ten-cent wings and late-night cable television. Pithy desk calendars. Air-conditioned hotel rooms. Emma's hips, her hair.

Waking from one such dream, in desperation I stole the paddleboat of a man who sold kebabs down the beach and set out for Saudi Arabia. I had no idea what I was doing, really. God knows what I would have told the Saudi military if they'd met me on the other side. I thought I was just borrowing the boat until waves began to slosh over the plastic bow. Moonlight shimmered on the water like barracuda skin. The front of the boat started to sink. I tried to turn back but the rudder had risen behind me and now cut uselessly through the air. The water in the bow reached critical mass and the boat dove below the waves, leaving me adrift three hundred yards from shore.

I swam back, huddled sopping and exhausted beneath my blanket, and slept better than I had in a month.

At daybreak, though, the anxiety returned, and I knew I had to leave, if only for a few days.

It was summer. The village had been at capacity for weeks, and Asif could not afford to lose me. But he studied my face for a moment, nodded as if satisfied with what he saw there, and said, This is fine. I'll have my wife's brother help while you're gone. He can use to learn what honest work is, anyway.

With the improvement in business Asif had insisted on paying me a salary in addition to room and board. I used this money to hire a nearly toothless Bedouin named Suleiman, who looked sixty but was closer to forty. He wanted to take me into the mountains—this was where most tourists went, he explained, because the terrain offered beautiful views and there were mud-brick huts along the route for us to shelter in. The desert, he said, was just that—desert. Nothing to see. Flat, lifeless, dangerous, the fact that his people had been thriving there for millennia notwithstanding.

I told Suleiman that was exactly what I wanted. I had no interest in watching the sun rise from Mount Sinai, or visiting St. Catherine's Monastery, or trekking through the Colored Canyon, or any of the other activities his usual clientele enjoyed. I wanted to be in the desert. I might only need two nights, or maybe three.

Suleiman, whose English was impeccable owing to years of guiding Westerners through the Sinai, nodded and laughed and said, Okay then. If we get in trouble, I guess we can always eat one of the camels.

The night my father died, I learned that real-life miracles do happen, and also that they're small and quiet and don't change anything. After I helped him trade in his truck because he couldn't drive it anymore, after I brought him to a store to find a recliner that had a machine inside it to help him stand up, after I heard his final confession, after I sat beside his bed and chafed his hand between mine during the last hours of his life, after I kissed his cold forehead and said good-bye, after the undertaker came and expressed regret and did his job and drove away, after my sisters and I stood for a while beneath the overhead light in the kitchen, staring at the floor and not talking while our mother wept on the sofa in the living room, I excused myself and got in my car to drive home. When I turned the ignition and backed out of the driveway that a few hours earlier had belonged to both my parents and now belonged just to my mother, the opening strains of 'Maggie May' came on the radio. Which wouldn't have seemed all that momentous, except that a couple of years earlier my father had, quite uncharacteristically, revealed a bit of his younger self to me that had everything to do with that song, and now it was playing as though someone had cued it up just for me.

Unbeknownst to me, of course, as I set out into the desert with Suleiman for the first time, my unfinished book, Emma's book, the last thing I'd written, that elephant man of a novel, was being shipped in huge quantities all over America. Booksellers were under strict orders—orders that carried the threat of legal action if violated—not to peddle a single copy until the ordained date. The first printing, an even 300,000 copies, was expected to be gone within a month or two. This of course did not take into account e-book and audio sales, themselves slated to be huge.

By way of comparison, the book I'd published while I was alive had sold fewer than ten thousand copies in hardcover. My baby. Staid, weighty, droll, ignored thing.

Emma's book would soon appear in over twenty other countries. A film version—adapted by Aaron Sorkin, directed by Sofia Coppola, bankrolled by Paramount—was in production and scheduled for release the following summer.

I would come to learn, eventually, that Emma's book had been sold (helped along by my suicide and the events surrounding it) as the tragicomic love story of our time. And its hero, a man whose circumstances, manner of thought, and big dumb heart all bore striking similarities to my own, stood as the contemporary answer to Goethe's young Werther.

And would be played, in the film adaptation, by a sulky Leonardo DiCaprio.

No delirious shamanic revelations or Earth-mother cleansings took place out in the desert, either on my first trip or the dozen or so subsequent ones. Which was fine, seeing as how that wasn't what I was after.

Suleiman's camels plodded. I got sunburned. At night we camped wherever we found ourselves, and I listened to the wind scour the desert while Suleiman cooked single-pot meals over fires made with dead acacia boughs, fires he stoked through the night to discourage the attentions of curious leopards.

I slept easily and without dreams. Sand gritted between my teeth for an hour after I woke, sticking fast even after water and a cup of Suleiman's strong, bitter coffee, which he brewed over the remnants of the previous night's blaze.

Suleiman, like most Bedouins I'd met, had an intense attachment to his family. They were all he talked about—and he rarely stopped talking. In the hail of syllables he explained at some point that this was the way he kept from missing his family too painfully while he was away—talking about them comforted him, especially in the long, black desert nights.

Sometimes he even sang about them, always after sunset, his voice high and sorrowful, drowning out the wind. His singing brought tears to my eyes. It did exactly the opposite of what I'd come out into the desert for: it made me feel. I wanted him to stop, but couldn't bring myself to ask. Then, on the fourth night, a curious thing: I no longer felt myself stirred by his singing. And this was how I came to discover a barometer for gauging whether my insides had gone still again. When Suleiman's singing no longer made me cry, I'd been in the desert long enough.

I told Suleiman the next morning over coffee, and he turned us back in the direction of the sea.

I will confess, there are moments when even a corpse grows curious about how the lives of those he loved have developed in his wake.

And if I'm being honest, a flicker of vanity persisted in me, and there were times when I found myself wondering idly, over a sink of greasy dishwater, how my friends had eulogized me, and what, if anything, had been written about me and my book.

Because it could be argued that people only really understand and express how they feel about you after you're fertilizer.

And maybe I allowed myself to hope that I was remembered fondly.

And maybe I wished, from time to time, that my first book would be read now by more people, and perhaps in a different light.

And maybe, in ugly little moments I'm almost too ashamed to confess to (and this should give you an idea of the quality of this shame, considering everything that I've confessed already), I hoped there were quiet moments in Emma's day when her thoughts wandered to me unbidden, and she felt the fact and finality of my absence.

I hoped, in other words, that she was in pain. I hoped that she grieved.

This is perhaps the least palatable facet of suicide: the fucking sour grapes.

Again, I'm not exactly swelling with pride when I tell you this, understand.

And when these thoughts came on me I went to Suleiman, and he brought me into the desert, and we wandered for three days, five, however long it took.

Toward the end of my father's life, he sat in his easy chair in the living room for days on end. He stared at the television without really watching. He stared at the walls, through them. We asked if he wanted the curtains drawn so he could look out the window, and mostly he didn't answer us, but we drew them anyway. Sometimes he would gaze at the snow outside in the yard, and the icy road beyond, and sometimes he wouldn't. He refused to go to bed. It was almost impossible for him to walk to the bedroom and he found it difficult to breathe lying down and was afraid he wouldn't wake up. So he sat in the chair. He smelled bad, because he didn't shower, and also because a sick, dying body gives off a subtle but indescribably bad smell. The smell of creeping terror, maybe, or of futility. So he sat in the chair, exuding that smell, staring at everything.

Then one evening he asked me, completely out of the blue, to take him to see a movie. My relief at his sudden desire to get out in the world nearly overwhelmed me, and I said yes, maybe a bit too eagerly.

We drove in silence, twenty minutes to the Flagship Cinemas in town, and I parked the car in a handicapped spot near the doors and went around to help him out of his seat, took small shuffling steps at his side as he struggled along with his walker.

In the lobby we stood together looking up at the list of films. It was late fall, a wasteland in terms of movie releases, and there wasn't much I had any interest in sacrificing two hours of my life for. But given that, at least in theory, I had a hell of a lot more hours left in reserve than my father, I decided to let him make the call.

He opted, inexplicably, for *The Game Plan*, a goofy-looking Disney comedy starring Dwayne 'The Rock' Johnson as a football player and gadabout who learns important life lessons when the young daughter he didn't know existed—a girl whose requisite good cheer and pluckiness made me want to strangle a bag full of kittens—comes into his life.

I mentioned, didn't I, that toward the end tumors had begun to grow in my father's brain?

I bought tickets and loitered at the snack counter in the hopes of missing the first ten minutes of the film. My father needed to sit, though, so into the theatre we went.

The inanity can be neither explained nor comprehended. The dialogue singed my synapses. The endless agonizing gags felt akin to sitting through the firebombing of Dresden. And the girl . . . good lord, the girl. She sassed her way through two hours—and since when are Disney comedies two hours long, by the way?—of pure pain, dropping one obvious wisdom-from-the-mouths-of-babes line after another, until I found myself wanting to shave her studiously cute head of hair.

I sat there, marking time. My father munched popcorn beside me, staring impassively at the screen, giving off that stink. It was impossible to know whether he was enjoying this, though I found it impossible to believe that he could be.

I actually began to feel sick to my stomach. My watch indicated that an hour and a half had crawled by, and still the film's easily foreseeable denouement hadn't begun to take shape. Happy as I'd been when my father had asked to go to the movies, I found myself fighting the urge to ask him if we could get out of there. But he was still my father, and one did not ask him to leave—if he wanted to he would decide all on his own, without input or suggestion from me.

A giddy tension mushroomed inside me until I felt on the verge of bursting into hysterical laughter, and not at the movie.

Finally, the credits rolled like a mercy killing. I walked at my father's side, holding his elbow lightly on the slight upslope out of the theatre and preparing myself for the possibility that, half-witted by the cancer in his head, he *had* in fact enjoyed the movie—and that I was going to have to pretend to have enjoyed it, too.

We didn't say a word to one another, all the way through the lobby and out to the car. I eased him into the passenger seat, my tension abating now, thinking that his ever-reliable silence would save me from having to discuss the movie at all.

Quiet in the car, still, until apropos of absolutely nothing, about ten miles down the road, my father, staring through the windshield at the cones of light from the headlamps, said: Well, that was a real piece of shit.

And all the laughter I'd bottled up in the theatre came out at once, until I was crying, until I had to slow down while I tried to gather myself and get my eyesight right again, and even my father, two weeks or so from being dead, cracked a rueful smile.

The ascendance of my book from an unfinished navel-gazer of a manuscript to the hottest literary commodity since *Harry Potter*, I would come to learn, began like this:

On the island, my landlord finally showed up with the keys. Chief Morales and his henchmen let themselves into the pink stucco casita and found, among my belongings, the suicide note. Case closed, as far as they were concerned.

The note was the thing that set it all in motion, you see.

Morales catalogued and packaged my things and put them in the mail to my mother—but not before giving the note to a woman who'd asked to read it.

This woman's name was Cecily Calder. Turned out all she had to do was ask, and Morales handed it over without a second thought. Again, crack police work.

Calder did not just read the note and give it back. My disappearance was big enough news in the town where I lived that the local paper had sent Calder to the island to report on it firsthand, and as part of her work on the story she transcribed the note word-for-word into her iPad, though she had both the professional and moral good sense to harbor no intentions of using it for the story.

She was simply struck by the thing—in particular the passages addressed to Emma, which had broken Calder down—and she wanted to preserve it for herself verbatim. Her affinity for the sentiments expressed in the note were such that, while none of it appeared in her own writing, it did heavily influence both the tone and content of the stories she wrote about my death. In addition to three straight news pieces, Calder ended up banging out, on spec, a lengthy Sunday feature praising my book and implying that there are circumstances under which suicide is not to be condemned, but understood, even celebrated.

This last earned her more than a handful of harsh rebukes, from psychiatrists and clergy and parents who'd lost their teenagers to suicide—but it also served as a harbinger of the phenomenon that would end with Leonardo DiCaprio doing a better than serviceable job of channeling my angst in theatres all over America.

Here was the first domino in the chain: after the minimal local dust had settled from Calder's feature, she emailed copies of my suicide note to several close friends, along with the somewhat naïve admonition not to share it with anyone else, given the nature of its origin.

In the prologue to his book *The Age of Spiritual Machines*, Ray Kurzweil uses an old episode of *The Twilight Zone* as an analogy for the Singularity.

A gambler has died and gone to heaven. Heaven, for a gambler, is a casino where no matter what game he plays, and no matter how long he plays it, he can never lose. For months he moves from poker to roulette to blackjack and back again; he hits his number every time, and he wins every single hand. At first, the gambler is pleased. He accrues great stacks of chips, and enjoys the attention of the many beautiful women in the casino. After a while, though, he starts to grow weary. He wouldn't, in life, have believed it, but this is monotonous, just winning and winning and winning. In its uniformity, winning has been stripped of its fun, of its very meaning. Over time he becomes desperate. He is buried under chips, drowning in his good luck. He goes to the angel who runs the casino and pleads with him: don't make me stay here, winning and winning and winning, any longer. I wasn't supposed to be in heaven anyway. Not the way I lived my life. I was supposed to go to hell.

And the angel tells him that, indeed, he was supposed to go to hell. Which is why that's precisely where he finds himself.

The point, as concerns the Singularity, is that it's easy to imagine that when perfection is achieved, it will lose its meaning. Without the contrast of imperfection, of strife and suffering and petty daily problems, there will be no upside to the upside. Which is actually true, when you stop to think about it. As Kurzweil says, we are more attached to our problems than to their solutions.

But when the Singularity occurs, Kurzweil argues, our inability to appreciate all the good things in store for us will be transfigured along with everything else. One aspect of perfection, after all, it stands to reason, will be that our need for imperfection will cease. Or, perhaps more precisely: that imperfection itself will cease to have meaning.

Sometimes when I grew restless and Suleiman was off in the mountains with Welsh tourists, or spending time with his family, I would lie awake in my hut, feeling my insides stir, longing for cheap domestic draft beer and Red Sox broadcasts and low-dose aspirin, and eventually I would rise and push open the door and go down to the edge of the sea.

I wouldn't bother putting on any clothes. If the sky was clear, in the moonlight I could make out the undulating backbone of Saudi Arabia across the black water.

I'd wade in slowly. The shallows stayed warm even in winter, because the reef offshore came up to just a foot or so beneath the surface and held the water in, and each day the sun created a sort of naturally occurring hot tub between the reef and the beach. When the water rose to chest level I'd turn and let my feet leave the sandy floor and float on my back, staring up at the moon, listening to the womb-sounds below.

And while the current was weak, in the right spots it would pick me up and pull me out gradually. I'd let myself drift, lungs filled with air for buoyancy, my arms and legs as slack as if I were quadriplegic. I'd know when I passed over the reef into deeper water, because the temperature dropped precipitously, sending a chill through me and making my muscles want to tense, but I would fight this. The discipline was like a physical manifestation of some Buddhist koan: struggling to stay loose, resisting in order to relax. And if I could resist as the cold numbed my limbs and sent exploratory tendrils into my center, if I could stay slack while my biology screamed its need to shiver, then I would feel my insides grow still again, however temporarily, and then I could breaststroke back to shore and go to my hut and climb underneath the mosquito netting and, cocooned in the damp softness of a single fleece blanket, tremble myself to sleep.

Coping strategies notwithstanding, there was no way, after a while, to deny that the blankness enveloping me on my arrival in the Sinai had become—like my life—a thing of the past. I abandoned Asif more and more often to disappear into the desert with Suleiman, and stayed disappeared for longer periods of time; so long, in fact, that Suleiman had started to complain about the absence from his family, and to sing ever more plaintively, a fact that made it more difficult for me to not respond to his singing—which of course meant we needed to stay in the desert even longer. And still I found myself in the water at least two or three nights a week, or so I estimated, having long ago stopped keeping track of the passage of time, which was to my mind a construct of use only to the living.

Perhaps the concept of the Singularity becomes less difficult to accept when you consider the fact that we are all, and always have been, machines.

We are made up of components—in our case, biological components, but components nonetheless—that interact according to strict and immutable rules involving chemistry, physics, and, by extension, mechanics. That we do not yet understand some of these rules doesn't change the fact that our bodies, and more important, our brains, obey them.

Stands to reason, then, that achieving artificial intelligence will be a fairly simple matter of gaining understanding of the rules of chemistry and physics that our brains obey, and then—in principle, at least—there should be no reason why we can't transfer those rules onto nonorganic materials that are not subject to acne, or hypertension, or bedwetting, or muscle fatigue, or staph infection, or pinkeye, or gout, or influenza, or diaper rash, or erectile dysfunction, or joint deterioration, or AIDS, or radiation sickness, or anorexia, or canker sores, or epilepsy, or halitosis, or IBS, or lead poisoning, or multiple sclerosis, or altitude sickness, or tennis elbow, or smallpox, or kidney stones, or rot, or heartache, or cancer, or cancer, or cancer.

Around the same time that Calder circulated my suicide note among her friends, two packages containing my belongings, along with the original note, arrived at my mother's apartment, the place she'd moved into after she was finally able to wrench herself away from the cherry trees and sell the house.

This is one aspect of my faux death that I feel nothing but bad about, and rightly so. My poor mother, still grieving hard for my father despite the passage of time, cutting open those boxes and believing, in a deep and concrete way reinforced by the sight, the feel, the scent of my things, that in that most agonizing reversal of the natural order she had outlived her son.

And then the manner in which I had 'died,' and her pulling the note from wherever Morales had stowed it—I never asked her, but I always picture it folded neatly at the top of the first box she opens—and having to read a fairly eloquent account of my cratered, smoldering interior landscape, a state of mind that itself was very much real, even if the suicide it indicated was not.

Of course at the time the suicide *was* real to her, and surely one's mother does not need to read in brutal detail about the mental horrors that led to it.

Maybe this was why she ended up giving the note to Emma. Maybe she couldn't stand the thought of those pages being anywhere inside her home, lurking in a drawer or on a closet shelf, a permanent account of her son's deterioration and end.

Or maybe she, like Calder, found herself most affected by the section of the note addressed to Emma—who, by the way, my mother was not a fan of after she'd kicked my ass on our first go-round, but who it turned out she'd warmed to in their shared grief after my death—and felt that it rightly belonged to her.

Whatever the reason, shortly after receiving the packages my mother tracked Emma's number down and called her. They shared a cry on the telephone. They shared another over cups of coffee when my mother drove down to meet her several days later. Then my mother handed over the note, and that was that.

My other things—clothes, iPod, books, shoes and flip-flops, handful of DVDs, backpack, set of dominoes—my mother sorted through, making a point to touch each item and let that touch linger for a moment. Then she placed them carefully back in the boxes, and the boxes themselves went into her bedroom closet.

She did not put away my computer, though, or my notebooks.

No, because she had reluctantly opened the notebooks and found portions of what was recognizable as a work in progress, and then she turned on the computer and found more of the same. And these things, to her mind, should not be stored away. But she didn't know what to do with them herself, so she called my agent.

And he said, Please, absolutely, if you don't mind, send them along, we'd love to take a look. He promised to return them exactly as they were received.

To my recollection, the only time my father ever hit me occurred when I was about five years old, when I'd been flipping through a pictorial history of Vietnam that he owned, and I put together what I knew about him and what I saw in the book's photos and asked him if he'd ever killed anyone. He reached back and slapped me across the face hard enough to knock me flat, and then left the room and the house and didn't come back again until the next day, or maybe even the day after that, it's hard to remember exactly, you know, time and memory being what they are.

And so it came to be that around the time I first went to work for Asif, my agent was busy poring over the two hundred thousand words I'd written since the last time I turned in a manuscript. The box arrived from my mother on a snowy Tuesday, winter's last stand that year in New York City. At my agent's request my mother had printed out the manuscript she'd found on my computer, put it together with the handwritten pages, and shipped the whole thing. The top of the box was dark with melted snowflakes. My agent is not a sentimental man, but he sat there for a few minutes just looking at the box, leaning back in his chair and considering it, thinking, allowing himself to hope a little. Then he slid a letter opener through the bands of tape my mother had used to secure the box top. He lifted the lid, peered inside. Read the title, sat back again, thought a bit more. Snow continued to fall lazily outside his office windows. His assistant came in with the *macchiato* he'd asked for. His assistant eyed the open box, thought to ask a question, then put the coffee down and left without a word. Finally, my agent reached in and removed the manuscript, set it on his desk, placed the box carefully on the floor. He really did mean to send it back to my mother exactly as he'd received it, including the box. He considered the title once again, decided it was okay but not great, flipped a page. Then another. At first he read with guarded optimism. The snow began to fall with purpose now, accumulating in wet piles on cars and awnings up and down 26th Street. My agent's optimism blossomed into satisfaction, then excitement. He read the manuscript in one sitting, eating lunch at his desk and staying there well after the rest of the office building was dark and empty. When he'd turned the last page he called my editor at home and told him they needed to meet for a drink, right away if possible, and then, glancing out his windows, my agent added that he should probably take the train, because the roads were a mess out there.

Keep in mind that my agent's excitement, and by extension my editor's, had nothing to do with the massive publicity that the book would eventually be published to. None of that had yet come to pass. Calder's friends were only now beginning to violate her admonition and distribute my suicide note among their own social circles. This electronic dissemination had not yet taken on its own momentum, and remained, for the time being, private, email to email.

So although there had been a good deal of short-lived publicity surrounding my disappearance and death, my agent and editor were not twisting their figurative mustaches over the prospect of exploiting it. They were, in fact, not twisting their figurative mustaches at all. Theirs was the pure and guileless excitement of book people who believed they found themselves with the opportunity to publish a great book. My botched ode to Emma, my incomplete hymn to obsessive love, my literary flipper baby, was quite simply, as far as they were concerned, a hugely compelling piece of art— well nigh a masterpiece.

After my mother gave her the suicide note, Emma took two weeks off from work and flew down to the island alone. Rented the pink stucco casita for twice what I'd paid for it, the extra tariff necessary to wrest the place away from another prospective short-term tenant. Discovered strands of her own long auburn hair in the sheets, and stuck to the shower wall, on the day she arrived. Slept alone for twelve nights in the bed we'd shared. Held the pillows to her nose, searching for a trace of me. Found my prized vintage Montblanc—apparently Morales and company thought it just another pen—and slid it into her messenger bag next to her journal. Ate at the same table at the resort where we'd had dinner several times, accepting a glass of Chianti from a man who said he couldn't stand to see a beautiful woman eating alone. Drove to all the beaches, sat in the sand with sunglasses on, sipping warm beers and staring at the water. Foiled men's gambits with smiles as frigid as they were polite, smiles that sent them scurrying in their minds and left them wondering, after, why they'd been so spooked. Went to Mosquito Pier, leaned against the makeshift repairs to the guardrail, watched old fishermen set their lines and grumble over tangled reels. Marveled at enormous, distant plumes of water as the Navy detonated stray ordnance they'd dropped into the bays thirty years previous. Wrestled guilt like a vengeful angel. Let it all go, in the end. Got on a plane and went home and added me to the list of heartaches she'd left behind. And good for her.

A couple of months before my father died, after it became clear that the surgery hadn't worked and the doctors gave up on chemotherapy and radiation and his body sagged and protruded with unchecked tumors, he went to Boston for what at that stage could have fairly been considered a pointless examination. I imagine machines spinning and analyzing my father's blood and urine samples, CT and MRI and ultrasound units bouncing X-rays and magnetic fields through his body and compiling, byte by byte, visual proof of what everyone already knew, what one could literally smell on him at this point, and I imagine heart and blood pressure monitors beeping and whirring as they transmitted, moment to moment, evidence of his continued existence—all these machines working tirelessly, with absolute dedication, despite the futility of their task.

Then I imagine my father's doctors and nurses, the actual human beings involved in his care, spending less and less time on him, knowing that he was the very definition of hopelessness, and that all this testing was little more than the formal constraints of care continuity. Maybe even, at their team meeting, giving his charts a perfunctory riffle, saying, This one's a goner, what's next, and casting his paperwork aside.

In other words, the doctors were unwilling to waste their own time on the myriad tests they'd wasted my father's dwindling time with. The machines, though, remained uniform and unflinching in their dedication.

So anyway he'd gone to Boston for these pointless tests, and started to have trouble breathing in one of the exam rooms at the cancer institute, so they called an ambulance to take him around the block, to the ER of the hospital next door. Where they discovered, after yet another series of tests, that his one remaining lung had become choked with blood clots.

They administered Alteplase, without much hope given how weak he was already, and told my mother to call whoever should be around in the event that he died.

My phone rang around nine that night. I'd been drinking, but I took a cold shower and threw a few things in a backpack and drove to my uncle's house. He looked at me and suggested he drive, and we got in his car and headed south on the mostly empty highway.

We talked about my father, but we talked about other things, too, and not without good humor. One of the peculiar aspects of ushering someone you love through a long illness is that everyday life, dull and unimportant though most of it is, inevitably intrudes upon and somehow obscures the high drama of looming death—so that you find yourself, at a bedside in a sick room, talking about last night's *American Idol*, for example.

And as we drove through the night toward what we believed and acknowledged out loud could be my father's corpse, my uncle and I discussed high gas prices, and the oddly warm October we'd had, and the Red Sox, who were blazing through the postseason on what would turn out to be their second world championship in just three years.

And I said, in reference to my father, You know, he could have waited to die until the playoffs were over.

These things come out of your mouth, sometimes. You get tired, or dumb, or just plain angry at someone for dying on you, though they obviously have no choice in the matter.

When we got to Boston just after one in the morning my father was still alive but sleeping, and we joined my mother and my aunt in the waiting room. None of my sisters, scattered about the continent, could get there in time. We sat for hours, talking in fits and starts but mostly quiet, listless. We flipped through old magazines, watched the sky brighten from black to a stolid autumnal gray outside the windows. Paced the ghastly fluorescent-lit halls. Received periodic non-updates from the nurses: Still sleeping. Doing okay. Seems to have stabilized.

Finally, after nine, we were allowed in to see him. He sat up in bed in a private room, some network morning show on the television, and I was struck by a plain and unmistakable fact: for the first time since he'd been diagnosed, my father looked *happy*. His eyes shone soft and peaceful, and while he wasn't smiling, exactly, relaxation had settled around his mouth in a way I'd never witnessed in thirty years of knowing the man, giving him a contented, sage look.

I sat there all day. My father talked in a gentle, friendly voice I did not recognize while doctors and nurses and family wandered in and out. I only rose from the chair at his bedside twice before sundown, both times to use the private bath attached to his room.

Who was this gregarious dying man, I wondered, and what had happened, while we sped down the highway and sat up in the waiting room all night, to create him from the raw material of the man I'd known before?

And then, during the Red Sox pregame show, it struck me: acceptance, was what had happened. His was the relaxed, friendly manner of one who has come to truly accept his own doom. The sort of enlightenment that dedicated Buddhists strive after their whole lives and often never achieve, right there in front of me, clad in a hospital johnny with graying mustache askew and eyes warm and calm.

Before the first pitch his dinner showed up, a dry greenish slab of something the attendant claimed was meatloaf, and my father was about to dig in happily (this was another sudden change, as weeks beforehand his appetite had abandoned him and more than once I found my mother in tears after trying and failing to get him to eat) when I stopped him.

There's a food court downstairs across the street, I said. Let me get you something edible.

He asked for a steak and cheese sandwich from Subway, and I left and went down in the elevator, feeling strangely light and happy as I jaywalked over to the Longwood food court. The place was filled with people in scrubs and white lab coats, sitting at plastic tables in groups of three and four, scarfing the same McDonald's burgers and Chinese takeout that had delivered many of their patients to them across the street.

I ordered a footlong from a plump, surly Puerto Rican girl in a mustard-stained Subway polo. My father had asked for nothing but the meat and cheese, no vegetables, and I watched as the girl plopped two tiny microwaved dollops of stringy beef into the hollow she'd cut from the bread. It didn't look any better than the meatloaf, and I thought to ask her to work on the presentation a bit, maybe add more meat, or at least spread it out in a way that didn't make so obvious it had been dropped out of a plastic cup—in short, to try a little harder—but then I didn't. Though I'd given myself the assignment of finding something good for my father to eat, at that moment I kept my mouth shut.

And then carried that limp, lukewarm bag back across the street and up in the elevator and into my father's room. He sat upright still, his eyes trained on the television. In the fourth the Sox were up 1–0.

I handed him the sandwich, feeling as though I'd failed in some small but vastly important way, and he smiled and said thank you— understand, again, that the warmth, the smile, were just this side of a shock coming from him—and unwrapped the sandwich, dug in with delight.

Later, after he'd fallen asleep during the seventh inning and I'd switched off the television and the light over the bed and gone out, I sat at a nearby bar thinking about how I'd never expected to learn something about joy, how to create and sustain it, from my father of all people.

And then smiled into my beer as one of my mother's favorite chestnuts came to mind: miracles, she liked to say, never cease.

True to the Bedouin custom of unflagging hospitality, Suleiman often invited me to share dinner with his family at their home, a mud-brick structure squatting gloomily amidst the dirt and broken rocks of the Sinai foothills. The invitation, however, was where many of the customs ended. His was a family of all women—a plight I could sympathize with, having grown up with three sisters in a house where even the cat and dog were female—and so, as Suleiman told me himself, even with a strange man in the house his wife and daughters had to appear at dinner, otherwise he and I would be dining alone. They ate not with their hands, but with a set of pearl-handled silverware given to Suleiman by a longtime client. The soles of bare feet were on constant display, both during the meal and afterward; the younger girls most flagrantly violated this normally sacrosanct rule, but did not once earn a rebuke for it from either of their parents. Suleiman's wife spoke openly and at length with me, smiled at my jokes, even ventured the occasional friendly grasp of my forearm. In these ways and others, Suleiman's was an extremely progressive household, by Bedouin standards. The fact that they had an actual household, rather than a tent, being yet another liberal deviation from custom.

One custom the family did observe, though, was an overwhelming interest in who I was, where I came from, what I did for a living, who I loved, etc. When asked these and other questions, I lied without hesitation. I started the ruse with a name: Henrik. This construct hailed from Minnesota, specifically that convergence of the Mississippi and Minnesota rivers known as St. Paul. He'd been a chef and sometime professional snowboarder, a detail which at first baffled the girls and then, once explained, fascinated them.

Lies all, of course. My name, obviously, was not Henrik; only in the Sinai could I, a swarthy Canuck of southern French descent, have used a Scandinavian handle and gotten away with it. I was from the Northeast, not the Midwest; in fact, I had never even set foot in Minnesota. And while I'd slung slop in more than a handful of kitchens before selling my first novel, I'd never been anything resembling what one thinks of as a chef.

The snowboarding? Please. I'd been tobogganing, two or three times, as a kid.

When the girls pressed me on the last question—who I loved—I formulated a lie to go with the others, but then this lie stuck in my throat. So instead, after a minute of obfuscation, I told them the truth about Emma. I figured, where's the harm? I laid it on pretty thick, too, and the girls were rapt, smiling and dreamy, adrift in pre- and mid-adolescent reveries of idealized romantic love. Their parents, side by side on cushions behind them, smiled indulgently beneath a cloud of smoke from Suleiman's cigarette.

For whatever reason I did not anticipate the obvious follow-up question: where on Earth was this Emma, light of my life, yin to my yang, the very purpose for which I'd been snatched from the black nothingness of pre-existence? How could I bear to be apart from her, if I loved her so?

I thought for a minute, gazed at the girls' expectant faces, their almond eyes intent and unwavering, and this time the lie came easily: She died, I told them.

The girls accepted this news with less sadness than I expected. But then, they'd seen two of their siblings go straight from their mother's womb into the stony ground; death here in the desert was neither surprising nor unbearable, even to children.

When I was a kid, one of the only things my father and I did together on a regular basis was have our hair cut. An old Marine my grandfather's age ran a barbershop the size of a broom closet in our neighborhood. He always smelled of whiskey and had an actual working barber pole out front. My father had been going to him since he was a boy. We'd walk in together, and my father would sit down under the Marine's scissors first while I perused back issues of *Field and Stream* and listened to them talk about the things men talk about when their wives aren't around. The place had one mirror, adjacent to the barber's chair, and on the wall beneath the mirror was a shelf crammed with containers of strange blue fluid, where plastic combs and clipper attachments floated in stasis. The floor was always littered with multihued piles of clipped hair, no matter the time of day.

I was thinking about that barbershop one afternoon, maybe a week before my father died, as I sat in the living room with him watching television. His eyesight and hearing had begun to fail, which made him easy to observe for long moments without him noticing your gaze, and I considered him as he stared at the TV. I noticed suddenly how unkempt he was. He hadn't shaved for days, and the hair on his head, which had come back spottily after the chemo, shot up from his scalp in ugly, uneven tufts.

On impulse, I asked if he wanted me to clean him up a bit. We'd gotten used to his bad hearing, and I knew that the first time I asked he would only hear that I was talking to him, but not the particulars of what I said, so I waited for him to turn his head and ask, What? I repeated myself, forming the words carefully, and smiled in a way I hoped was encouraging rather than condescending. He thought for a minute—everything with him was so slow now—and then, as if realizing suddenly that he still occupied a world in which people cut their hair and shaved and felt good about it, he nodded with all the vigor he could manage, gratitude splashed across his face like some kind of abstract art.

I draped a towel around his shoulders, tucked it tight into the neck of his shirt. I oiled the clipper blades and set them to his scalp. I used my free hand to turn and tilt his head gently, this way and that, and for a few minutes we talked about the things men talk about when their wives aren't around.

In a moment of bold inappropriateness that even in Suleiman's progressive household would have earned her severe punishment, his oldest daughter Noora came to me alone in the yard post-dinner, while I stood gazing into the hills and smoking.

She was sixteen. I was a grown man, no relative to her, and a Westerner to boot. We stood without chaperone in the near-dark. I wondered frantically at Noora's intentions, felt the sudden suffocating danger when a girl is still young enough that everything is play, but old enough that she's eager to play with people instead of toys.

Emma is not dead, Noora said. She smiled and pressed a hand to my shoulder, a gesture so unspeakably improper that it sent a reflexive thrill of excitement through me. I don't know why you lied, but you lied. She is alive somewhere.

Then Noora was gone as quickly as she came. And I was left with concurrent waves of fear, one receding, the other cresting: that Noora meant to seduce me, and that she would somehow find me out.

Around the time my suicide note was going viral, Emma attended a fund-raising reception for Planned Parenthood of Maine on an August evening thick with humidity and, it would turn out, fate.

She stood in the ballroom at the Hilton drinking rum and tonic, draped in a thin black cotton dress that clung where indicated and flowed where indicated and dropped away in the back to showcase her strong, elegant shoulders, a dress that I can to this day close my eyes and conjure a dulcet vision of. I can hold that vision as long as I like, as though the image in my mind were in actuality a photograph in my hand. I do so more often than is probably good for me.

And on that evening, another man shared my appreciation of this image.

But because playing pick-up artist at a Planned Parenthood fund-raiser was bad form, and because Peter Cash was quite shy besides, he did not approach Emma directly, or send a waiter over with a drink. Instead he situated himself near where Emma stood among colleagues from her office, and made sure he had a line of sight to her.

Emma was easily distracted—when we ate dinner she always sat facing the wall so as not to have her attention sapped by compulsive people-watching—and her eyes wandered the room as she talked. Eventually they settled on Peter Cash, who had been waiting for just such a moment, and he held her gaze for as long as his bashful nature would allow, which was about two seconds.

The moment repeated itself several minutes later, and again Peter held her gaze, for a bit longer this time.

Emma, who'd been repelling the overtures of bolder men for months, but who'd by now had three drinks and found herself amused by Peter Cash's timidity, sought him deliberately the third time.

I know how he must have felt when those eyes, full of intent, fell on him.

Much later, Emma herself would tell me that though Peter didn't remember it, or even necessarily realize he'd done it, the thing that really grabbed her the third time their eyes met was the way that, now suddenly emboldened, he smiled and cocked his head to the side in slight inquiry, reminding her of the hundreds of times she'd seen me do the very same thing.

Many believe the Singularity will take place when the Internet becomes self-aware. Some even think that the Internet already possesses a version of what we think of as consciousness: the ability to store, process, remember, and convey information with a degree of autonomy.

If you're skeptical about what the Internet will do in the future, though, consider what it could accomplish even back then, while I was erased in the Sinai and, as simply as the universe itself began one day, Emma met a shy but kind man named Peter Cash: it took an obscure American novelist, a writer whose level of fame lay somewhere between that of the shortstop for the single-A Hickory Crawdads and the Rotato Express Potato Peeler, and based on the dissemination of a mere five thousand words or so of his writing made his name more recognizable among certain demographics than that of the current U.S. president.

You know what it was about that suicide note? The reason why millions were compelled to post it in chat rooms and on message boards, to put it up on Facebook and MySpace and Tumblr and reddit, to email it to their parents and brothers and sisters and girlfriends and aunts and coworkers and yes, more ominously, to old lovers who'd jilted them, to film themselves talking about it and post the videos on YouTube, to hyperlink, to blog, to hashtag, to tweet and tweet and retweet ad nauseam? The reason why my suicide note not only persisted but thrived in the face of competition from cute animal pictures, videos of skateboarders snapping their forearms and people being mauled by sharks, the Twitter feeds of basketball players and reality television bimbos, the minutiae of friends' lives updated by the nanosecond, the massively multiplayer online games, the virtual tours of the Louvre?

Simple, to my mind. Of course it seemed simple only in retrospect, after I spent a lot of time thinking about it, marveling in a sort of nauseated way, and then reaching this conclusion: what people found so compelling about the note was its naked, abject honesty.

Because I'd jammed more earnestness into a single line of that note than existed in the whole of my first book. And in a world where people daily put on false indifference along with their deodorant and makeup, where they girded themselves in irony between sips of coffee, where the morning newscasters winked at them while relaying the latest news, where their politicians did the same while telling them what they wanted to hear, where they told friends their babies were beautiful when in fact they were sort of nauseating to look at, where they told spouses they loved them when they no longer did, where they pretended not to know that the sun would one day expand and consume the Earth, where they smiled brightly at people they loathed, where they took Dexedrine to begin the day and Xanax to end it, where they ate when they were tired and fucked when they were hungry and slept when they were horny, where they willfully believed in television characters as a panacea for their loneliness, where they preferred this loneliness to the vulnerability that could relieve it, where they felt with their brains and thought with their hearts, where they seethed and feigned calm, where they feared and feigned courage, where they hungered and feigned satiety, where they almost never said how they really felt for fear of being perceived as strange or weak or plain crazy, where they each and every one continued to perpetrate this massive, ravenous lie upon themselves, they each and every one felt themselves, moment to moment, trembling for something true.

And I was no better. Like everybody else, I had trembled my whole life for something true. I had hidden, and called it living. In my suicide note, at last, I'd finally stopped hiding. And this, to my mind, is the reason why that archaic thing, words on paper, in the form of my suicide note, carved out a section of the Internet's burgeoning consciousness all to itself.

Ever more alarmingly reckless, Noora took to sneaking away from her father's house after dark to visit my hut on the beach. She stole into Habiba Village silent and shoeless, her feet tough from years of passing unshod over dust and rock. The first time she came, I woke from a dead sleep to find her hovering over me like an assassin, her hand on my cheek, and for a moment, in my confusion, I thought she was Emma, waking me in the bed on the island, tracing the scars and bruises on my face, demanding to know what had happened to me.

I told her, that first night, that I would not tolerate her touching me again.

What will you do? she asked, grinning impishly. Tell my father?

Just don't do it, I said.

You should shave your beard, she said. I want to see your face.

Her head uncovered, immodest child. Her hair long and dark and slightly kinky, shining in the moonlight outside my hut.

I folded my arms over my chest. Stared across the water at the Kingdom's bumpy silhouette. Said nothing.

Noora obeyed my wishes, did not venture to touch me again. But every time she came to my hut she wore a little less clothing. Never anything racy by Western standards, certainly, but nonetheless. She went from the traditional *thobe*—a garment that resembles nothing so much as a tent—to jeans and loose long-sleeved blouses, to T-shirts that clung to her new breasts, to chino shorts that revealed strong brown legs and dusty ankles.

Couldn't you be stoned to death, I asked, for dressing like that?

She laughed, and I shushed her, terrified someone would hear and come to investigate. Her eyes: shining, obsidian, mischievous. The plain facts of her body revealed in nightly increments, the Bedouin equivalent of a striptease. It moved me, and she knew it. I bobbed in the Red Sea while she sat on the beach, waiting, my one blanket folded in her lap.

Through manipulation of our cognitive structures we will be able, post-Singularity, to make sex more unpleasant than a drug-free root canal. To transform it into literally the last thing we would want to do. To make naïvely manipulative and physically precocious young women less appealing than an IRS audit.

And then of course there were the dinners at Suleiman's, nerve-rattling affairs now. I sat guilty and trepidacious, ate little. Suleiman smoked and laughed, unsuspecting to the very end. Noora's eyes twinkled. She was not evil, though, or even conniving. Just young, spirited, at odds with the constraints imposed by the accident of her birthplace, and by her limited knowledge of who I was.

Thus prepped for the expansive earnestness of Emma's book by the abbreviated earnestness of my suicide note, people bought hundreds of thousands of copies.

I think if not for the phenomenon of the suicide note going viral the novel would have been a commercial flop, dead on arrival, as most books tend to be. It would have been too sad, too serious, too self-involved, despite the happyish ending tacked onto the manuscript by the ghostwriter hired to finish it. It would have been, above all, too damn earnest.

But the suicide note had hit some great neglected nerve, and people came to bookstores as if on a pilgrimage, forking over thirty dollars apiece to bear witness to a devotion undiminished by death.

Everyone still believed I was dead, remember. That was the thing. That was the fulcrum around which their reverence turned, gained momentum, grew to a fervor.

The critics, though, were largely unmoved. One particularly snarky fellow said the book put him in the mind of nothing so much as 'Nicholas Sparks with a thesaurus.' To which I say, now: fair enough, sir. Fair enough.

Noora asked many, many questions. At first I refused to answer, but she wore me down and I started to talk. Sometimes I lied, and sometimes I told the truth. It became a game for her, accruing answers and trying to figure out where they didn't jibe with one another.

When were you born?

You already asked me that.

Yes. I'm asking again.

Nineteen seventy-seven.

She stared. Last time you said nineteen seventy-five.

For whatever reason, I'd decided to tell the truth that time.

Either way, you are very old, she said. It was clear she found this appealing. And you were born in St. Paul?

I've never been to St. Paul, I told her.

Why did you say you lived there? Why did you lie to my family?

Because I don't want you to know who I am.

Why?

Noora, I said. You have to stop coming here.

Just a few days before he died, my father called two of his sisters, my aunts, to his bedside. Theirs was to be a private talk, but I hovered in the room because he needed constant tending. In my role as caregiver I was less like a person and more like a fixture, as insensate, to outward appearances, as the bedside lamp, so their conversation went as though I weren't even there. It wasn't a long conversation. My aunts, grown women, knelt beside his bed. My older aunt held my father's desiccated hand. He told them he was sorry, neglected to specify for what, exactly. Apparently they all knew what he meant. Then he cried, and they cried. I blinked tears away myself, fiddling with my father's morphine vaporizer. He was breathless to begin with, and the crying left him gulping for air. I turned the vaporizer on and pressed it to his lips, grateful for the mild hissing sound it made, grateful for the task itself, more grateful than I have ever been before or since for the simple blessing of having something to do.

And that was it, really. My aunts stood, wiped their eyes, took turns leaning over to press themselves against his prone form in an approximation of a hug. One of them used the word 'forgive,' though I don't remember exactly how. Then they left, and he went to sleep again. I never asked what he'd apologized for. I don't have any idea, to this day.

I had a dream about Noora. In the dream she did amazing, improbable things, and her body turned out to be exactly the marvel of youth and sound breeding that the T-shirts and chino shorts implied. The next morning I woke up to the rare tap of rain on the thatch roof, found my belly coated with flaky, dried sperm.

I'd never had a wet dream in my life, up to then. Which was part of the reason why I didn't entirely trust that it had been a dream in the first place.

I never asked Noora. If it had been just a dream, I didn't want her to know about it, and if it'd been more than a dream, then *I* didn't want to know about it.

Remember at the beginning of all this, when I vowed that I would not lie, either by substance or omission? Here, for the first time, I have violated that promise. Now I have to come clean.

Because when I said I had no idea what my father apologized for, that was not the truth. I have an idea. In fact, I know exactly what he apologized for. But I won't say it. I was named for him. I am his first and only son. Even today, people comment all the time about how much we look alike. His shame is my birthright, and my secret to keep. So please, don't ask me to say it. I can't. Let my admitting to the lie be enough.

It took two years, but Noora finally figured out who I really was.

The irony being that after she'd stalked my true identity so fervently and for so long, it came to her completely by accident.

Irony: God pinching our backsides, waiting until we turn to see who just goosed us, then tweaking our noses for good measure.

The accident: Noora bought the Arabic translation of Emma's novel during a trip to Cairo with her mother. She had no idea, at first, that I'd written the book. She bought it simply because it was the hottest read going at the time, especially among teenage girls. On the long bus ride back to the Sinai she got about halfway through the book before flipping to the back and taking a good, long look at the picture of the guy who'd written the thing.

At this point I was older, obviously, than my author photo, and wildly bearded, and much thinner, having not set foot in a gym since before leaving for the island. Nonetheless, Noora realized without a doubt who had been breaking bread with her family for the last four years.

By then, Emma and Peter Cash were engaged. My mother, still fleeing my father's ghost, had moved apartments three more times. Suleiman's wife was pregnant again, with what would turn out to be their first surviving son.

Oddly, for whatever reason Noora did not approach me with her revelation. It was Suleiman who came one morning as I stood in the kitchen at Habiba Village before breakfast, drinking coffee and try-ing to shake the fatigue from a long night spent drifting back and forth over the reef.

He placed a hardcover book I did not recognize on the prep coun-ter. He flipped the book over and put the tip of his index finger on a black-and-white photo of me smiling more widely than I could con-ceive of.

My daughter tells me, he said, that you are dead. This is news to you, I'm sure.

I started slightly at the mention of Noora, made a show of sipping my coffee. So the jig was up.

Not exactly, I said.

At this point, not having learned to read Arabic, I assumed that the book was a copy of my first novel—an edition had been published in Egypt.

And also that you are quite famous, Suleiman continued.

Though I didn't laugh much those days, I couldn't help but chuckle. That, I said, would be news indeed.

You must be fairly well-known, Suleiman said, having written two books.

One, I corrected him.

Two, he said. He opened the book on the counter, flipped a few pages until he found what he wanted, then translated: Also by Ron Currie, he read, and then spoke the title of my first and, to my knowledge, only book.

This, of course, was the moment when I began to wonder pretty vigorously just what the hell was going on.

Though I can't imagine a scenario in which the Singularity is a bad outcome for us, there are those who can. Ray Kurzweil and others worry, in particular, about self-replicating nanobots—machines the size of molecules, intended for use primarily in medicine, bucking their programs and making copies of themselves endlessly.

It sounds silly, I know. The very word: nanobots.

Then again, there was a time, not too long ago, when words like 'cyberspace' and 'spyware' seemed pretty goofy, too.

Perhaps it would be easier to take seriously if I approached the idea obliquely. So think, if you will, of malignant cells. Of cancer. Because that, in essence, is the threat that self-replicating nanobots would pose.

Imagine that the whole world has cancer. The Earth itself. Incurable, late-stage, almost instantaneously terminal cancer. This is what we're talking about. Tiny self-replicating machines, convinced that their only purpose is to create more copies of themselves. In this singular ambition they consume everything, spreading across plains and through forests, devouring cities, plunging into the oceans' deepest trenches, in the same way that cancer invades adjacent organs and bodywide systems, seizes an ever-larger portion of the blood supply, co-opts oxygen and calories for itself.

Among people who think about and discuss such things, this theoretical phenomenon is known alternately as ecophagy—Greek *oikos* ('house') and *phagein* ('to eat')—and the Gray Goo Problem.

Either of which, depending on one's perspective and mood, might be an apt way to describe cancer as well.

Back in 2003, Prince Charles made the mistake of publicly asking the Royal Society to examine the potential threats posed by nano-technology.

Headline: CHARLES IS BLASTED OVER GREY GOO FEARS. Also: PRINCE CHARLES AND THE ATTACK OF THE GREY GOO.

Et cetera.

So then I made a trip to Cairo myself, spent eight hours on the bus, staring out at all that sand with my forehead pressed to the window and an unwelcome curiosity welling in me again. Beyond curiosity— I'd started to piece together in my mind what had happened, though I couldn't begin to imagine the scope of it, and as I thought of Emma's book having been published, God help me I *wanted* things again. I wanted the book to be loved. I wanted to be famous. I wanted my words to redeem and validate me in the view of strangers and friends alike. I wanted, most of all, for Emma to have read the book and understood how I felt about her, in a way I couldn't have explained in ten lifetimes merely by talking.

All these wriggling desires, again, after so long.

I didn't realize how accustomed I'd become to Sinai's enveloping quiet until I deboarded the bus into the crush and stink of Turgoman station. I fought through a riptide of locals clamoring toward the loading bays and found one of Cairo's ubiquitous black-and-white taxis, asked the driver for the nearest Internet café. He negotiated a series of filthy backstreets at alarming speeds, dropping me finally at a place called Sector 7, where I went inside and bought an hour's worth of Internet access on a computer that looked like it had been obsolete when I'd first come to Egypt.

I would end up needing four more hours to take in all the ways in which my life had changed since I'd died.

I've given you the broad strokes, of course. But imagine me becoming aware of all this for the first time, after four years in the sensory deprivation of purgatory. The fact of the book being published in the first place. The phenomenon of the suicide note, and what it spawned.

There were uglier aspects, of course.

When I searched my name on Google, the third hit was a website that kept a running count of how many spurned lovers, inspired by the note or the novel or both, had taken their lives. This was not merely a neat, sanitary list of names and dates, lifeless data. No.

Each suicide had its own page, with a photograph of the deceased and a detailed narrative of how they'd loved and died. Casey, a woman of twenty-eight, pretty brunette, with the sad but hopeful eyes of a dog that's been beaten with a broom its whole life: asphyxiation. Rhea, an RN from Quebec with dubious self-esteem who'd nonetheless found the will to demonstrate her chagrin to the dozen or so playboy doctors who'd used her throughout her career: pills, predictably. Paul, a middle-aged loan officer whose estranged wife would, according to his own suicide note, 'withhold (her) love for weeks, on a whim': leapt from the Golden Gate Bridge. Elliott, a bartender and singer/songwriter in Memphis: drove into a concrete overpass support. Yvette, UNC undergrad: pills again. Rob, merchant marine based in Maryland: jumped at sea. Carrie: slashed her wrists. Sunny: gunshot. Dustin: hanging. Liz. Jesse. Molly. Self-immolation. Suicide by cop. Starved self.

A sufficient horror, to be sure. But there was more.

Page after page of Google results revealed how the American celebrity machine had reached for Emma time and again, and how Emma had tried, with varying success, to avoid its grasp. She'd refused myriad interview requests, from *Vanity Fair* all the way to *Penthouse*, not to mention every cut-rate online venue. She'd shunned offers of television appearances, as well as one bit movie role. She'd changed her phone number at least twice, and during the height of her notoriety, around the time the book was published, took to wearing large-brimmed hats and sunglasses to thwart photographers, both professional and casual.

She was either adored or loathed; everyone, it seemed, had an opinion, and there was no middle ground. I knew that Emma being Emma, neither extreme could suit her in the least. Her instinct was to be anonymous except among friends and family; before the book, an Internet search of her name would have revealed exactly three items pertaining to her, and each of those related to her work and had nothing whatsoever to do with her personal life.

Images of her were numerous now, of course. At first I resisted looking, then decided who was I trying to kid, and not only looked but pored: Emma in her car, Emma pushing a cart through the produce section at Whole Foods, Emma striding into a movie theatre. I clicked through to enlarge the photos, then studied each one for long moments. How can I explain it to you? If you've never been this inexplicably moved by a set of eyes, or the dainty dual points of a woman's upper lip, then it won't make any sense. It will seem like hyperbole, or the ramblings of the delusional. But I'm telling you, the only conclusion that makes sense is that my love for her is encoded in both of us at the genetic level: hers the signal, mine the receiver. And you can't fight that, brother. I gave up trying a long time ago.

In the end, in my greed, I perused one too many images, coming across a shot of Emma walking arm in arm with a man down a Manhattan avenue, and when I clicked through to the webpage—

Star magazine, it turned out—I was greeted with this caption, in a large, bold font:

Emma Zielinski leaving a SoHo coffeehouse with fiancé Peter Cash.

What do YOU think of Emma's impending nuptials? Should she stay faithful to the memory of Ron Currie? Or should she get on with her life? Make your opinion heard in the comments section below!

I don't know what I'd expected. It'd been four years, after all.

Still, I just sat there for a while with my hands in my lap, and when the attendant came and asked in warped English if I wanted more tea, he had to repeat himself three times before I looked up.

Asif insisted I had to resurrect myself and go back to the States.

We stood in his kitchen post-lunch, eating leftover rice and thin-sliced flank steak straight from buffet pans.

I thought he was going to take Roberto's tack, tell me I couldn't let Emma get away, that love was all, the Alpha and Omega, trumping every other consideration.

But it turned out Asif didn't really give a toss about romantic love. Ever practical, his concerns lay elsewhere.

He used two fingers to scoop rice from the pan, asking me, Did you leave a will?

A will? You're joking, right?

Of course not. I am serious.

No, Asif. I was too busy faking my death to worry much about estate planning and power of attorney.

He cocked his head, stared at me quizzically.

Never mind, I said. No will.

Then you must go back, he said.

Why?

You have a family, yes?

I don't have *a* family. Not in the way that you mean.

But you have family. Parents. Brothers and sisters, nieces and nephews.

All of that, sure.

How many nieces and nephews?

I thought for a minute. Ten, all told, I said. I think.

Asif stared, exasperated that whatever obvious truth he offered continued to elude me. Then you must go back, he said, holding his hands out, a plea for reason. You have no choice.

Can you explain to me why, exactly, I have no choice?

Your family. You must take care of them.

I wasn't exactly taking care of anyone before. What makes you think I will now?

Listen, Asif said, sitting in the chair he normally used only when peeling vegetables over the trash can. This book of yours, it is selling very much, yes? Making a lot of money?

Certainly seems that way.

And that money is going somewhere. But where? You have no will. So who takes the money? Not your mother. Not your nieces and nephews. Who?

This was a question that I hadn't considered. Who *was* getting all that money? I had no idea how such things worked.

They won't get it if I go back, Asif, I said. It'll go to me.

Yes, yes, he said, but then *you* control it. *You* decide where it goes, now and after you really are gone. You could give it to them yourself, if you don't want it. But you must take care of your family. It is most important. More important than books. More important than you. How you treat and care for your family. This is the thing.

I nodded. Difficult logic to argue with, though I still was not entirely convinced.

I see that you have never even thought about this, Asif said, and now his voice was tinged with reluctant accusation. In his view, a man who did not take care of his family was no man at all.

I felt my cheeks go hot.

It makes me sorry to learn this about you, Asif said.

One thing I didn't learn during my long narcissistic cruise on the Internet was that Hankie had died. Killed, finally, by the narcolepsy that had stalked him for years. I found out from Dwayne, who picked me up in Boston on my return to the States. This was after the Egyptian authorities deported me and the U.S. authorities questioned me for five hours, determining that while in faking my death I'd certainly done something odd and probably heinous, I had not, in fact, done anything illegal.

We'll get to that in a minute.

But so Dwayne waited for me just outside the secure area at Logan Airport, along with half a dozen reporters and what seemed like a thousand of my new fans, many of whom held copies of Emma's novel. This crush was held back by grim-faced state troopers, who created a cordon for me to walk through. Behatted, sunglassed, head down, listening to my name being called from twenty directions at once and feeling my whole body vibrate with the unwelcome energy of these supplicants, I no longer wanted to be famous in the least. I wanted to be nameless. I wanted to be erased, again. I wanted to be on my back in the Red Sea, naked beneath that twinkling emptiness.

At the end of the cordon stood Dwayne. I reached him, and he took my bag without a word. The bulk of the state troopers held the throng inside the terminal while a pair accompanied the two of us out to the parking garage. I kept waiting for Dwayne to speak, but he remained silent and so I kept my mouth shut, too, not having the faintest idea what one says to friends when one returns from the dead.

We paused outside Dwayne's car, and suddenly he turned and hit me square on the mouth, the same spot where the caballeros had relieved me of my teeth years before. I went to one knee as the troopers fell on Dwayne. They pinned him against a concrete support with his arm twisted behind him at an impossible angle, the offending fist clenched between his shoulder blades.

It's alright, I said to the cops, wiping blood from a cut on my lower lip. I deserved that. Let him go.

Not your call, one of the troopers told me as he fastened a cuff around Dwayne's wrist. He's going in for that.

I stood up. Fellas, come on, I said. That wasn't assault. That was business between friends.

The troopers looked at me, then at each other, while Dwayne breathed hard with his face mashed against the support beam. Finally they relented, after a bit more posturing and a few awkward moments of uniform straightening during which no one really seemed to know what to do.

On the ride north we didn't talk much. There wasn't any need. It had been a while since we'd shared the sort of common experience that inspires easy conversation. Aside from that, I couldn't explain what I'd done or why, and Dwayne (like most people who had known and loved me, it would turn out) had no real interest in an explanation regardless.

He broke the silence, finally, as we crossed the lazy green arch of the Piscataqua River Bridge into Maine.

Hankie's dead, he said. In case you didn't know. Really, in actuality, dead.

An ignoble if unsurprising end for Hankie, and painfully ironic, too, I thought as I sat there in the passenger seat and listened to Dwayne, ironic because here was the one guy I knew in his thirties who occupied his life with ease and grace and comfort, who took unqualified satisfaction in both his work and his family, who loved his wife more than he had when they were married, who would lay down in traffic for his son and daughter, but who also had fun where he found it and slept soundly each night and through the tectonic changes of marriage and fatherhood had nevertheless remained the happy cooler-than-thou spike-haired punk he'd always been, inveterate smart-ass with a big tender heart, a guy who quite simply liked his life and wanted it to continue. And now he was gone.

He'd fallen asleep at the wheel of his pickup, driving home from watching the Sox game with Dwayne. Clipped a deer—it had dragged its shattered hind end into the grass, where the police found it dead the next morning—then careened into an old maple on the roadside. He hit the tree driver's-door first, sixty miles per hour of force negated with great violence on the very spot where he sat.

As my high school physics teacher used to say, it's not the speed that gets you, it's the rate of deceleration.

This was a bit that Hankie himself would have found endlessly funny, not in spite of the fact that the joke was on him, but because of it.

I sat there in the car, the news of Hankie's demise having been transmitted and the two of us silent again, and it occurred to me that Asif had been right, but now I had several families to take care of: mine, and Suleiman's, and now Hankie's.

So I've told you that my father and I shared a name. I am, or was, a junior. Which raises a question I've wondered about since he died but haven't yet found an answer for: does one continue to be a junior after the elder shuffles off? The distinction, at that point, seems to lose its utility. And then there's what I know from having published in England, where they removed the suffix from my books altogether, explaining that the British audience wouldn't understand what it meant. One imagines that the British make a habit of naming children after themselves just as we do, and given that, one wonders how they distinguish between the father and the son.

Sharing a name with my father presented a minor inconvenience at times throughout my life—my overdue phone bill would show up on his credit report, for example, and we each could rely on occasionally receiving the other's mail. This was harmless, for the most part, and occasionally funny, as when a copy of his AARP magazine came sliding through my mail slot in my twenty-eighth year.

After he died, though, it was no longer funny. It was, on occasion, like having a ghost brush up against me. A nice woman from Ford ESP Premium Care called to ask if I was happy with the extended warranty service on the car my parents bought right before my father died. The state wrote to inform me that I owed payroll taxes for the last two years that my father's lawn care business existed. *Golf* magazine address-corrected and sent me nearly a year's worth of issues before I finally called and told a customer service rep who bore no responsibility for my grief that my father, being dead, no longer played golf and, further and besides, in my estimation golf was a grotesque, elitist waste of real estate, thereby making their publication a grotesque, elitist waste of trees.

But the ghost of my namesake was and is inside of me, as well. In traffic, I drum my index and middle fingers on the dashboard exactly as he did, and will do this for several moments before I catch myself and my fingers freeze in the air above the textured leather. When I clear my throat, sometimes I hear my father instead of myself. Likewise when I yawn, or whistle. It's always sublinguistic sounds, nonsense noises. And I've become convinced that this is not me aping my father, not subconsciously mimicking behaviors I saw him exhibit a thousand times or more, but something deeper and more fundamental than that—something genetic, in all likelihood. My father's ghost, imprinted on the simple proteins of each cell in my body, as well as on every piece of mail I'll ever receive for the rest of my life.

So: how I came to be deported from Egypt.

I've got a few regrets here and there, but none greater than this.

Because I chose to ignore what Asif told me, chose to believe I could not return home, chose to insist on remaining dead, and I went to Suleiman that afternoon and told him I had to be in the desert right away, and that it might take a long time, longer than ever before, but I was asking him as his friend, not as his client, to do this for me.

Suleiman, whose wife was hugely pregnant by now, looked at me for a long moment, and beneath the wispy graying beard his mouth was set in a line that bespoke both obligation and anticipated regret.

And I saw this, but I could not find a way to set myself aside and let him and his family be, let him welcome his son into the world. The next morning we set out.

God pinching our behinds, again: Suleiman himself had cautioned me, over and over, that Egypt held more unexploded land mines in its deserts than any other country on Earth, many going as far back as World War II, when the British and the Germans were Rochambeauing each other across North Africa. This comprehensive blanketing was supplemented years later by the Egyptians and Israelis, who laid down thousands of toe-poppers over the course of several wars. The minefields were mapped and mapped again, Suleiman told me, but the problem, and the danger even to experienced Bedouins like him, was that the mines refused to stay put. They migrated in the loose sand as though seeking victims, and occasionally they found one. Suleiman's own nephew, a young man in his teens who had just begun guiding tourists in the mountains, was lucky to have survived after being relieved of his left leg by an ancient Nazi mine.

We'd been in the desert for a week, and nothing was working, nothing could still my longing—not the heat, not the infinite featureless horizon, not the omnipresent crunch of sand in my mouth, that previously reliable flavor of nothingness. I still felt everything. I still wanted everything. At night when the camels bedded down and we sat Indian-style before the fire, Suleiman sang with an intensity and feeling I had not heard before on any of our excursions, the plain and plaintive sound of a man who fears he will miss the most important event in his life, a man who prays that this will not be so. While he sang I turned my face away from the flames and swiped tears from my cheeks. And in those moments I knew it was over, knew that I could not empty myself out any more, that I could keep Suleiman away from his family for a year and it would make no difference, on the 365th night I would still be wiping tears away as he wailed—in short, I knew that I would be full to bursting, again, from now until the end.

Still, I couldn't admit this to myself, and so each morning when Suleiman asked me if it was time to return I told him no, onward, and we trudged farther north, toward a horizon that refused to draw any closer no matter how much ground we covered.

Suleiman's camel tromped on the mine near sundown on the eighth day. The desert was so quiet that evening that we could hear the whisper of the camel's hooves in the sand. In the stillness I had begun for the first time to feel more calm, however temporarily. And then that calm exploded around me, and when I looked up from where I'd landed, facedown in a dune, I saw the sand stained with the mingled blood of Suleiman and his camel, and then I saw Suleiman himself, halved cleanly by the blast. His eyes were closed, and below them his face was cratered, tattered and crimson, the lower jaw obliterated. My first confused thought was that no plaintive sounds would ever come from his mouth again, and this, initially, was what saddened me. Not the fact of Suleiman's death, but its consequence: his now-endless silence.

If the mine had been of the anti-personnel variety, Suleiman may have lived to meet his son. But this mine, like many in the Sinai, was designed to stop a Soviet T-62 tank, one among millions of gifts of high explosives from the United States to Israel. It could blow a hole through an inch and a half of steel and still retain enough force to kill everything on the other side. A man and his camel didn't stand a chance.

I lay there through the night. Though not badly hurt, I likely would have died; even if I'd found the motivation to rise and move on, I could not have navigated back to Habiba Village. But the next morning a half-dozen Bedouin men arrived astride camels, the wind flattening their white robes in folds against their bodies, curved knives at their waists and bandoliers slung across their shoulders. They'd heard the blast from miles away and come to investigate. Without a word they took in the scene and collected what remained of Suleiman, loaded us on the animals and headed south. They asked questions I didn't understand, and in response I told them, over and over, where we had come from. Which was where, after four days of steady, direct riding in fair weather, they deposited me and Suleiman and his remaining camel.

At Suleiman's home I stayed outside for three days while his wife wailed, first in grief, then in labor. I was in the midst of digging a grave when her cries ceased, and that peculiar desert silence marked the birth of Suleiman's son.

The pickaxe recoiled from stony soil, throwing sparks with each swing. The spade handle cracked, then snapped in half. A full day and night passed before I had a hole deep and broad enough to bury what was left of my friend.

I did not dare go inside the house. Noora took mercy in the searing daylight hours, bringing water and strong, aromatic sherbet to revive me. She did not speak. Her eyes had lost their twinkle, and she kept them trained on the dirt. I imagined she felt responsible for her father's death, and I wanted to tell her that God had not taken Suleiman as punishment for her flirtations. But then, what did I know, really? Maybe He had.

With Suleiman interred there was nothing left to do, so I sat down on the ground and waited. I didn't know what I was waiting for, until the governorate police showed up in their Jeeps.

They brought me to the precinct, a concrete block of a building just outside Tarabeen. Their manner was courteous, even friendly; I was allowed to sit uncuffed in the front of one of the Jeeps, and at the precinct they offered bottled water, tea, and cola, insisting with the good humor of proper hosts that I accept one of the three. I opted, in the heat, for water. I sat in the chief's office, a windowless room with only a small oscillating desk fan to move the air. The chief himself, a thin, ashen man whose face remained coated with a sheen of sweat no matter how often he mopped at it with his handkerchief, asked the questions. They did not believe I'd done anything wrong, he told me, and they certainly had no intention of charging me with a crime. The Bedouin who'd rescued me had gone to him after, explained the scene they'd happened upon, and he was satisfied that Suleiman's death had been an accident. But it was incumbent upon him to confirm details with the only witness—me—or else he could be accused of shirking his duties.

I sipped water and told the chief that whatever questions he wanted to ask, I was happy to answer.

Things went well for an hour or so. When he'd exhausted his queries the chief smiled and stood up and offered his hand, saying, Thank you for being so cooperative, and I met his hand with my own and said I only wished that there'd been no reason for us to talk in the first place. I was about to leave when he said, Oh, I'm sorry to keep you any longer, but there is one more thing.

I turned to face him again.

A formality, he said, smiling, his head bowed a bit in apology. For our paperwork, we must confirm your passport information.

It was the first time I'd had to use the fake passport from Roberto's fixer since coming to Egypt, but I assumed if I'd managed to get past immigration officers in three countries on my way here, there was little chance a provincial police chief in the Sinai, especially one so eager to perceive and treat me as a friend, would smell a rat.

Naturally, I was completely wrong in this assumption.

I should preface this next by saying that I understand how strange and perhaps even creepy it will sound. It's not lost on me. I contend, though, that what we now define as 'strange' and 'creepy' will, like everything else, undergo such a transformation at the moment of the Singularity that the words themselves, suddenly signifying nothing, may well fall out of use.

So here it is: when the time comes, I will occupy Peter Cash's experience.

There's little point in speculating about the details—it could be a virtual reality created by nanobots in my brain, hatched whole cloth but no less real for that, or it could be a direct feed from Peter Cash's mind, assuming he chooses, as many will, to stream his sensory and emotional experiences onto the Internet, in the same way that people stream video of their bedrooms and work spaces today.

These are only two of innumerable possibilities, and again, the details don't matter. What matters is that, one way or another, I will be able to see, feel, smell, and taste the things that Peter Cash sees, feels, smells, and tastes. Whenever I choose to I will enjoy, as though I were there myself, the sight of Emma walking about her bedroom in the morning before work, viewed from the perspective of someone lying in bed with his head propped on a couple of pillows. Emma dressed, for example, in nothing but a snip of black panties, standing at the door of the closet with her hands on her hips, considering what to wear to the office that day, her breasts pert and pale, the nipples stiff against the chill of an early spring morning. Or else talking to Emma over a Sunday morning beer on the deck at the Port Hole, seagulls wheeling about in the sky above her, fishing vessels smeared with diesel soot bobbing against the docks below.

Or, yes, okay, sex with Emma.

I mean, imagine it.

But experiencing Peter Cash's life in real time is just the beginning. I'll also be able to cast back in his mind and draw on, for example, memories of the pleasant rush of his courtship with Emma, the effortless way in which they fell into one another, as if every prior moment in their lives had occurred solely for the purpose of bringing them together that day in the Hilton ballroom, and I will be able to experience these memories as seamlessly as if they actually belonged to me. And not only will this give me the ability to enjoy life with Emma whenever I care to, but—and here's a critical detail—I will experience it as if I *were* Peter Cash, rather than just my own consciousness occupying his body and circumstances. I will become him. I will lose myself and know, finally, what it's like to be perfect for her.

I hope I live long enough to see it.

The last time that I saw Emma, as I waited in the coffee shop for her arrival, nervous as I'd ever been in my life, and through the window I caught a glimpse of her sauntering up the sidewalk in a scoopneck blouse and denim skirt, the sun behind her highlighting little wisps of hair that had escaped from her ponytail, I was reminded of the time I first laid eyes on her, when I'd been in eighth grade, and she in seventh.

I had known even then. At first sight, as they say. Trying out for the junior high cross-country team in a frigid autumn rain, shivering in tank tops and flimsy running shorts. All of us thin-limbed, gawky with pubescence. Clutching ourselves against the cold while we waited for the coaches to indicate it was time to move. The more serious runners, those with real ambition who trained on our own over the summer, engaged in self-conscious demonstrations of that seriousness, kicking our legs out to loosen the thighs, squatting to double-knot laces on expensive, cleated shoes. Emma stood out from both the serious runners and the tourists. She was not self-conscious in any way. She hugged herself like the tourists, sure, but while they stared apprehensively at the coaches, squeegeeing rainwater from their foreheads with shaky hands, trapped each in private misgivings about their legs, their lungs, their decision to come here in the first place, she gazed placidly out below us, to where our little town unfurled in the valley beneath the cross-country course. She was attentive—when the word came from the coaches, she would fall in with the rest of us—but not on tenterhooks. A vault of self, even at age eleven. I glanced at her, then stared, then gaped, and I forgot about the cold and the rain, forgot about the twelve minutes flat I'd hoped to run on the 3K course, a time I'd been chasing all summer with the goal of being the best runner on the team. Forgot myself, never to recover. We were young, but it didn't matter. The common notion that romantic love among children is fleeting, insubstantial—not true, at least in this case.

Here we were now, approaching forty, and as Emma opened the door to the coffee shop and stood in the entryway searching the room, her face broadcasting ambivalence, this was the memory that sprang to mind: the two of us half-formed, trembling in the rain, our ambitions no greater than to be the best among a group of thirty or so.

Who can make sense of it?

Speaking of running, and getting back, for a moment, to the creation of superhumans via nonorganic enhancement—imagine a time when an athlete whose lower legs were amputated when he was one could be banned from international competition because he had an *advantage* over whole-bodied competitors.

And then imagine no longer, because this very thing happened, way back in 2008.

His name is Oscar Pistorius. He was born without bones in his lower legs. Now he runs on prosthetics called 'Cheetah Flex-Feet.' In terms of mechanics, these are simple devices, J-shaped blades of taut carbon fiber that act as springs. We're not talking bionics, here, or even robotics. There are no moving parts. There aren't even joints. But the Cheetah Flex-Feet are, nonetheless, a triumph of engineering. So much so that they earned Oscar Pistorius a ban from the IAAF, who cited their belief that because of his prosthetics, Pistorius uses less oxygen and fewer calories than whole-bodied athletes traveling the same speed. The Flex-Feet also earned him, tellingly I think, the label of 'pioneer on the posthuman frontier' from a bioethics think tank at Johns Hopkins. For the purpose of running 200 meters as fast as possible, the Cheetah Flex-Feet are superior to the lower legs you and I were born with.

What's more, they point the way to the future. Listen to Hugh Herr, a scientist at MIT and friend of Oscar Pistorius: 'We're going to see a point in this century when the running times, the jumping heights, in the Paralympics, are all superior to the Olympics. The Paralympics won't constrain technological development. So what's going to happen is the Paralympics will be this exciting human-machine sport like race-car driving. It will make normal human bodies seem very boring.'

I hadn't anticipated how angry everyone would be.

In retrospect it's more than a little ridiculous, that I thought I could fake my death without anybody getting pissed off when the ruse was up.

First there was Dwayne, punching me in the mouth at Logan.

My mother was furious as well, angry to a degree I didn't know she was capable of. I would have expected her to come to the airport on my arrival from Egypt, to insist on it even though Dwayne would be there to drive me back home, but no. She did not come, and for more than a week after I returned she let my calls go to voicemail, and did not answer her door when I knocked on it.

Eventually she relented, of course, and when she did her tears were copious, her embrace fierce as ever.

Still, if my mother were that angry with me, what could I expect from the rest of the world?

Many of the hundreds of thousands who'd bought Emma's book, upon learning that I was actually alive and well and returned now to the United States, felt as though they had been misled. No, not misled: lied to. In a world that had taken God from them and replaced Him with talk of nucleic acids, pilfered from them the rush and hum of love and replaced it with explanations of brain chemistry, they felt robbed of the one thing that they'd ever been able to bring themselves to believe in with their guts and hearts as well as their brains. And as a consequence, they became angry as hell.

Maybe rightly so. Maybe it wasn't at all unreasonable for them to wish I'd stayed dead. Maybe it was even okay for the angriest among them to threaten to make me dead again, this time for good.

Because really, what have I done for anyone other than myself? I wrote down some words. That was it. Look at my apolitics. Look at how I squander my wealth. Witness the uselessness of my profession, the inward focus of my one talent, and look how devoted to it I was, to the exclusion of all else. If no man is an island, I am at least an isthmus. Being dead is clearly the best thing I've ever done for the world. Maybe I should have stayed that way.

Which highlights another unfortunate aspect of Hankie being gone: he, among all the people I knew, would have been the only one to find me faking my death funny. He would have thought it hilarious, in fact. Had he still been alive, he would have bought me a beer by way of thanks and congratulations. He would have thumbed his nose at the people who didn't get it, the thousands demanding (and receiving) refunds from my publisher when they learned I was alive. He would have strode unrepentant beside me, his shitkickers clopping the sidewalk, and when the haters got in my face he would have shoved them aside, told them to fuck themselves with their mothers' dicks, would have done for me what I could not, in his absence, do for myself.

As it stood, though, with Hankie buried for real and no one else willing to defend me, I played the penitent and came by it honestly, hung my head, received spit on one cheek and turned the other for the slap, sought out and read every word of vitriol, accepted every media request and sat patiently through eviscerations in newsprint, on television, in podcast, on glossy page.

More than one interviewer, hot with the righteous anger of multitudes, shoved photos of suicides inspired by the book in my face and asked me what these people had died for, now that the world knew the example they'd followed had been a sham.

This was one of several questions, repeated over and over, for which I had no answer. And when I had no answer I simply looked at my feet and waited. There was nothing to say that would be equal to the loss, and thus there was no point in offering regret, or pleading that there was no way for me to know the book would be published in the first place, let alone have the sort of hypnotizing and tragic effect that it had.

So instead of talking I stared at the floor, and hoped people did not mistake my silence for indifference. And though I agonized, I did not ever wish for it to be done, which was fortunate, because it seemed America's appetite for celebrity was matched only by its appetite for punishment, and the hits, as the deejay said, just kept on coming.

And God, the lawsuits. To this day, you know, people imagine I'm ridiculously wealthy. It's not as though I don't continue to make money, of course. But the lawyers turned me upside down, and I'm still hanging there by my ankles. Some of the lawsuits had to do with the book itself, readers who claimed mental anguish and the like as a result of my still being alive. The majority, though, were wrongful death cases brought against me by the families of suicides. All these coalesced into two class-action suits, and both require that I pay in perpetuity and allow for new plaintiffs to be added after the fact.

We're talking millions.

Not that I care about the money. What I cared about was sitting in the Moynihan courthouse in Manhattan and listening to statements from the loved ones of people who had killed themselves.

The judge granted an audience to any and all who wanted to speak. It took over two months.

It would have been fascinating, if not for the heartache that filled the courtroom each morning promptly at nine. Fascinating for the emotional range with which people presented their grief. One could spend years studying sociology, or psychology, and not come away with the insight into human behavior that I earned in that courtroom. It turned out, for example, that parents of suicides, of all those who came and spoke about those they'd lost, were most demonstrably upset while on the stand. Parsed further, mothers cried more often and more wrenchingly for lost sons, and fathers for daughters.

On the other hand, the spouses of suicides tended to be dry-eyed, their chief emotion fury rather than sadness. This was the demographic that fixed me directly with their gazes most often, and held those gazes longest. They sat on the stand with a brittle stillness, as if fossilized by grief. They rested their hands in their laps and never moved them, not even to emphasize their words or wipe away the few tears that did come.

And then there were the children of the departed.

During recesses I vomited into the hoary new porcelain of the Moynihan courthouse toilets. At night I shut down my synapses with whiskey. Over those two months I woke more often on the sofa of my hotel room, or on the floor, than in bed.

One afternoon in the courtroom I glanced over my shoulder toward the gallery and swore that I saw Emma. The barest glimpse—she disappeared when the man in front of her, who'd been leaning forward to fiddle with something on the floor between his legs, sat back up.

I stood and turned to see if it were actually her, but the judge, who took no pains throughout the trial to hide her disdain for me, bade me take my seat again.

Shortly thereafter she called a recess for the day, and I pushed my way through people as the multitude in the gallery rose and filed out. I walked all the way to the top of the courthouse steps, scanning faces, but if it had been Emma in the back row, she was long gone.

Soon I would see Emma in the courtroom without doubt or question, as a witness for the plaintiff. But of course I had no way of knowing that, at the moment.

The day my father died we all knew that the time had arrived. We didn't really understand how we knew, and we didn't discuss it. No one said, Today's the day. It was intuitive. He'd been very sick for weeks, but that morning there was a lethal hush in the bedroom he shared with my mother, a quality as unmistakable as it was impossible to define. We knew.

The telephone rang and rang, and all day the house teemed with the arrivals and departures of relatives and friends, people who milled around the kitchen and smoked in the yard, crushing cigarette butts against the icy walkway with the heels of winter boots. The coffeemaker gurgled nonstop. As the day dragged on the entryway became splattered with mud and slush, and dirty mugs piled up beside the sink. All these visitors were conspicuous in their lack of anything to do but displace air and wait, while those of us who'd spent months ushering my father to his death tended to the last few things.

There wasn't much for us to do either, really. My final interaction with my father consisted of me leaning over him with my thighs pressed against the side of the mattress, prodding him with a hand on his shoulder, trying to get him to focus on me, then asking if he wanted a drink of water. He scrunched his face up, trying to understand from within the haze his sickness had trapped him in, and when understanding blessed him—such modest revelation, to grok the sort of inquiry any dog can grasp and respond to: *do you want some water?*—he nodded gratefully, his mouth slack and making loud ragged noises. A few other people had accompanied me into the bedroom, wanting a chance to say good-bye to him while he could still realize they were there. Two uncles, an aunt by marriage, and a friend who had served with my father in Vietnam. They watched with quiet, awkward reverence as I lowered a glass to my father and aimed a bendy-straw at the collapsed strip mine of his mouth. He wrapped his lips around the straw gingerly, and the effort of drawing water left him exhausted.

Months later I ran into one of my uncles at a hardware store. I was measuring out a length of heavy-gauge steel chain, but I don't remember now what I needed it for. We said hi, chatted for a few minutes. I asked after his wife, who had recently had heart surgery. He invited me to the lake sometime, to seek out smallmouths and pickerel. And then, seemingly out of nowhere, he said how proud and impressed he was at how well I had taken care of my father. The tenderness with which I'd asked my father if he needed a drink of water and then given it to him, my uncle said, was a quiet sort of heroism that he'd found really moving.

And it was nice, hearing that, though I had the sense that my simple, inconsequential act seemed impressive to my uncle only because he was one of the many people there who had nothing to do but sip coffee and smoke cigarettes and watch my father thrash his covers and expire. If I'd wanted to, I could have told my uncle about a hundred times during my father's illness when whatever courage I possessed had abandoned me, and I'd turned away from him and toward whatever petty distraction was closest at hand: a television, a bottle, a woman.

Instead, I told my uncle that yes, I would like to get together and take his boat out on the lake one evening and catch some fish. But we never did.

The lawyer who represented me in the class-action suit has said repeatedly that I could, if I wanted, have the whole thing tossed out with a minimum of effort and near certainty of success.

Here's the thing: the reason the judge hated me wasn't because of what she heard in testimony from the hundreds of plaintiffs who accepted her offer to sit on the stand. It was because she shared many of their sentiments, having once been a fan of Emma's book. The judge counted herself among the betrayed, the hoodwinked.

All this became public knowledge after an anonymous source with intimate ties to the judge talked to the *New York Post* for an article written in the wake of the judgment against me.

The anonymous source, incidentally, was anonymous only insofar as everyone agreed to pretend they didn't know it was the judge's estranged husband.

Somewhat less incidentally, the anonymous source provided the *Post* with audiotape of the judge saying, over the ambient clink of crystal and fine flatware at the Four Seasons, that she wished mine were a capital case so she could 'fry [me] like a Hebrew National' and 'write the ending as it should be.'

Needless to say, she should have recused herself.

My attorney called at three o'clock on the morning the article went to press—he'd read it online before actual newsprint hit the streets—and the sound I heard on the other end when I answered the phone can only be described as panting.

I'll file the paperwork this morning! he said. That unbelievable bitch! That frigid little cooze! By the close of business today you'll be off the hook!

I listened to him champ at the bit for several minutes, then told him that I had no interest in being off the hook.

He was, of course, flabbergasted. Are you out of your mind? he asked. He paused, rendered momentarily mute by his incredulity. Then he spit out: This is millions of dollars!

I've got enough left over for your fee, I said. Don't I?

It's possible—maybe even likely—that the Singularity is nothing more or less than the afterlife we've been promised for so long.

I mean, it would be difficult not to notice the theological implications of everything I've told you so far.

But beyond that, look at the basics of what Judeo-Christian mythology says about the afterlife: I was told, as an altar boy, that my finite mind could not comprehend the joys of eternity. I was told that corporeal existence is the gauntlet through which we pass on our way to heavenly enlightenment. I was told that my dying body will be transformed into a body that shall never die. I was told, finally, that in heaven no one suffers or grieves. That there will be no pain, and no end, that this dulcet perfection will go on forever and ever.

The principal difference between Scripture and the Singularity, as far as I can see, is that admission to the eternal life of the Singularity will not be conditional upon one's faith in it.

What my lawyer was by profession and probably temperament incapable of understanding is that, as I told you, I didn't care about the money. They could have it. It was theirs to begin with, after all—they'd paid for the books and filled my coffers, and really all I did was return that money to them in a perfect circle of commerce and atonement.

Here's the thing: I didn't have to be in that courtroom at all. These were civil suits. I could have sat out the duration under a mango tree, earning 5 percent in a country without an extradition treaty. But I wanted to be there. I wanted to hear what these people had to say to me, and I wanted to do whatever they felt necessary in terms of penance, and I wanted them to be as satisfied as they could be, and then I wanted to fade from their minds and hearts, like a raw image on film, burning blank in the sunlight.

The right to be forgotten.

What I did not want was to go through all that for a second time. Which is exactly what would have happened if we'd had the case thrown out—it would have been reloaded with a different judge, and I'd have had to sit and take in all that pain, all that ire, all over again.

After Emma testified for the plaintiffs, I asked my lawyer if she had approached him about testifying for us.

This was outside the courthouse, during a short recess immediately following Emma's testimony. She'd left without saying anything to me. A cigarette smoldered between my fingers, but I was still too stunned to actually smoke it. The cigarette would eventually burn down to the filter, stinging my knuckles, and I would toss it away without having taken a single drag. For lack of anything better to do, my lawyer had bummed a cigarette from me. He didn't smoke his, either, not because he was stunned at Emma's appearance and testimony, but because he didn't actually smoke.

When I asked if Emma had approached him about testifying, he looked at me, then looked at the cigarette held in his right hand, then back at me. Yeah, he said. He gave the cigarette an unpracticed, awkward flick, nearly snapping it in half. She did. Before the trial started.

And why didn't you say yes?

He looked at the cigarette again, as if trying to figure out what he was supposed to do with it. Jesus, I don't know, he said, shrugging. We were fucked anyway. I figured there was no point in getting you all worked up.

If I imagined the judge hated me, though, if I imagined the families of the departed wanted my blood, nothing, but nothing, could have prepared me for the wrath of the plaintiff's lead attorney.

Professional, well-compensated hatred often being more withering than the personal variety, in my experience.

My lawyer thought I was insane for agreeing to take the stand in the first place. But it was just another whistle-stop on my world tour of contrition, as far as I was concerned.

Determined though I was to speak, I still trembled while ascending the stand. Being called up there—the new courtroom's warm lighting, tasteful oil paintings, and plush area rugs aside—was like walking into a meat locker.

Before me stood the plaintiffs' attorney, her arms folded over her chest as I settled in. She held her face turned slightly away from me, toward the jury. She managed to appear both furious and grief-stricken at once, her mouth a tense red line turned down at the corners, her eyes refusing to acknowledge my presence.

I have to say, the attorney began, still not looking at me, it is difficult for me to talk to you because I feel really duped. But more important, I feel that you betrayed millions of readers. I think it's such a gift to have millions of people read your work, and that bothers me greatly. So now, as I stand here today I don't know what is true and I don't know what isn't. So first of all, I wanted to start with the question that everyone wants answered: why did you tell us that you were dead when here you are, very much alive?

Well, not that this excuses anything, but I did actually try to kill myself, I said.

And you failed. Curt, accusatory.

No sense in denying it, I said.

And then your book was published and sold three million copies. And counting.

I didn't know it would even be published, I said. I certainly didn't *mean* for it to be published.

Please just answer the question.

I paused a moment, unsure, then said, Yes, over three million copies. According to my last royalty statement.

My lawyer, who had by now abandoned all hope, scribbled on his notepad, then held it up so I could read: IXNAY ON THE OYALTIESRAY.

Counselor, the judge warned, glaring at him.

Let's assume, the attorney continued, that we believe you when you say you never intended for the book to be published. Nevertheless, the book *was* published, and published to great success. A success due in no small part to the lie of your suicide. Would you agree that this is the case?

Well, sure, obviously, I said. The book would most likely have been ignored, if not for the fact that everyone believed I was dead.

My lawyer tore compulsively at the corner of his notepad, making bits of yellow legal–ruled confetti.

So you *wanted* people to think the suicide note, and by extension the book, were true. So that people would buy the book.

I wanted people to think the suicide note was true. That I don't deny. But the book was, and remains, a work of fiction. A novel.

The attorney straightened her blazer. So you expect us to believe, after all the things you've said and written that we know now were lies, that you meant for this . . . *novel* to be read as fiction. As not true.

Well I don't mean to quibble, I said, but a novel is, by definition, not factual.

Your honor? the attorney said.

Witness will answer the question, intoned the judge.

Okay, I said. That's correct. But the thing is, from the perspective of a novelist there is a brand of lying that feels more honest than the actual facts of an event. Lying as a way to move closer to the truth, or to illuminate how something actually feels in a way the mere facts cannot. It's all sort of abstract and difficult to defend, but, uh, no less valid for that, I don't think.

I was dying up there, and I knew it. I had expected to die up there.

I'd even wanted to die up there. Nonetheless, sweat started to run in rivulets down the small of my back.

Did I mention that I was drunk? Sad but true. My testimony started at eleven in the morning, and I went out there absolutely soused on whiskey. I'd tried to clear up my eyes with several doses of Visine, in addition to giving myself borderline frostbite on both cheeks with a baggie of ice intended to reduce the alcoholic protrusions of my face. Despite this, I still looked like I'd just crawled out of a Dumpster, and what was more I could sense precisely how bad I looked, which did nothing to alleviate my burgeoning anxiety.

But also, I continued, once again I have to make the point that the book was and is a *novel*. I'm happy to admit that I'm as guilty of casual duplicity and lies of various size as anyone else who's spent a few years on Earth, but I never meant for this story to be interpreted as what people generally think of as the truth. It's a fictional representation of very real experiences and emotions that I had. That's all.

A 'fictional representation'? the attorney asked, eyes narrowed. That sounds evasive to me. That sounds like exactly the sort of vague language someone would use when they've been caught in a lie.

I don't deny lying, I said. I haven't all along.

The attorney sighed and shook her head. She strode slowly back behind the plaintiff's table. Fine, she said. You don't deny lying. Fine. Then let me ask you this: *why* did you lie?

I looked at her. Why did I lie?

Yes. This is your opportunity to come clean. So please, tell us why you lied.

I hesitated. Is this a trick question?

No, it isn't. It's an honest question, and I'm expecting an honest response.

Well . . . I mean, I lied because that's what I'm paid to do. I realize this isn't the answer you're necessarily looking for. But I don't know what the answer is that you're looking for, and in lieu of that answer this is the only one I have.

The attorney repeated my words slowly. You lied . . . because that's what you're *paid to do*?

As a novelist, I added, trying to be helpful.

Then the attorney completely lost her cool. She leaned forward and jabbed one finger at me, using her other hand to brace herself against the plaintiff's table. I think you're missing the point here, she said. I think you're missing the point entirely. Because people don't care about the difference between a novel and a memoir. What people care about is being led to believe in something, and then finding out that what they believed in is a goddamn lie.

I'd recoiled without realizing it, but nevertheless did not drop my defense entirely. 'Novel' and 'lie' could probably be considered synonymous, I said.

Details! the attorney said. Semantics! We believed you, and you lied to us. That is what matters, here.

I paused for a moment. Took a deep breath, thinking about how I wanted this to go. I could remain meek and contrite and most likely get out of there alive. But on the other hand, what did I really have left to lose? Not even my dignity, that tattered artifact. So fuck it, I thought.

If I hadn't been drunk, I almost certainly would have stuck with meek and contrite.

Okay, I said. Let's say for sake of argument that I did write the book as a memoir. That I meant for everyone to interpret it as a factual record of events. That was how you took it, yes?

The attorney looked to the gallery, a sea of multihued ovals nodding in unison. She turned back to me, nodding herself.

And when you believed the story to be true—and understand that I'm not conceding for a minute the definition of 'true,' that's a different discussion altogether, but for the sake of expedience I'm trying to get us all on the same page—so when you believed the story to be true, it meant a great deal to you. You found it heartfelt and moving and above all *honest*. It would be fair to say, even, that it changed your life.

Nodding again, more vigorously now.

So what I'm wondering is, why should the story suddenly mean any less to you just because it isn't factual? It's a ridiculous distinction to begin with. Consider the popular cliché 'there are two sides to every story.' Perception is singular and faulty and unreliable. I will remember today's events differently than you will. We could both write down our impressions of this hearing, and it's more than likely that our accounts will differ. Does this mean that either of us is lying? Of course not. But if neither of us is lying, then neither of us is telling the truth, either. We're incapable of it. We are not reportage machines. We're perception machines.

I paused, thought for a minute. Also, I continued, we're not even getting into the stickier issues of whether or not what we define as 'reality' actually exists. A lot of debate about that, you know.

The multihued ovals stared at me, suspicious, unconvinced, and I decided to try another tack.

Or maybe, I said, maybe think about the stories we loved, the stories that got inside us and tumbled around and melded with our DNA when we were kids. All fiction. All lies, by your own definition. Can you imagine a four-year-old stomping out on story time when he discovers that the Wild Things are made up? How silly would it be for a second-grader to march into Barnes and Noble and demand his money back on finding that it indeed may be Cloudy, but there is not, and never will be, a Chance of Meatballs?

We all exist in fantasy worlds, even as adults, I said. How many of you whiled away the drive here daydreaming about something or another? Singing along with a song on the radio and imagining yourself onstage? How many of you close your eyes when making love to blot out the sight of your spouse, conjuring in his stead the image of the checkout boy at the grocery store, or the beau of your newly divorced best friend, or your coworker's wife?

The multihued ovals exchanged glances, and even the attorney's veneer slipped ever so slightly, revealing a glimpse of something human and vulnerable and found out.

These things are counterfeit, I continued, complete and utter make-believe, and yet you find them satisfying—perhaps, in some instances, more satisfying than your real lives. So why, then, have you turned on me for providing one more deeply satisfying lie?

The attorney stood stock-still behind the table.

I'm not mad at you, I said. I don't even think you're wrong. I just don't quite understand it. The story I wrote—the story you fell in love with, the story you believed—is true. It had to be, because otherwise there is no way that it could have moved you so. I felt, and continue to feel, all that I wrote. Facts notwithstanding.

Of course neither the attorney nor the jury were particularly moved by my monologue.

When the torches are lit and the pitchforks handed out, it follows that someone has to be lynched.

And anyway, by the standard they set and refused to budge from, I deserved to be lynched. I had lied, and as a consequence people had lost their lives. That was never in dispute. I didn't take the stand in search of absolution. Like I said, if it hadn't been for the whiskey I would have just sat there and accepted my punishment, without explanation or complaint.

My lawyer hadn't known that Emma would testify for the plaintiffs, because she hadn't been declared as a witness at the beginning of the trial. The plaintiff's attorney brought her as a rebuttal witness. To rebut, specifically, my testimony.

So we were all the picture of surprise when she strode into the courtroom, dressed for work in dark wool slacks and a sleeveless white blouse open at the neck, the usual admixture of sensibleness and sensuality. Her vault of self welded shut under the prurient gaze of those assembled. She walked past the defense table without a glance in my direction, but when she took the stand she looked straight at me, shrugged her shoulders almost imperceptibly, offered a slight smile.

And then proceeded to tell the truth, the whole truth, etc.

Which was bad news for me, legally speaking, though I couldn't have cared less. I watched her mouth, those eyes. I noticed a shift in the courtroom's silence, as those assembled went from lewd rubbernecking to rapt, malleable engrossment. She made people forget to breathe. For twenty minutes, at least, they were all as deeply in love with her as I was. And like that, finally, they understood.

When the plaintiffs' attorney had finished, my lawyer declined, with a weary wave of one hand, to cross-examine Emma. The judge was about to dismiss her, but Emma asked if she could say one more thing.

Not as a rebuttal witness, Ms. Zielinski, the judge told her. You're limited to answering specific questions.

Is there any way around that? Emma asked.

The judge considered for a moment. You could make a victim impact statement, if you like, she said. It wouldn't be sworn.

Your honor? the plaintiff's attorney said from behind her table. The judge ignored her.

I would like that, Emma said.

The judge nodded. Go ahead, she said.

Emma gazed out at the courtroom. You should all be ashamed of yourselves, she said. She looked at the plaintiffs' table. You there, she said, pointing at the attorney. And all of you, she said, indicating the gallery.

Those assembled were mute.

Is that it? the judge asked.

That's it, Emma said. That's what I really came here to say.

Which brings us, more or less, to the coffee shop where I sat and waited for Emma, where I watched her come up the sidewalk with the setting sun at her back, where I found myself transported to a cold rainy day twenty years previous, then hauled back to the present when she stepped inside and those eyes scanned the room, once again, for me.

Nothing had changed. Nothing ever would. Inside me cars were overturned and buildings set ablaze, after so long. Five years, give or take. A death, a stint in purgatory, and a forced rebirth. On her left ring finger a new band of white gold, nestled against an engagement ring of more than respectable carat and style. Nothing too flashy, but certainly not cheap. Perfect, in other words, for her.

She spotted me, walked over to the table where I sat stiff and straight and upright. Her expression did not at all resemble that which you would expect to see on the face of someone engaged in a happy reunion.

This impression was confirmed when, now within range, she hauled back and slapped me across the mouth, much as her mother had slapped her in front of me all those years previous—with great sincerity, swinging from the hips, no concern at all for the fact of an audience.

I turned my head from side to side, flexed my jaw. Silence and stillness from the coffee shop's other patrons.

Welcome home, Emma said.

I thought that we would talk, first, about my disappearance, the how and why of it. I imagined that we would not be able to talk about anything else until that subject was punctured and exhausted. I was sure it would stand in the way of anything else we might try to communicate to each other.

But as was so often the case when it came to her, I was wrong. Because she wanted to talk about anything but that.

She told me she'd bought a sewing machine, an interest she'd expressed and not really understood when we'd been together, and she'd begun fashioning clothes, for herself and for Peter Cash, that sometimes fit and sometimes did not.

I told her that I'd recently gone to Mass for the first time since just before I was supposed to be confirmed but instead, willful boy, had renounced the hymnal, the rosary, the cheap Chianti passed off as lamb's blood. She asked why I'd suddenly decided to attend Mass after so long, and I said I didn't know. I wasn't looking to get reacquainted with God, or to be convinced anew of His existence and benevolence. The only clue I had regarding my motivation, I told her, was in the way I clung to the rituals from my childhood. The dipping of fingers in holy water, and the crossing of oneself. The genuflection. The exchange of blessings with my neighbors in the pews. There was something in these acts as ceremony that I wanted, though I had no idea what that thing might be.

She favored me with a guarded smile and said, It's nice to see that you're still making as little sense as possible. That you're sticking with that strategy, despite everything it's cost you.

Emma glanced out the window at a couple passing arm in arm on the sidewalk, then tucked a strand of hair behind her ear and looked back at me. Her eyes were blazing suddenly in that way I'd come to know and fear. At first I had no idea why she was so angry. We'd spent the previous twenty seconds in silence, fiddling with napkins and teaspoons, and then, seemingly apropos of nothing, she was on fire.

You had it all right here, she said to me.

To demonstrate what she meant, she held one of her hands out over the table, palm up, fingers flexed slightly as if cupping something. Right here, she said, poking her palm with the index finger of her other hand.

I didn't respond. I had no idea what to say.

Goddamn you, she said, but her eyes were cast down at the tabletop now, and her tone was not entirely unkind.

Are you happy? I asked her.

I am happy, she said.

Good, I said. You got what you were after. Your white whale.

I meant it. I wasn't trying to be an asshole.

She nodded and smiled, looked in her coffee cup. It's not perfect, she said.

It never is.

You were a better lover, she said.

Life is full of trade-offs, I guess.

It is, she said. It is.

Sitting there as the day ended outside and people abandoned the coffee shop for home, or the bars, or wherever, I found myself thinking about a conversation we'd had years before, after particularly violent coitus, when we lay contused and content with our arms and legs braided together, and Emma had said, still somewhat breathless, You do things to me that no one else has done.

I was pleased to hear this, of course, and I guess it was one of those times when it's easy to believe that you will stay that safe and happy forever. And I did believe. Despite what I knew about the width and depth of the world, and how people get lost in all that empty space, I sank down under the weight of her body, wiped a crust of blood from the corner of my mouth, breathed the tang of our spent sex wafting up from under the covers, and I believed.

We didn't touch at all, there in the coffee shop, except once when she shifted in her seat and her booted foot made brief accidental contact with my shin under the table, then immediately retreated.

There came a moment, unbidden, when suddenly I knew every-thing there was to know about the woman. Currently it takes Google about .25 seconds to produce between 70 and 80 million re-sults, and it took me about the same amount of time to suddenly, if temporarily, become aware of the millions of bits of minutiae that constituted Emma's life and times. On my father's grave, this actu-ally happened. I thought that perhaps the Singularity had occurred, but it only lasted a moment. I knew, though I could not see, that Emma had a bruise on her right thigh, in the soft flesh just below her hip, and that she'd incurred this bruise the previous morning, when she'd risen to go to the bathroom before sunrise and whacked her leg on the armoire. I knew her blood type was O-negative. I knew that her hair had inexplicably turned clown-wig red and stayed that way for two years, between the ages of three and five, and I knew that after this period it had returned just as mysteriously to the subdued auburn shade I associated with her. I knew, also, that as she sat across the table she was filled with the urge to go some-where private and have sex with me, and I knew that this urge had begun and blossomed independent of any thoughts about Peter Cash, and that, far from being uncomfortable or otherwise a bur-den, she found the urge warm and comfortable—because she had every certainty that she would not act on it.

I'd like to be able to say that we left the coffee shop and went to my place and made love one last time, a physical testament to the permanence of our feelings for one another despite the impossibility of being together, but that isn't how it went down at all. There were a couple of moments during our conversation when I half-listened while I tried to drum up the impetus to take her hand and say simply Let's go and walk her outside and get into a cab and take her home under cover of darkness and give her a look that broadcast unmistakably Damn the consequences and have her return that look and lead her up the stairs by the wrist and unlock the door and leave it open behind us and fall onto the bed and take her clothes off and have slow passionate cinematically lit sex and let our love lie in repose for a bit afterward and then put our clothes back on and agree to never speak of it to anybody and say good-bye and maybe never see one another again.

But it just wasn't there. I wanted to be impulsive and passionate in a wildly inappropriate way, but nothing happened inside me, and to commit such an act without a genuine mandate in my gut would have been beyond horrible. Because look, it was just really nice, being there with her. We floated in the peculiar calm and sexless affection that blossoms when there's nothing left to prove or salvage. Neither of us looking for an apology, or to be proven right at the other's expense. No anxiety to make it better than it was, no yearning toward something more. No dramatic conclusion at all. Just an array of loose ends, wrapped in a bundle of memories, all tied together by the sinew of regret—regret that we could both ultimately live with.

I paid the bill. We paused at the table for a moment, looking at each other in silence, and then both stood at the same time and went out onto the sidewalk, where we paused again. She said, Alright, well I guess I'll see you, and I said, Okay then. There was another moment of quiet during which neither of us moved, and then

I said: Good-bye, Emma. And these were the words that dislodged us from one another, finally, when no other words would. She turned and went back in the direction I'd seen her coming from earlier. I did not watch her go, but turned away myself with my hands jammed in the pockets of my jeans, and I walked and walked.

I understand how unsatisfying an ending that is. Believe me, I understand better than you do. But that's life, right? I mean real life, the kind of messy conclusionless non-narrative we all write a page of every day. I could tell you a story in which things wrapped up very neatly between me and Emma, if I wanted. But that's just not how it happened. And besides, the story isn't really over yet. I haven't seen her since that day, but who knows? We're both still drawing breath. Peter Cash could step in front of a bus. I could show up under her window with a boom box. We could both live to see the Singularity. For a while I despaired of making it all the way there myself, but recently I quit smoking again, so I'm feeling optimistic. The nicotine patches, once more. They tether me to life, keep me from my father's fate, grant me time and, by extension, opportunity. As I wrote in the final line of my first novel, the one nobody read: '. . . anything, anything, anything is possible.'

Speaking of messy and conclusionless: I did eventually speak to the detective with the curly hair and the predatory manner, and he of course found no reason to hold or even suspect me in the fire that destroyed Emma's house way back then. No reason at all, my alcoholic paranoia notwithstanding. They never made an arrest, and the detective very quietly deactivated the case, and that's how the whole thing ended—with a shrug, basically.

Or, if you insist on a natty conclusion, how about this one: my father got sick and died and that was it. Nothing followed but silence. No insight or revelation, no evidence of anything beyond that last breath. We paid someone we did not know to transform him from a man full of love and hate and fear into three pounds of ash, which is just about as neat and tidy as it gets, if you like neat and tidy so much.

It has seemed, since then, as though he never existed.

Nothing left to say about all of that, except: The End.

Now that we've spent all this time together, now that you know everything there is to know, now that you know the capital-T Truth, when the moment comes I hope I'm here in this place with you. I hope you're the one sitting there next to me and I can say: Did you feel that, just now? Like the smallest, briefest earthquake? Just a slight shifting of the ground, underneath the floor, underneath the chairs that we sit on at this moment? Raise your glass with me. That was the Singularity. Please, raise your glass. Here's to perfection. Here's to the end of all suffering. Here's to being mastered with infinite benevolence. Here's to being exterminated by our own creations. Here's to never needing to solve another of our own problems ever again. Here's to living for as long as the machines can keep our universe from decaying into a featureless void. Here's to loving for that long, too, and loving perfectly, without error or sorrow, held forever on the edge of madness by our desire, but never tumbling over. Salud.